EDGE
OF DARKNESS

by
Jove Belle

2008

EDGE OF DARKNESS
© 2008 By Jove Belle. All Rights Reserved.

ISBN 10: 1-60282-015-5
ISBN 13: 978-1-60282-015-9

This Trade Paperback Original Is Published By
Bold Strokes Books, Inc.
New York, USA

First Edition: May 2008

THIS IS A WORK OF FICTION. NAMES, CHARACTERS, PLACES, AND
INCIDENTS ARE THE PRODUCT OF THE AUTHOR'S IMAGINATION OR
ARE USED FICTITIOUSLY. ANY RESEMBLANCE TO ACTUAL PERSONS,
LIVING OR DEAD, BUSINESS ESTABLISHMENTS, EVENTS, OR LOCALES
IS ENTIRELY COINCIDENTAL.

THIS BOOK, OR PARTS THEREOF, MAY NOT BE REPRODUCED IN ANY
FORM WITHOUT PERMISSION.

Credits
Editors: Jennifer Knight and Stacia Seaman
Production Design: Stacia Seaman
Cover Design By Sheri (graphicartist2020@hotmail.com)

Acknowledgments

My thanks to Margie for pointing the way, Tara W. for challenging the weather, Andi M. for cleaning it up, Len for signing the contract, and Jennifer for suffering through the edits.

Writing is a gift, and without the support of my partner and oldest daughter, I'd never have been able to carve out the time between work and diaper changing. Thank you, Michelle, for the hours of babysitting and for making me so damned proud of you as you grow and evolve into a fine adult. And to Tara, my heart, thank you for juggling the many pieces of our lives and for agreeing to grow old with me.

Visit us at www.boldstrokesbooks.com

Dedication

For Tara—you are my true north.

PROLOGUE

There was no light. Only the heavy pounding of Ali's feet against the soft, plush carpet as she ran blindly, driven forward by the haunting voice behind her in the dark.

"Ali." The singsong tone was laced with acid. "You can't escape. You know this. Why do you make me chase you?"

She stopped running and pressed herself tight against the wall. The hammering timpani of her heart continued and she feared the roar of it would betray her location. She could no longer hear Ricardo's voice above her own labored breathing.

A distant scratch of metal against adobe startled her into moving again. When he captured her, as he always did, he would stand over her, a sneer on his icy face, watching as she polished the scrape marks out of the wall.

"Why do you try to run, my beautiful girl?" he would ask.

If she moved too slowly or hesitated to answer, he would rap the wall with his open palm. The leather shackles—her shackles—would dangle loosely from his other hand, the morning sun glinting off the brightly polished buckles.

She had to find the door. It was right here yesterday. She frantically swiped her hands over the surface of the wall. "Ali." The natural rhythm of Ricardo's voice was hypnotic. "Stop hiding from me, poppet. I'm worried about you."

The melodic warmth created a false sense of security and Ali stifled the urge to call out to him. She knew what awaited her if she was found, yet she was overwhelmed by the desire to comfort him, to assure him she was okay.

"Please, angel, tell Ricky where you are."

A bolt of panic raced down Ali's spine. The soft sympathy in Ricardo's voice promised love and affection, absolute forgiveness. It was the same voice he used when he branded his name on her thigh with a lit cigarette.

"Ah, don't squirm, poppet," he'd said. "This hurts me as much as it hurts you."

He had watched her closely as he pushed the hot embers into her exposed flesh. Both her hands were gripped tightly together in one of his and held high above her head. His voice and hands were at war in an exquisite dichotomy, one comforting, the other torturing. The sadistic gleam in his eye made Ali tremble with fear. The smell of burning flesh had filled the air.

Ali gulped back tears. She could feel him getting closer. The fine dinner of curried prawns and rice rioted in her stomach, working its way up. He was right. There was no escape. She slumped against the wall, defeated.

Warm breath tickled her ear a moment before his vise grip closed around both arms. Ricardo pressed his body fully against hers, crushing her into the cold, hard wall. He ground his pelvis into her, deliberate and slow, his arousal evident and straining against her.

"You're mine, Ali." He ran his tongue along the outside curve of her ear. "I'll never let you go. Never."

Ali awoke with a violent start, the sound of her screams echoing in the room. Sweat ran down her face as she rocked back and forth. It was always the same. No matter how many times she killed him, he still found her trembling in the dark like a frightened child.

CHAPTER ONE

Lightning ripped across the night sky and flashed on the steel blade of the katana. Ali Sandoval dropped to one knee and took the weapon from the man crumpled on the floor. Looking down at the lifeless face of her victim, she ran her hand over his eyes, closing them forever. A spreading pool of scarlet seeped into the thick, cream carpet at her feet. Beyond a wall of glass enclosing the study, the faint glow of yard lights failed to brighten the slate patio that skirted an oversized lap pool. By daylight the crystal blue waters bore testament to the man's wealth and decadence. Now, with the sun's descent, the liquid surface was transformed into an eerie dance of reflection and unreadable blackness.

Ali slid the bloodstained sword into its sheath with a deadly rasp and slipped out the door into the night. The dark, unforgiving sky hurled teardrops of rain onto the hard pavement. She flicked the brim of her hat with two fingers and watched the haphazard arc of water join the deluge pouring down from the heavens. The dull roar of a thousand liquid pellets hitting the ground assaulted the peace that only exists in a veil of 3:00 a.m. quiet. The late summer storm did nothing to calm the beast raging inside her.

Stretching her hands above her head, she tipped her face toward the moon and invited the downpour to cleanse her restless soul. The voices of past sins clamored at her from all sides, pleading for redemption. Above the cacophony, she could hear the rising scream of police sirens as they drew closer.

The black-and-white chariot of justice careened around the corner into North Astor Street, stopping just short of the closed gate designed to protect the Stewart family from harm. Ali retreated into the shadows of the city moments before the crimson and cerulean lights reached her. She would wait until the stench of corruption called her to action again.

❖

Diana's phone rang as she stepped into the dim light of Bernie's Fish Shack. The line to order reached almost to the door. The hulk of a man in front of her made a show of inching forward to allow room for her. He threw a disdainful glance over his shoulder as her cell phone rang. Diana smiled brightly. The circus music she'd chosen for a ring tone was likely the cause of his irritation. It made some people crazy. She took the phone from her front pocket with a look that mixed accusation and acceptance. *What are you going to do? Damn cell phones. Have a mind of their own. Ringing at inappropriate times.*

The man scooted even closer to the person in front of him. Diana snorted a laugh and flipped open the phone.

"You're late." She wasn't chastising, just making a simple observation.

"I know. I know." Brigitte, the youngest of her three siblings, sounded rushed and more than a little pissed off. The noise of city life roared in the background. "I got a call right as I was headed there. Protect and serve and all that."

Brigitte had followed in their father's footsteps and entered law enforcement. To top off her compulsive need to place her life in danger, she'd opted to patrol downtown Chicago rather than the suburbs where they grew up. Diana had no idea how Brigitte reconciled the extremes in her world—diapers and bottles at home, and prostitutes and drug dealers at work.

She heard Brigitte open her car door, then close it a moment later, shutting out the madhouse of activity that lived and breathed every day on the streets of Chicago.

"You gonna make it?" Diana asked.

Ahead of her, the line moved forward at a steady pace. Nobody else had entered the restaurant. Lunch hour was winding down. She could have lagged slightly, but she kept pace with the line.

"I'll be there. But why don't you order for me?"

"The usual?" Diana suppressed a sarcastic comment. Yet again Brigitte had tricked her into buying lunch.

The sound of a siren, presumably the one on top of Brigitte's patrol car, came to life on the other end of the phone. "That'd be great. I'll be there in record time."

"Ciao, baby." Diana closed the phone and forced it back in her jeans pocket. Not an easy task. It was time to hit the gym and hit it hard, or buy a bigger size of clothing. She sighed.

Surprisingly few people remained inside Bernie's. Most had elected to take their meals to go, which meant it was Diana's lucky day. She and Brigitte might actually get to enjoy their lunch on one of the ever-popular outside tables. It was still pretending to be summer, but the balmy September weather wouldn't last for long. A few more weeks and the tables would be moved inside until spring.

Hulking Man placed his order and tossed Diana one last disapproving look before heading off to the table with his friends. Diana made a kissy-face at him and stepped up to the counter. It was a good day. Yes, indeed.

A bored-looking girl with pieces of metal stuck in her face droned, "What'll ya have?"

Her attitude was part of the ritual at Bernie's. The employees looked as though they couldn't give two shits about you; then, if you didn't leave a fat tip in the big mason jar on the counter, they would accidentally trip on the way to your table. Fish and fries be damned. You could then wait thirty more minutes while they sorted out what went wrong, or you could eat the stuff that landed on the floor. Neither option was desirable. Both the fish and the service were legendary at Bernie's. Only one of them was any good.

Diana placed her order, including a pint of lager. She hated drinking beer while her sister drank water, but not nearly as much as Brigitte hated getting caught drinking beer while on duty. The girl behind the counter popped her gum loudly and went on with the difficult task of looking bored while she waited for Diana to pay.

Diana handed her two twenties and made a show of putting all the change in the tip jar. "Did my friend over there leave you guys a tip?" She gestured toward Hulking Man's table.

Metal-face gum-popper arched an eyebrow. "Sure. If you call two bucks a tip."

Diana pulled out another twenty and slipped it into a jar. "Thanks for the upcoming floor show." She smiled wickedly and retreated to the opposite corner of the room. Great view.

That was when all hell broke loose. Or, more accurately, burst through the door. A skittish man wearing a black shirt and black pants charged into the restaurant. Hell, he even had on black boots. Could it get any more clichéd? To top it off, he had a ski mask bunched on top of his head, which he had clearly forgotten to pull down over his face. A pistol-waving maniac in all his glory, he pointed a shaking gun at the no-longer-bored clerk.

"Money!" he screeched. "Now!"

Charming. This place was just full of articulate men. Diana weighed her options. If she didn't intervene, the crew would be rattled and then distracted by the police. She'd never get her fish. If she stopped him, the crew would still be rattled and then distracted, and she'd never get her fish. But at least with the second option she'd get to hit someone.

She'd always hated the gaudy, dark red flower vases that adorned the tables at Bernie's. Using one as a weapon would be a public service. She snatched one off the nearest table on her way to the counter. The closer she got, the wider the über-pierced girl's eyes got. Not good. When she was less than two steps away, the man with the gun whirled around to face her.

Oh, hell. Diana abandoned her plan to club him with the vase in favor of throwing it. The short distance between his head and her outstretched hand didn't allow for proper execution and the vase bounced off his head with little effect.

"Don't move," the man stammered, confused and outraged all at once. "Don't you fuckin' move."

"Okay." Diana tried to appeal to his sense of logic. "But don't you want me to put my hands up?"

"I've got a gun here!"

Diana made a show of inspecting the weapon from a respectful distance. The small .22 was completely engulfed by the man's meaty hands. Diana could see enough to pick out that the firing pin was not engaged and the safety was still on.

"Yes, I see you have a gun. It's very nice." Trying her best to look sincerely helpful, she held out her hands, palms up. "Why don't you let me hold on to it until the police get here?"

The gunman wavered. He started to hand Diana the weapon, then apparently thought better of it. "No, no police. I'm here for money."

Why don't they ever just agree and play nicely? Diana nodded with understanding. "If that's what you really think is best."

Before he could shake the confused look off his face, she lunged. Fifteen years of martial arts training, yet her instincts still told her to scratch his eyes out. Her right fist connected squarely with his jaw. There was enough force behind it to knock out a small pony. Not that ponies deserved to be knocked out, but it would take some doing.

Diana hopped around like a madwoman, shaking her hand. "Ow. Motherfucker! That hurt." She always forgot that making contact hurt the hand as much as the other person's face.

The gun dropped to the floor and slid under a table. The man shook his head hard and glared at her. "Fuckin' bitch! I'm gonna kill you."

Great. Crazy man with a steel jaw. Diana edged backward, toward the door. She didn't want to end up pinned in a corner.

Before the armed robber could move in on her, Hulking Man stepped up behind him and crashed a chair over the gunman's head. Perhaps he wasn't so bad after all. Now that they had a common enemy, maybe he could overlook her musical cell phone and they could be friends.

The chair splintered and flew around the man in a hail of jagged pieces, right at Diana. A flat section caught her just below the eye. She clutched her face and sat down with a thud on the nearest open bench.

"Christ! You could have blinded me." So much for gratitude. Now her face hurt.

"That's all you have to say to me?" the man snarled. "I saved your life."

The gunman lay crumpled on the ground, moaning, bits of chair lying around him.

"Saved my life?" Diana leapt to her feet and jabbed Hulking Man in the chest. "You didn't save my life. You gave me a black eye!"

Red and blue lights reflected on the walls inside the diner, and Diana heard a car door open and close behind her.

"Diana! Jesus, Mary, and Joseph! What is going on here?" Brigitte went immediately into cop mode. She handcuffed the man on the floor, then radioed for backup and EMS. All the while she glared at Diana. "I can't trust you to do even the simplest of tasks. All you had to do was order fish, for Christ's sake."

Diana stood contritely, waiting for a lull in her younger sister's explosive outburst.

"Well?" Brigitte demanded. "Are you going to explain yourself?"

Diana smiled hopefully. "I did order fish. I was waiting for it to be delivered when this brainiac"—she nudged the unconscious man on the floor—"came in waving a gun around like Jesse fucking James. What was I supposed to do? Let him take the money?"

"Yes! For the love of God, Di, he had a gun."

"He didn't know how to use it." Diana pointed to the gun. "Take a look at the safety. He was more likely to drop the cartridge out than shoot me."

Brigitte looked no less irritated, but slightly relieved. "What happened to your eye?"

"The big guy over there smashed a chair over this idiot's skull. One of the pieces caught me in the face."

Brigitte's shoulders convulsed with laughter. "You got clipped with flying debris? You've got to be kidding me."

"Keep laughing and I'll tell Mom what happened to that bottle of rum your sophomore year."

Brigitte's face transformed instantly. Their mother was not to be trifled with. "I'm more interested to know what you're going to tell Russell on Tuesday morning."

Russell was their six-year-old nephew. For some unfathomable reason, he had asked Diana to come to his school to talk about her career. It wasn't career day or anything like that, just show-and-tell. But how could she say no to puppy-dog eyes?

"That's almost a week away. It'll fade by then."

"You'll still have to explain it to Mom and Dad on Sunday."

"Fuck." Diana wondered if Bernie's would supply her with a bag of ice.

The would-be bandit moaned from his manacled position on the floor. Brigitte eyed him warily. "Christ. We'll have to wait for EMS to take him in."

Diana's stomach rumbled and she debated the virtues of eating while waiting for help to arrive. She decided against it. No reason to appear crass. She sidled over to an open table near the door. Brigitte wouldn't sit, not while she was in official cop mode. That would be disrespectful to her uniform and, therefore, her position as peacekeeper. She took her duties seriously, just like her father.

"They're sending Ramirez," Brigitte said.

"Angel's coming?" Diana flinched at how pathetic the question sounded.

Angel Ramirez was Brigitte's ex-partner and hell on wheels. She looked better in a uniform than any one woman had a right to. She was also responsible for throwing Diana's tender heart on the 'L' tracks right as a train was passing by. Amazing in bed and liked everyone to know it firsthand.

"I radioed for backup. She responded."

As if on cue, Angel slanted her car into the open space in front of Bernie's, leaving room for the ambulance on her tail.

She walked—a cocky little strut that always made Diana think exceptionally naughty thoughts—up to Brigitte, her cop face firmly in place. Her skin was darker than usual. Summertime did that to her. Blond hair that should have been brown was pulled back in a ponytail and her teeth shone with their customary white brilliance.

Absolutely wonderful. Still beautiful. And evil. Don't forget evil.

Before they could discuss the situation, EMS muscled through the door and descended upon the handcuffed patient. With choreographed precision, they checked his vitals, stabilized his neck, and rolled him onto a stretcher. Then they were gone.

"That was quick." Brigitte looked mildly shell-shocked. "They're never that quick."

"There's a fire over on Rampart. They've called for all available EMS," Angel explained.

Diana didn't wait to hear the rest of their conversation. There was a paid-for beer summoning her from behind the counter. All she had to do was convince the girl o' many piercings to snap out of her daze long enough to pour it for her. Hell, maybe she could still get some fish after all. She approached the counter with what she hoped was a comforting smile.

"How about that fish?"

The girl nodded, mouth agape. She collected the order from under the warming light where it had been forgotten and mutely handed it to Diana.

"Thanks, you're a doll." Diana gave her a quick wink before walking outdoors where Brigitte had migrated with Angel.

The battered wooden picnic table Diana chose sported many names carved into the surface, in testimony of everlasting love. She realized she'd chosen to sit in the exact spot where she'd added her inscription: *D.C. + A.R.* within an uneven heart. She had been very naïve. Angel and Brigitte stood a few feet away reviewing Brigitte's notes on the incident.

"I forgot the drinks. I'll be right back." Diana stood abruptly and retreated to the safety of Bernie's.

When she returned, Angel was leaning against the back of Brigitte's patrol car with the same casual sensuality that had lured Diana in four years ago. They turned in unison as Diana set Brigitte's water on the table. She took several gulps of her lager and clutched the half-empty pint like her life depended on it. Seeing Angel always left her nerves a little tilted on edge. The cool glass and light amber liquid had an illogically calming effect.

"Diana," Angel said in greeting, "you look good. Except the shiner, of course. How you been?"

"Fine." Diana marveled at her ability to speak. Unbelievable. "And you?"

Okay, so it wasn't sparkling conversation or witty repartee, but at least words came out of her mouth. Words that didn't include things like: *You evil, heinous bitch! How can you stand there looking so good and acting like nothing happened?* It was a proud moment.

Angel turned back to Brigitte, all business again. "I'll follow up at the ER. That way you can enjoy your fish."

"Works for me. I'll do the paperwork when I get back." Brigitte held the top edge of Angel's door as Angel swung her legs into the car.

Angel tilted her head toward Diana. "Good to see you again, Di. I've missed you."

Diana simply arched her eyebrows in disbelief. That easy charm wasn't going to work a second time. Not a chance. She gave a little half wave as Angel pulled away from the curb and watched the retreating car until it rounded the corner three blocks up.

"Sit down and stop staring. You look like a fool." Brigitte drank some water.

Diana dropped roughly into her chair.

"I can't believe she still gets to you like that. How long has it been?"

"Not long enough." Diana drained her beer and wished for another.

Brigitte snapped her fingers in front of Diana's eyes. "Focus on me now. How often do we get to enjoy lunch, just the two of us, without the rest of the family popping up?"

That was a good point. She and Brigitte saw each other every Sunday at their parents' house when the entire family gathered to share a meal. The tradition had started when Diana's oldest brother, Maxwell, moved out years ago. They all should have been grateful for the extra room in the house created by his absence. Instead, the loss upset the balance of organized chaos that made their home function. The advent of Sunday dinner didn't eliminate the sadness they all felt, but it lessened it. Her parents said if they had their way, all of their children would stay at home forever. Empty-nest syndrome took on a whole new level of meaning in their close-knit Irish-Catholic family.

"Focused." Diana forced her eyes wide open and stared directly at Brigitte. "On you. Talk to me."

In response, Brigitte threw a fry at Diana's face, smacking her in the exact spot the chair had earlier. The swollen flesh screamed in protest. Diana winced and clamped her hand over her eye. "I have got to get some ice for this thing."

"Do you want to file assault charges against…" Brigitte consulted her notes. "Duane Ronaldson?"

"Are you serious? Of course not. He was trying to do the right thing. My face just got in the way."

They paused as footsteps approached their table. Pierced girl stood a few feet away looking for all the world like a scared twelve-year-old.

"I thought you might want this." She thrust a bag filled with ice at Diana. "For your eye."

Diana thanked her and took the bag. The girl retreated, stumbling as she attempted to walk away while still staring at Diana.

Brigitte laughed. "I think she likes you."

"I think she's scared of me." Diana held the ice gingerly to her face and took a bite of halibut. Even at room temperature the fish tasted wonderful. "Tell me about work. Any interesting cases?"

"The detectives are talking about a possible serial killer," Brigitte said with an air of satisfaction. She liked impressing her big sister with "inside" information.

"Really? Here? In Chicago?" Diana knew that her fellow citizens of Chicago were killing each other off at an ever-increasing rate, but a real-deal serial killer…that was a severe escalation from your average crime of passion, and still rare.

"Yeah. Hold on." Brigitte reached through the open window and grabbed the newspaper from the front seat of her patrol car. "Here's the write-up on it."

The paper was folded over to page three, where a short article discussed an ongoing investigation into several murders the police felt might be linked. The victims were all male. The most recent had happened two nights ago. This victim's name hadn't been released yet, just the fact that he'd been stabbed to death in his home.

"I'm surprised it doesn't say more," Diana remarked. "The media lives for this kind of thing."

Brigitte popped a piece of fish in her mouth. "I couldn't believe it either. But so far that's it. How 'bout you? Anything interesting going on in the world of insurance fraud?"

"I'm wrapping up one case now. Typical stuff. Guy gets in a bad spot financially. Decides to make a quick buck off his insurance. This guy was smarter than most, though. He actually hid the merchandise and didn't involve the police."

"I thought no one could get paid without a police report."

"I didn't say he got paid. But he's not in jail, either. You people respond to false police reports, unlike false insurance claims."

"Ah, he dodged that bullet. So he's only half stupid."

"On that note, I should get back to the office. See what other dastardly deeds I can uncover."

Diana gave Brigitte a brief hug and dropped the evidence of their lunch, including the melted bag of ice, into the nearby trash can. Diana's phone rang as she got into her car. She flipped it open. "Collins."

Her boss, Jeter, never wasted time on small talk. "I need you back at the office. I have a new case for you."

"On my way." She blew a kiss at her sister and pulled away from the curb. It was proving to be a very interesting day indeed.

Chapter Two

The obituary notice was small, without embellishment. It didn't mention the way Charles Stewart lived his life and certainly didn't describe the way he died. Ali pulled her hair back into a loose ponytail as she read the details. She no longer expected her demons to die along with the predators she tracked down. The best she could hope for was to smother her overwhelming despair and regret for lost innocence. She took a deep breath, inviting the cleansing scent of sage to chase away her unwanted emotions. A familiar detachment washed over her and she was ready to begin.

The eleven by eleven scrapbook was almost full. Ali had selected it because of the rich, black leather cover. She'd bought the album from a vendor on Canal Street. Solid and sturdy, it inspired confidence and promised to keep her secrets within. The pages bulged with the burden of her history, and it was time to add one more testimonial. She smoothed latex gloves over her hands and snapped the cap off the razor-sharp blade of an X-Acto knife. With quick, precise motions, she cut the short piece from the newspaper and held it up to the light to inspect the edges. Satisfied that there were no rough bits and no burrs, Ali set the square of paper on the table next to another, slightly larger piece of newsprint. She moved her attention to a second newspaper, repeating her motions to secure an identical set of articles. One for her scrapbook, the other for delivery tomorrow.

The first article conveyed that the police had discovered the body of Charles Stewart lying in a pool of blood. The scene was described with cool indifference, no attention given to the possible cause. The police, the article said, had no suspects in this apparent crime of passion.

The newspaper said nothing about Charles Stewart's twenty-year-old stepdaughter, who did not attend his funeral. It also didn't comment on the three fifty-five-minute therapy sessions she participated in each week and that the reason for the treatment was the systematic sexual abuse she'd endured, starting at age ten, from the only man she'd ever called Daddy.

Ali pasted the clippings into her scrapbook and returned it to the top shelf of the bookcase, a floor-to-ceiling monstrosity built into one wall of the small apartment. Aside from her scrapbook and a small, framed photo of her parents, and another of her sister, the unit was completely barren.

She returned to the table, took a plain sheet of white paper from a ream of printer stock, and wrote in large, even block letters with a fat, black marker:

He Will Have No More Victims

She folded the paper and slid it, with the clippings, into a long envelope. On the front, she wrote the name "Mona Stewart." For a few seconds she stared down at the name, and Mona's tear-streaked face swam over the page. She traced her index finger over the letters in a ritualistic tattoo. Three weeks ago, when Mona had checked into South Lake, the scars on her body had burned their way deep into Ali's subconscious. Ali had vowed then that Stewart's days of terrorizing his stepdaughter were over. That would be completed with the delivery of her package.

The act of committing her promise to paper strengthened the connection she felt to Mona. Ali placed the envelope on top of the neatly wrapped package sitting on the table and reflexively moved her right hand from her forehead to her chest. The sign of the cross was ingrained in her consciousness, but she stopped herself from completing the symbol. God was dead. If not, he had forsaken her long ago. She would not worship him now. Unable to completely deny her parents' teachings, she offered up a reluctant prayer that Mona Stewart be granted the peace Ali could never find.

❖

Diana was a few steps away from the elevator when the doors began to close. She lunged forward and thrust her hand into the quickly narrowing gap. If she missed this elevator, she would be forced to contemplate the benefits of huffing and puffing her way up sixteen flights of stairs rather than riding in comfort in the oh-so-speedy express elevator. Tight pants or not, she just wasn't interested in making that kind of tough decision this late in the day. Best to get upstairs and see exactly what reason Jeter had for summoning her.

"Jesus H. Christ! Hold the elevator."

The doors closed tight on her hand, clamping down hard enough to make her wish she'd never conceived of the idea of putting her hand in their path in the first place, then they popped back open with an indignant ding.

The elevator was already filled to overflowing, but Diana was not one to be easily deterred. She pointed to the large number fifteen on the capacity placard with what she hoped was a knowing smile and pushed into the crowd. She had no idea how many people were actually jammed in the metal box, but took a chance that no one would take the time to count.

"Ya know, Collins, a normal person would wait for the next one." Kyle Dempsey, an admin from her office, stood closest to the elevator buttons. Sixteen was already lit.

"Why in the world would I wait for the next one when this one wasn't full yet?" Diana pressed herself tightly against the closed door. The man behind her was in desperate need of some remedial personal hygiene lessons, and her nose violently protested the cramped quarters. Perhaps waiting would have been better. "Besides, Jeter called me in. You know how he doesn't like to wait." Diana tried to hold her breath.

The car jarred to a halt at the tenth floor and Diana moved aside to let the smelly man depart, along with three other passengers. When the doors slid shut again, Diana let her breath out with a whoosh. She heard several other people do the same.

"So, why'd the big man summon you?" Kyle asked.

Diana turned slightly to face him. "I don't—"

"Holy shit! Di, what the hell happened to your eye?"

Diana examined her face in the mirror and frowned at her reflection. "There was an unfortunate incident involving an idiot with a gun, coupled with an idiot with a chair." She gingerly touched her cheek. "My face got in the middle of it."

The doors slid open on the sixteenth floor and Diana stepped into the lobby of Carter and Lowe, the fraud investigation group she worked for. Kyle followed her out of the elevator.

"From anyone else that explanation would just raise more questions. With you it makes perfect sense," he said dryly.

They headed down the long corridor that led to the admin bullpen and the investigators' offices. Kyle veered off when they reached the large open space in the middle of the floor that housed the administrative staff. Carter and Lowe had adopted an open floor plan for this area several years ago for efficiency. Not for the first time, Diana said a silent prayer of thanks that her office had four real walls and a door.

"Later." She gave Kyle a salute with military precision. Five-star generals would be jealous of her form.

"Try to avoid guns and chairs for the rest of the day."

Diana winked over her shoulder at him. "Sound advice. You do the same."

She'd almost made it to her office when her boss called out to her from an open conference room. "Collins! Get in here."

Splendid. He was obviously having another one of his good days.

She stepped into the room and said, "What's up, boss?" He liked it when she called him boss and, given his current mood, flattery couldn't hurt.

Two senior investigators, Braxton Rinaldi and Bob White, were seated at the large, oval table, reviewing a case file. The sight of them evoked a mental gulp from Diana. She'd been summoned to a meeting with the two heaviest hitters in the firm. Occasions like this generally proved to be career defining.

Jeter Lewis gestured for her to sit. He did a double take and stared at her for several seconds. "What in the hell happened to your face?"

Diana sank into the plush leather chair next to Braxton, a friend and mentor. "Well, you sure know how to make a girl feel pretty."

Braxton and Jeter had transferred to the Chicago branch of Carter and Lowe from New Orleans. Jeter worked hard to hide his accent, but Braxton let hers flow like wild honey.

Braxton slid a folder in front of Diana. "Pay him no mind, sugar.

Give this a good going over. You're not here to entertain Jeter with stories of your wild life."

"That's exactly why I'm worried," Jeter said. "I have to send her to do an interview and she looks like she's been in a bar fight."

Diana's ears perked up. "I'm doing an interview?"

After seven years with the firm, she had built up a reputation for being relentless when it came to recovering her target. She was not, however, known for her interviewing skills. Braxton and Bob were experts. She flipped open the file, wondering where all this was going.

"We've got a particularly bothersome case, and you seem to be the best person to conduct this interview." Jeter smoothed his thumb and forefinger over his mustache, a habit Diana found supremely annoying. "First, tell me what happened to your face."

Diana barely stopped herself from rolling her eyes. To avoid having to ignore this question every ten minutes for the next several days, she answered, "I stopped a robbery in progress at Bernie's. Then there was an incident with a flying chair."

Jeter did not appear impressed. That was okay. Neither was she by his stalling tactic.

"Why me?" she asked. "The other people in this room are infinitely more qualified to do an interview."

Jeter straightened his tie and squirmed in his seat. "You and the subject share…ah…common interests."

Common interests? That could mean anything. They were both women, they both grew up in cop families, they both had a thing for fast cars, they both recently stopped a chair in motion with their face. The possibilities were endless.

"What exactly does that mean?"

Braxton patted her hand. "Sugar, let me explain. I did the original interview with the mother. High maintenance, that one. While I was there, I met the daughter. In my very hetero perspective, I think she plays for your team. This horse's ass thinks that means the two of you will instantly bond."

She flipped through the open file and guided Diana to the picture of both mother and daughter. A young woman with peroxide blond spiky-dykey hair stood next to an older woman with shoulder-length brown hair and soft laugh lines around her eyes. Unless Diana's gaydar was malfunctioning in a major way, Braxton was right about the daughter. Still, Jeter's immediate conclusion that they would have some sort of instant camaraderie was asinine at best.

"So she'll spill her guts or something?" Diana asked, her head spinning with the insanity of Jeter's logic. "Hell, odds are I already know her, right?"

Jeter nodded enthusiastically. "Yes, that's it exactly."

Diana searched for a fact sheet on the young woman. "What's her name?"

"Mona Stewart. *Do* you know her?" Jeter's face was the perfect blend of sincerity and triumph. Braxton smothered a giggle in her hand.

Diana decided to play with her boss. Not a smart career move, but Jeter was being so blatantly stupid that he deserved some grief. She abandoned the file in favor of her PDA, opening it to her calendar.

"Mona? Are you sure?" She dropped her PDA on the table. "Holy shit, I slept with her last weekend."

"Seriously?"

"No. For the love of Christ, Jeter. I don't know every dyke in this city and I sure as hell haven't slept with all of them."

Braxton slapped her hand against her leg and laughed long and loud. Jeter had the decency to turn red.

Bob snickered. His testosterone was running amok through the room. "Collins does the interview, but I want to watch."

Diana considered her options. Fly across the table and introduce Bob to her manicure, up close and personal? Nah, her hand was still aching from the last time she couldn't control the urge to smack the crap out of someone. Sarcastic rejoinder? Definitely a better choice.

"Why don't you interview the girl, Bob? After all, she just needs a good man to turn her around, right?"

Braxton patted her hand. "Now, now, sugar, play nice."

"Diana, listen." Jeter pulled his tie loose. "This case is big money. High profile. We can't afford to fuck it up."

The room was heavy with serious quiet. They all broke rules, acted inappropriately, said things they shouldn't. But when it came to the bottom line, there was no more dissension. They would do whatever it took to protect the firm's reputation.

"If there is any chance at all of breaking this nut open..." Jeter sighed. "Well, let's just say I'm not ruling anything out."

"Sugar, I got nowhere with the mother. We need whatever edge we can get with this case, even if it means exploiting the lesbian connection."

Diana considered Braxton's observation. When Diana joined the firm, she had been very open about her sexuality. Braxton had immediately taken her under her wing and provided guidance throughout her career. Never once did the fact that Diana was a lesbian come into play. For Braxton to bring it up now showed how desperate they were with this case.

"Tell me what I need to know," Diana said.

Braxton summed up the Stewart family, starting with the origination of the insurance policy for the ancient jeweled katana and ending with its theft and the death of Charles Stewart. Her rundown was professional and succinct. It also offered no insight beyond the paper in Diana's hand.

"What else? Give me something to work with."

"She's twenty years old, a business major at the University of Chicago. The policy holder turned murder victim, Charles Stewart, was her stepfather." Braxton took a sip of water. "About a month ago she moved out of her parents' house. Kind of odd."

"Why? I moved out when I went to college, too." Diana's childhood home was not big enough to hold her entire family. Two parents and four children crammed into a three-bedroom ranch style. She'd left to keep from killing Brigitte. They'd shared a room starting three months after Brigitte was born, and Diana's threshold of tolerance for her annoying younger sister had been sorely taxed.

"Yes, but she moved in the middle of the summer quarter, and your parents don't live on North Astor." Braxton referred to a street filled with mansions in one of Chicago's most affluent neighborhoods, Gold Coast. Diana's family home in Norwood Park was worlds apart from where Mona Stewart grew up.

"I see your point. Anything else?"

"I asked for a spare picture of Mr. Stewart. The only ones they had didn't include Mona." She shrugged. "It just seemed strange, that's all. There were pictures of her with her mom, but none that included him."

Now that was interesting.

"Don't suppose you asked about it?" Diana knew it was too much to hope for, but she had to know for sure.

"No, sugar, I didn't."

Jeter looked skeptical. "So Mr. Stewart was the official camera holder. Nothing unusual about that."

Diana made a notation to ask about it. "Hmm. Perhaps." She tapped her pen against her front teeth. "What else?"

"I really don't know anything else about the daughter. The mom is a real head case." Braxton made a circle motion with her index finger next to her temple, the universal sign for looney-tooney. "She filed the claim before contacting the morgue about her husband's body. If I were in a similar situation, I'd be thinking about funeral arrangements, not insurance policies. She's very wound up in herself. Not a whole lot of room for anything else."

"Do we suspect that she took the sword?" Diana asked.

"We don't think she's a suspect, but we really have no idea. The police aren't sharing that information." Braxton flipped through the file and pulled out a glossy photo of a gold katana. The handle was encrusted with diamonds and rubies, and the blade had a highly detailed etching of a flying dragon battling a tiger.

"Wow, the details are amazing." Diana flipped the photo over. "Eight hundred thousand. For a sword." She blew out a low whistle. Seven years and she still wasn't used to the astronomical price tags attached to the property they insured. "To think, I was happy with my Hot Wheels collection."

"It'll be worth more now." Jeter's voice took on a gleeful, Scrooge McDuck quality.

The other investigators nodded their heads sagely.

Diana hated it when they acted like that, smug and all-knowing. The sword's value would appreciate naturally over time, of course, and there would be an immediate spike due to the theft. That always happened. Still, her colleagues seemed to be overdramatic. "What am I missing?" she asked.

"The police believe this weapon was used to kill him," Jeter explained.

That would definitely influence the value. A tainted history always upped the ante for weapons. Still, if the sword was evidence, that should end their involvement.

"It'll go right into evidence lockup when we recover, so why are we still pursuing this?" Diana took the optimistic view that recovery was certain. With the talent in this room, failure wasn't on the agenda. This was a new scenario for Diana. She'd tracked down stolen property before, but never a weapon that had been stolen and then used in the commission of another crime.

"That's true," Bob said. "But finding the sword saves us from paying out a settlement. It's left to the original property owner, in this case Charles Stewart's widow, Traci, to petition the court for the return of her property."

Braxton scooped up the papers and returned them to the file. She flipped the cover closed and rested her hand on top. "You have the basics. I want you to form your own opinions about the Stewart family, then we can compare notes. If there's anything inconsistent, we'll catch it."

"Hell, no." Diana reached for the file. No way was she going in to that interview without more information. "I need to be properly prepped."

"Calm down, shug." Braxton refused to release her hold on the file. "The cold, hard reality is that interviewing isn't your greatest skill, prepped or not. We just want you to talk to the girl."

Ouch. "Thanks for the vote of confidence." Diana didn't like Braxton's succinct summary of her shortcomings, but the assessment was accurate. Dammit.

Jeter stepped in as the mediating voice of reason. "You know Braxton didn't intend that as an attack. Your strengths just lie elsewhere."

Diana nodded once in acknowledgment. That was all her ego would afford her. "So, where is Mona living now?"

"In an apartment on Lansing Street."

So maybe she wasn't crazy about her mom, either. Some people would move home after the death of a parent, even a stepparent they didn't like. Especially under scary circumstances like home invasion and robbery. To choose Lansing Street over a mansion on North Astor was a sure sign that there was more going on than Mona stretching the wings of independence while attending college.

Diana stood. "Come on, Bob, let's go introduce ourselves."

Braxton lightly touched Diana's arm, stopping her from rising. "Wait a minute, shug, why you bringing Bob to the party?"

Bob was out of his chair like a shot. "Too late, Braxton, your protégé just invited me to the prom and left you standing on the wall." He made a tsking noise. "And after you got all dressed up and everything."

That's when Diana noticed that Braxton was wearing her tailored ivory suit. It was one of two she wore when she conducted important interviews. The other was peach. She said gentle colors threw people off, encouraged them to reveal more than they intended.

"You're getting ahead of yourself, Di." Jeter redirected them. "Bob has a job of his own to do. He'll be looking for the sword in all the usual places." He snapped his portfolio closed and stood. "Braxton, you're with Diana."

"Come on, shug." Braxton led the way out of the conference room. "Time to put a suit on you."

After Diana quickly changed into one of the three suits hanging in her office closet, they headed across town to Mona Stewart's Lansing Street apartment. Diana had no idea what Jeter thought she'd have in common with a rich baby dyke hiding out in a downwardly mobile neighborhood. One who might or might not have information about a missing sword and her newly dead stepdaddy, no less, but she was about to find out.

Chapter Three

Lansing Street was a run-down collection of broken windows, broken streetlights, and broken dreams. Diana hadn't seen the house Mona Stewart grew up in, but she knew the locale. She couldn't begin to imagine what would motivate a young woman to move from an upscale area to this part of town.

"Nice place." Braxton stepped over a pop can bong lying on the sidewalk. At least it wasn't a crack pipe.

"Are you sure it's safe to leave my car on the street?" Even though the Mercedes was a company vehicle, Diana was reluctant to see it chopped for parts. There would be a never-ending pile of paperwork to complete if that happened.

"Look at it this way, They'll go after that Jag first." Braxton inclined her head toward the XKR convertible parked two spaces up.

Diana used a pen to push the intercom button that would alert Mona to their presence. She made a mental note to toss the pen when she got back to the office. She had a high tolerance for yuck, but this whole neighborhood went well beyond her boundaries. A buzzer sounded and the electronic lock on the entrance to the building disengaged with a loud popping sound.

Diana raised an eyebrow. "After you."

Mona's apartment was on the top floor of the four-story walk-up. The baby dyke from the photo held the door open about three inches, the chain still in place. Diana wondered who she thought that chain would stop. It granted a false sense of security at best. Braxton took the lead and introduced herself, producing a business card for the girl to inspect. Finally Mona closed the gap, slid the chain free, and invited them into the one-room apartment.

An older version of Mona stood next to the couch. Traci Stewart.

"Mrs. Stewart, how lovely to see you again." If Braxton was surprised by her presence, she didn't show it. "This is my colleague, Diana Collins."

Diana extended her hand to the mom first. "Mrs. Stewart. It's nice to meet you, though I wish it were under better circumstances."

Traci Stewart had one of those wimpy "I'm too delicate to grip anything" handshakes. "Please, call me Traci."

She giggled in a way that some would no doubt find demure and enticing. Diana found it nauseating. "And you must be Mona." She smiled and shook Mona's hand. It was a nice, firm handshake, filled with dyke confidence.

"I was just trying to talk some sense into Mona. It's time for her to move home now." Traci jingled her keys nervously in her left hand. The Jaguar emblem flashed in the late afternoon sunlight. As if it had finally occurred to her that the investigators must have some reason to come calling, she asked, "What are you doing here? I thought we'd answered all your questions."

Diana flipped open her file and referred to the notes. "Actually, Traci, it says here that you were interviewed, but never your daughter."

"She doesn't know anything else." Traci spoke with an extra dose of sweet, complete with batted eyelashes.

"I'll tell you anything you want," Mona said. "Just make her go away."

Traci whipped her head around to face her daughter, her eyes bulging. "Watch your mouth, young lady."

Mona's spunk was impressive. She wasn't afraid to talk to the big, bad insurance investigator, or a close facsimile, alone. Diana turned to Braxton and Traci. "Perhaps it would be better if I spoke with Mona alone."

Traci frowned at her daughter, her brows furrowed tight. "I don't know—"

"Mom, it's not like I know anything anyway. Just go."

Braxton, on cue, held open the front door and gestured for Traci to precede her into the hallway. "We'll just grab a cup of coffee."

"Well," Traci was hesitant in spite of her daughter's reassurances, "if you're sure."

Mona patted her mom's hand and for a brief moment looked every bit the loving daughter. "I'm sure, Mom," she said gently. "It's okay. You can go."

Diana saw them out and chose the kitchen table as the place to conduct the interview. Hard surface. Easier to take notes. "Okay, Mona, let's get down to business. Tell me what you know about the robbery and your father's death."

Mona went to the dorm-size refrigerator in the corner of her studio apartment and pulled out two bottles of water. She handed one to Diana and cracked the other one open before sitting at the opposite side of the table. "Let's get one thing straight before we go any further. My father died eighteen years ago when I was two. That man Charles Stewart was not my father. He was an asshole."

Diana eyed Mona levelly across the short expanse of table. Maybe she was better at this interview thing than she thought. Mona obviously knew all sorts of things about her stepdad that her mom hadn't shared with Braxton. Maybe she even knew a little about a missing sword. Diana allowed the silence to fill the room. Extreme declarations, like the one Mona had just made about her stepfather, were inevitably followed by a flood of explanation. Braxton had taught her that. In fact, Braxton had taught her everything she knew about interview technique. There was no way she'd be sitting in this room alone with Mona Stewart, conducting what Jeter believed to be a critical interview, without Braxton's endorsement. No fucking way, and that weighed heavy on Diana.

She watched Mona squirm in her chair and chew the earpiece of her sunglasses. The silence stretched and grew. Diana wanted to rush in and rescue Mona from the pressure of full disclosure. More than that, however, she wanted Braxton to be proud of her. So she waited, trying hard to look cool, like she wasn't about to crawl out of her skin. She didn't blink and she didn't flinch. She stared calmly at Mona, knowing eventually she would crack. Everybody did.

Mona took a wobbly breath and pointed at Diana's eye. "You look like you lost the fight."

Diana's cheek throbbed but she forced her hands to remain still, to deny their inherent need to comfort the bruised flesh. She contemplated

Mona's statement and wished for an ice pack. *Respond? Don't respond?* Before she could arrive at a conclusion, Mona spoke again.

"It didn't start out that way, you know?" A tear trickled down her cheek and she pulled a brushed silver cigarette case from her pocket. She opened and closed it rhythmically, the steady click of the clasp digging at Diana's brain.

"No, Mona, I don't know." Diana stretched out a hand, indicating the case. "May I?"

Mona seemed a little surprised, but dropped the silver into her open palm. Diana resisted the urge to hurl the annoying thing out the window. Instead, she pulled out an unfiltered Gitanes Brunes. The fire-cured tobacco had a bite most Americans couldn't tolerate. She'd never been cool enough to smoke—the acrid burn sent her into fits—but two weeks with a foreign exchange student named Monique had taught her about the dark tobacco wrapped in textured paper. Diana held the Gitanes out to Mona and pulled the matching silver lighter from the case. She needed Mona to relax, get comfortable, and tell her all about Daddy the asshole. She flicked the lighter once and held it up in a move she'd perfected during too much time spent at seedy little bars, before the ban on indoor smoking. More than once it had earned her a playmate for the night.

Mona held the tip to the flame and inhaled long and deep, her eyes half closing as a haze of smoke gathered around her. She blew out a long plume of smoke and relaxed back into her chair, all her previous tension gone. Diana returned the lighter to the case. *CRS* was engraved on the top. *Interesting.*

"What do you want to know?" Mona held her cigarette between her index and middle fingers of her right hand. The pose looked practiced, intended to be ultra-cool. It might have worked if her voice didn't harbor a slight tremor.

"Everything." Diana pushed Record on the digital recorder in her pocket, another of the little details Braxton had taught her never to overlook. "Everything you want to tell me." She waited for Mona's eyes to meet hers. "And everything you don't."

That was a good line. Diana made a mental note to remember it for later.

"My mom married him when I was three, a year after my real dad died. I don't even remember him. Charles adopted me. Mom says he was a dream come true. It's hard for a single woman with a baby to find a good man." Mona's eyes darkened. "Harder than she knows."

The blend of wounded little girl and proud woman battled across Mona's face and chilled Diana. The realization that her interview subject might not be an innocent bystander in all of this tugged at her brain. "Mona, before we go any further, there is something I need to know." Diana paused a moment, weighing the consequences of her next question. "Did you kill your stepfather?"

Diana heard a key in the front door. What the hell was Braxton doing coming back so soon? She looked behind her and saw the door had cracked a scant inch but didn't open any further. She could hear voices, presumably Traci and Braxton, discussing something, the tone low and urgent.

"No. I didn't kill the bastard, but I should have." Mona stared at the gap between the door and the frame, never blinking. She seemed to be challenging her mother, daring her to deny an ugly reality.

Diana wanted to look away, give them a moment of privacy, even if it was interrupted by space and a façade of separation, but she couldn't. She stared at Mona, waiting for the train wreck she knew was coming, unable and unwilling to stop it.

"He didn't do anything until I turned ten. Do you remember my tenth birthday, Ma? How happy I was? You guys gave me that horse, Raven. Remember? That night he came to my room. On my fucking birthday." She bit back a mirthless laugh. "Fucking. That's right."

A muffled sob reached in from the hall through the crack in the door, followed by Braxton's voice urging, "Let's wait out here a moment, Traci."

Diana wondered fleetingly if Traci already knew about the crimes committed against her daughter. Had she found out and taken action? Diana doubted it, and that gave her a moment's pause. Protecting your children should be a mandatory clause in the mother-child contract.

Mona stood and moved closer to the door, addressing her mother through the wood. "You were mad as hell because I never rode that damn horse. Never. I couldn't. The price was too high. Didn't matter. I still paid."

The cigarette glowed red at the tip, behind a long, dangling ash. Its fragile purchase faltered and the ash floated to the cheap linoleum in slow motion, scattering on impact. Mona took another shaky drag.

"You never believed me. Never. And he never stopped. He laughed when I cried. He taunted me. He said you loved him more and that you thought I was a dirty, lying whore. I was thirteen when he said that." Mona let her head fall against the wall with a dull thunk. "Thirteen. That was the last time I cried over him."

The silence ratcheted clean over oppressive and landed somewhere between smothering and downright homicidal. Diana squirmed.

Mona turned away from the door abruptly and faced Diana again. "So I didn't kill him. But I'd sure like to thank whoever did."

Before Diana could respond, Traci Stewart burst through the door, her face twisted with hurt and accusation. "You ungrateful little bitch. How can you say those terrible things about your father? He loved you."

Mona snorted. "Yeah, he loved me all right."

Traci lunged at her daughter and Diana barely had time to position herself between the two women. She placed both hands on Traci's chest and pushed her back, away from Mona. The door was directly behind Traci and still open. Diana said a prayer that Braxton would take control of the flailing woman.

Braxton's head appeared over the top of Traci's and she wrapped her arms around Traci's midsection from behind. Braxton was not a large woman, but she did her time at the gym. She steered Traci into the room and flung her onto the couch. When Traci attempted to get up, Braxton pushed her back down. "Get a hold of yourself."

Braxton cleared her throat and lifted one finger toward the opposite corner of the room. Diana understood the message instantly. It was time to stop focusing on the disgraceful spectacle Traci Stewart was making of herself and pay some attention to the sobbing girl in the corner. She was sitting on the floor, her knees pulled in tight, her shoulders shuddering violently.

Cursing her lack of sensitivity, Diana knelt next to Mona. She didn't know how to comfort the wounded child before her. Every training class she'd ever gone to echoed in her brain. Never, *never* touch someone when conducting an interview. She ignored the warning bells and instead heeded the compassionate advice of her mother: When someone is hurt, you do what you can to help. Period.

She pulled Mona into an embrace, and Mona buried her head in the crook between Diana's shoulder and neck. They sat there long enough for Diana's legs to cramp up and then go numb. The fabric of her shirt grew damp with Mona's tears, and for once, Diana didn't feel compelled to carry the conversation or even make small talk. Traci sat immobile, watching her daughter seek comfort in the arms of a stranger. The fight seemed to have drained from her, flowing out with her silent tears.

Diana's heart ached for both women. Maybe Traci had always known, if not consciously. Maybe not. Now, however, the illusion of normalcy was shattered beyond repair.

Mona took a deep, unsteady breath and turned a tear-streaked face to Diana. "Thank you." She placed a warm, gentle kiss on Diana's cheek and attempted to stand. Her legs quivered and Diana swiftly steadied her.

Porcupine pinpricks screamed up her own legs as she rose. "Mine don't want to work either."

Mona offered a weak half-smile. "I don't know who killed him, and I don't know who took the sword."

Diana nodded with sorrowful understanding. She'd delved into this young woman's painful past for nothing. Still, the professional Diana, the one who collected a paycheck from Carter and Lowe, reflexively pulled a business card from her pocket and held it out to Mona. "Please call me if you think of anything that might help us."

The look on Mona's face said "fat chance." She was grateful her stepdad was dead. Even if she had information, Diana had a feeling she wouldn't share it.

"I'm not a cop," she said, "My job is to recover stolen merchandise. Period."

A light flickered in Mona's eyes and she looked like she was about to speak, then it dimmed and she shook her head. She took the card and said, "Thanks."

Diana knew she should press harder. Braxton would have. But she couldn't bring herself to do it. This young woman had been through more than enough emotional upheaval for one day. Hell, more than enough for a lifetime, if her story was true, and it certainly looked that way. Diana couldn't erase her suffering. She could only offer a reprieve for the moment.

"Call me if you think of anything." She hesitated, knowing she'd already crossed one line today. "Or if you just want to talk."

Mona nodded and retreated to the only other room in the apartment, the bathroom.

Diana slid her notepad and file into her attaché. "It's time to go."

Braxton helped Traci up with a look that promised there was no option but to go with them. As they filed out of the apartment, Diana caught a glimpse of herself in the wall mirror. Her eye was purple and puffy and getting worse by the minute. She gently touched the abused skin. The bruise would heal eventually, but the kind of scars Mona carried might never go away.

❖

Ali placed her hand on the long package in the passenger seat next to her. It was wrapped with tight precision in nondescript brown butcher paper. A legal-size envelope was taped to the side. The first time she'd made a delivery like this she was an excited, uncontrolled mess. Too eager to wait and make sure it was safe, no witnesses. She'd ducked behind a corner in the nick of time, barely escaping before the police arrived, package undelivered. She'd sneaked back later, under the cover of darkness, and left it at the door. That night had taught her patience.

She grabbed a crumpled pack of Marlboros out of the console and set the alarm on the car before heading over to the battered picnic table a few feet away. The park across the road from Mona Stewart's apartment was a haven for prostitutes and drug dealers. Parents were afraid to bring their children here to play, and all that remained of a once-vibrant playground was the skeletal remains of a defunct swing set, a teeter-totter that had long ago rusted in place, and several wooden tables. They were big and heavy, the kind used in state parks for families on vacation. Now they were the tableau for more than one illicit business transaction.

Ali lit her cigarette. It was a perfect place to wait.

When the front door of Mona's building opened some time later, three women exited. Traci Stewart, Mona's mother, walked between two strangers. They had a brief conversation before she stalked over to her Jaguar. The other women waited next to a Mercedes until she drove away.

The younger one carried herself with the cocky self-assuredness of an athlete, her movements both graceful and aggressive. The combination was unsettling, yet intriguing. She opened the driver's door and looked directly at Ali, her eyes challenging from across the street. The heavy Chicago air grew razor sharp between them. Ali held her ground, refusing to blink, until the door of the Mercedes closed and the tinted glass blocked her view.

She took a long drag on her cigarette, inviting the smoke in like an old friend. It was the hazy constant from her youth, the only thing she'd brought with her when she fled Colombia. The memory of Ricardo's long cigarillos mixed into the smoke and stayed with her into the night. She chased them away with a wave of her hand and a shake of her head, but they always returned. She wondered what she would do if they ever stopped visiting her after all these years.

The horizon changed from blue to golden orange before fading to black. No one else entered or left the building. Under the cover of night Ali left her sacrificial offering at the altar of Mona Stewart's closed door. She rang the bell and walked away, satisfied that Mona would be the one to find it.

CHAPTER FOUR

Heavy, static-laden buzzing sent Diana's thumping head into orbit. And it wouldn't stop. Finally she ripped the cord out of the outlet and flung the offensive noisemaker across the room. It shattered against the wall and covered the light blue carpet in fractured plastic and electronic pieces. She flopped back down against her pillow and threw an arm over her eyes. She promised, not for the first time, that she would stop drinking if the pounding in her head would just go away.

"Morning," a sleep-and-honey-laced voice greeted her from the other side of the bed. Oh hell, she wasn't alone.

"Morning." Diana peeled back one eyelid and peered out cautiously. Wild, curly blond hair, freckles, cute as hell smile. What was her name? Chrissy? Connie? Carrie? Fuck it all, she couldn't remember. She lifted the blanket, and what started out as a quick peek turned into a nice long look. They were both bare-ass naked. Nice tits and a tattoo low on her abdomen, off to the right a bit. The wheel of life.

The details of the room began announcing themselves to Diana, demanding recognition. Bright blue paint, glow in the dark stars on the ceiling, a giant aum painted on the wall opposite the bed. This wasn't her bedroom.

"Um. I think I broke your clock." Good thing she wasn't looking for an invitation to come back. Breaking essential electronics was no way to woo a woman.

Cami—that was her name—threw her head back and laughed. "It would appear so."

Diana threw back the blanket and climbed out of the bed. There was no time for modesty. She was meeting Braxton first thing, and tardiness was on the list of unforgivable sins in Braxton's world. She scooped her clothes up off the floor. She'd grab a shower and a fresh set of clothes when she got to work. Thank God for the gym in the building.

"I really need to go." She shoved her legs into yesterday's jeans, sans underwear. Her panties were nowhere to be found. She plucked her bra from the corner behind the door and struggled into it.

"Me, too." Cami smiled.

"Last night was great...I think." Diana pulled her white T-shirt over her head. "And I'd love to stay, but I have a meeting first thing this morning. I can't miss it."

Cami stretched and crawled out of bed. Naked, her long sleek limbs effortlessly graceful, she sauntered across to Diana. Her half-open blue eyes were dark with renewed lust as she traced the line of Diana's jaw with her forefinger. Sweet Jesus. Diana watched in awe as Cami captured her bottom lip between her teeth and released it slowly. She was late, late, late. Braxton was going to kill her. But all she wanted was to suck on that lip for days, see if it tasted as good as it looked.

Cami stopped just shy of brushing her lips against Diana's. Instead she placed a light kiss on the pulse point at the base of Diana's neck, holding her lips there as Diana's heart tumbled around inside her like an ambitious gymnast. Diana closed her eyes and tilted her head to the side, inviting Cami to linger just a little while longer. Warm breath tickled her skin, teasing her to sharp awareness. Cami's tongue trailed up until her lips were pressed against Diana's ear. Diana savored the tingle that raced down her spine. Damn, this woman was hot. She cursed her alcohol-induced amnesia. Thanks to Jose Cuervo and his friends salt and lime, she didn't remember a thing beyond ordering her first round. The details of picking Cami up at the Closet were well beyond her mental grasp.

"Last night was great. You enjoyed yourself," Cami whispered as she laced her fingers into Diana's. She brought Diana's hand to the apex of her thighs and exhaled. "You enjoyed me."

Diana skimmed her fingertips over the trimmed fair hair, evidence that Cami was a true blonde, all the while ignoring the voice screaming in the back of her head. She needed to go. Duty called. Her less conscientious self, the one that melted every time Cami's exhaled breath caressed her skin, dared her to go just a little farther. Why not enjoy the way this oh so fuckably hot woman felt under her touch?

Cami's breath was smooth, bordering on teasing. Diana took that as a personal challenge and stroked just a little lower, dipping her finger into the hot, wet folds of skin. Just barely enough to announce her intentions. Leaving enough room for the electric current to race between the tip of her finger and Cami's obviously eager clit. She liked the way Cami's body fit against her, pressed tight, clinging and begging for just a little more. She wanted to see her with her head thrown back, glistening with sweat as she cried out Diana's name.

Circus music rang out from the night table where her cell phone lay. Cami's fingers felt delicious tattooing dirty little secrets onto her back beneath her shirt, and Diana twitched with need. The phone kept ringing. *Fuck it all.* She released Cami and picked up. "Collins."

"Diana? Where the hell are you?" Braxton was angry. She only called Diana by her name when she was rightly and truly pissed off. "It's after eight."

The lust-induced haze instantly lifted. "What? Oh fuck."

"Sugar, kiss the flavor of the day good-bye and haul your sweet ass into work. Now."

Diana smiled. She loved it when Braxton talked dirty to her. "Sorry. I'm on my way." She stuffed her feet into her shoes without untying the laces. No socks in sight.

Braxton didn't say good-bye before disconnecting the call.

Diana turned her attention back to Cami and all her glorious nakedness. "I'm so fucking late. I really have to go." She pressed a fiery, unrepentant kiss against Cami's mouth. "Keys. I have keys somewhere." She patted her pockets and heard a familiar jingle. "Please tell me I drove here."

"You did."

"Thank God." Diana didn't want to contemplate being so drunk she didn't remember driving. She could lecture herself on her recklessness and disregard for the safety of others later, when she wasn't painfully hungover.

"Call me." Cami scribbled her number on a scrap of paper and slipped it into Diana's breast pocket.

They shared one last pounding kiss before Diana ran out the door.

❖

Diana tapped the steering wheel impatiently and cursed the traffic.

It never failed. The cars around her moved the slowest when she was in the biggest hurry. Damn Murphy and his laws anyway.

A Lincoln Navigator roared up next to her and merged into her lane without the courtesy of a blinker. Diana slammed her foot on the brake and her hand on the horn. "Motherfucker! Where the hell did you get your license?"

The driver of the giant SUV smiled pleasantly and waved. Diana gave her the finger. "Diana, are you there?" Her sister-in-law's cool voice was laced with concern.

Diana slid the cell phone into its holder in the dash and hit the speaker button, all without taking her eyes from the road. "Yeah, I'm here. Sorry, Grace." She kept a wary eye on the Navigator. "What's going on?"

Through the phone, she could hear strains of Chopin in the background. The romantic piano was in stark contrast to the churning noise of traffic.

"Hope I didn't call at a bad time?"

"No, it's not a bad time. I'm on the way to the office and traffic is a bitch."

"Maxwell and I wanted to talk to you all about your parents' anniversary." Grace's voice faltered.

Diana forced herself to focus on what Grace was saying. "I thought we were all going to talk about it on Sunday."

"We wanted to talk to you without the others."

"Yes?"

"Forty years is a really long time. Long enough that we think they deserve more than the usual party."

Diana could hear Grace tapping her pencil against her desk, a sure sign that she was nervous. "Just say it, Grace, and get it over with. It can't possibly be that big a deal."

"We want to send them on a cruise. It's not cheap, and the others don't have the financial resources to contribute the way we can, what with the kids and all. So we thought we should all pay according to our ability. If you want to send them on a cruise at all, that is." The words came out in a jumbled whoosh and landed in a heap in Diana's head.

"A cruise? To where? When? How much does it cost?" The rapid-fire questions left Diana's mouth as quickly as they entered her head. She knew from experience that Grace would be able to keep up with her and wouldn't be offended by the lack of formality.

"Wherever and whenever they want to go. I don't want the others to feel bad. Maxwell and I are in a better position to do this, that's all. And you don't have kids either."

As the official financial advisor to each of his siblings, Diana's brother Maxwell, Grace's husband, would definitely know who could afford what.

"Yes, it makes sense for us to pay the bulk of the expense, regardless of what gift we choose." Diana forced herself into the carpool lane and blew past the SUV. She flipped the driver the bird one more time as she slipped back into her original lane in front of the gas-guzzling kiddie-mobile.

The Navigator looked exactly like the vehicle her other sister-in-law, Rebecca, drove, and Diana felt a fleeting ripple of guilt. She wouldn't want Rebecca on the receiving end of her temper when driving, but Diana knew from experience that her sister-in-law's driving style resembled that of Mario Andretti not Mother Teresa. A closer look in the rearview mirror confirmed that the woman behind her was definitely not Rebecca. Her momentary concern passed and she tapped her brakes just to see if she could shake the peaceful smile off the other driver's face.

"She's got to be high," Diana muttered. "Nobody is that happy in this kind of traffic."

"What?" Grace was clearly confused. "You still with me, Di?"

"Sorry." Diana focused on what Grace had said. Cruise for her parents' anniversary. She actually liked the idea a lot. "I think it's a great plan. What's the problem?"

Grace sighed. "You know how sensitive Lucas is about money. Remember what happened last time we all went for dinner?"

Diana chuckled as she remembered the men battling over the bill. They both refused to relinquish their grip and, as a result, the check had torn into two pieces. They'd both stared at each other in chagrined disbelief as Diana and Grace snatched the dissected bill and paid the tab before they could continue to argue about it any further. "I say you and I talk to Brigitte and Rebecca without Lucas and Calvin present."

"Brilliant. I knew there was a reason I called you first."

Diana cut across two lanes of traffic and vowed, not for the first time, to turn in the company vehicle and pick up a pass for the 'L.'

Memory of a well-intentioned experiment with the city's elevated train—specifically the other passengers—kept Diana from making good on that promise. The one time she'd used that method of transit, two warring gangs had picked her train car to live out their own version of *West Side Story*. She was all for blowing off steam now and again, but she couldn't see the point of trying to kill someone just because he wore the wrong color. Thankfully no guns had been involved that day and Diana had made it out unscathed. Brigitte assured her that such confrontations were not the norm. Still, Diana didn't care to test the theory.

Her freeway exit was surprisingly clear of traffic, a phenomenon that rarely happened, and Diana sailed up to the light. Two blocks to go and she'd be at the office.

"Di, I have another call. We'll firm up the details on Sunday."

"Gotcha. Ciao."

Diana hit the End button on her phone as she pulled into the basement parking garage. One short elevator ride later, she stepped into the lobby of Carter and Lowe.

Fran, the receptionist, gave her a frank once-over. "Rough night?"

Diana tried unsuccessfully to smooth the front of her shirt, then tucked it into her jeans. "I wish I remembered."

"I'll take that as a yes." Fran giggled behind her hand.

The double doors leading to the office area swung open and Braxton stepped out into the lobby. "Sugar, you look like shit." Never breaking stride, she threw Diana's gym bag at her.

Diana caught it reflexively.

Braxton held the elevator. "Well, you coming?"

Just once Diana wanted an encounter with Braxton to not leave her with whiplash. "I thought we had a meeting." She half jogged to catch the elevator.

Braxton dropped her own gym bag on the floor at her feet and punched the button to take them up to the floor that housed the fitness facility. "Had is the operative word here, sugar. It ended fifteen minutes ago."

Even though the answer was obvious, Diana still had to ask, "So, where are we going?"

"I thought we could spar a little. I can brief you while I kick your ass."

Oh, the joy. Anyone who didn't know better would lay odds on Diana doing the ass-kicking, not the other way around. Diana, however, had sparred with Braxton many times. She never came out on top.

The elevator doors slid open, revealing a room full of sweaty people making use of the weights.

"Braxton, I could live without the full contact sport today." Diana gingerly touched her bruised eye.

"Don't play up that sad excuse for a black eye. It won't work on me." Braxton marched off to the dressing room, not checking to see if Diana was following. "You show up for work an hour late wearing yesterday's clothes, don't think you'll be getting any sympathy here."

Diana realized she was only putting off the inevitable by dragging her feet. Braxton was not likely to be dissuaded when she got into a mood like this. But she just couldn't convince herself to move with any speed at all. By the time she reached the locker room, Braxton had stripped down to her bra and panties and stood, one hand on her hip, studying two outfits she'd laid out on the long bench. She ruffled her short brown hair, which was shot through with a healthy dose of gray, as she vacillated. Both outfits consisted of shorts and a T-shirt and Diana didn't understand her hesitation. Not that it mattered. She didn't really care why Braxton was standing there half naked, she was just grateful for it.

Scolding herself for thinking impure thoughts about a woman who was old enough to be her mother, she struggled to open her locker. Her gaze darted back and forth between Braxton's brazen display of skin and the small numbers on the spinning lock face. Braxton turned her face slightly and grinned wickedly. Diana had been caught staring and they both knew it.

"See anything you like, shug?" Braxton motioned toward the clothing, but she clearly was suggesting a bit more.

The locker popped open, mercifully, and Diana peered inside. No way out of the conversation in there. Hell, not even a set of workout clothes. At least there was a clean pair of jeans and a pressed button-down shirt. "Does your husband know you torment me?" she asked as she unzipped the gym bag. She found shorts and a tee inside. One of life's little victories there.

Braxton's laughter rang out through the locker room. "Know about it? Shug, he fantasizes about it."

Diana stripped and replaced yesterday's shirt with the fresh one from the bag. "Enough, Braxton. Get dressed."

She rummaged through the bag, remembering she'd left Cami's house wearing no underwear. No spare set. She made a mental note to remedy that when she restocked after doing her laundry this weekend. She pulled the cotton shorts on and hoped Braxton wouldn't notice the missing article of clothing. No such luck.

"Commando, huh? That's a new look for you."

Diana's mother had worked hard to impart the lesson that if you have nothing nice to say, say nothing at all, so Diana refrained from telling Braxton to go to hell. A diversionary tactic was in order. "How'd the briefing go this morning?"

"You mean the one you missed?" Braxton gave her a scathing look. "Truth be told, you didn't miss anything. Bob came up empty with the usual fences. Could be that he lacks finesse. He's going to try some…alternate methods of persuasion today."

Diana sat on the bench to tie her shoes. She thought it was silly that she had to wear them across the hundred yards to the room where they would spar, just to take them off again, but it was a gym requirement. "What's our plan for the day?"

Braxton made a leisurely show of dressing for Diana. It was almost cruel, but Diana loved every minute. Very few women could pull off a reverse strip show, but Braxton did it with ease. "Our job is to talk to the cops. There's more there than they've given the other investigators. We need to dig deep."

Dig deep. That could only mean one thing. "I'll try."

"You gotta do more than try, shug." Braxton, now fully dressed, patted her on the shoulder. No longer the temptress, she was back in friend mode.

"Okay." Diana pulled her cell phone out of her locker. At least by making the call she could postpone the ass-whupping Braxton intended to dish out. She punched the numbers into her phone and waited for the familiar gruff announcement.

"Talk to me."

Diana smiled. "Hello, Oscar."

She kept her voice steady. She didn't want her dad's old partner to know exactly how nervous she was to be calling him. "Collins." Oscar paused a moment. Diana could picture the scowl of concentration and disapproval etched on his brow. "What can I do for you?"

"Can we meet?" It had been several months since she'd last called on Oscar, and that encounter didn't end well. She waited, her breath caught in her throat, for him to speak.

"Do you have names for me?"

Diana rolled her head from side to side, stretching the overly tense shoulder muscles. "Only one. Charles Stewart. I need the works."

Oscar whistled long and low. "You're not asking for much."

Diana sat forward, her curiosity piqued. "What do you mean?"

"Two o'clock this afternoon," Oscar said roughly and then disconnected the call.

Two o'clock. Diana glanced at her watch and contemplated her options. It would only take thirty minutes to drive to their usual meeting place, so she had no reason to skip the workout.

She turned to Braxton and smiled halfheartedly. "Let's get this over with. We've got a few hours to kill."

Chapter Five

Traffic was at that manageable lull between the morning and afternoon rush hours as Diana navigated the streets on her way to meet Oscar. Not to say it wasn't infuriating, but rather than leaving Diana homicidal, the delays and inconsiderate driving simply encouraged thoughts of extreme violence.

Braxton sat at languid attention in the passenger seat. Her displeasure about not being in the driver's seat became apparent when she pressed her foot to the floor as Diana turned a corner. The absence of a brake pedal didn't stop her from going through the motions. Generally, Diana gave in and let Braxton drive. For this trip, though, she'd insisted on taking her own car, a little stab at retribution for being forced into a reunion with Oscar before she was ready.

Oscar wouldn't recognize Braxton's car, which meant they had to take Diana's. So, by default, Diana got to drive. She figured it was probably the first time Braxton had felt unhappy about being issued a higher-grade company car than Diana's. If they drove the same model, they wouldn't have to worry about Oscar spotting the car and Braxton would be happily sitting in what she believed to be her rightful place behind the wheel.

"What's her name?" Braxton asked, her voice tense as she clutched the "oh shit" handle above the door.

"Whose name?" Diana was focused on her upcoming conversation with Oscar and couldn't for the life of her figure out who Braxton was referring to.

"The reason you missed the meeting this morning." The roll of Braxton's eyes carried over into her voice.

Diana kept her eyes on the road. Even during non–peak traffic time there were still plenty of stupid drivers. She allowed herself a little smile as Cami's face popped into her mind. It was the freshly fucked hair that got to her. She loved that look on any woman, especially when she was the one responsible for it. "Cami." The name rolled out of her mouth, comfortable and easy. A rush of desire settled low in her belly, and she resisted the urge to check her pocket for Cami's number. She'd have to give her a call later.

"Cami," Braxton echoed. "How long have you known her?"

Diana debated how much to share and decided this was a case of less is more. "We met last night."

The central precinct came into view as she turned onto South State Street. She passed the police station and turned into the parking garage on the opposite block.

"Look at you. You spend the night with her once and you can't stop smiling. Is she really that special?"

"Special?" Diana snorted. "Hardly. Like you said, I spent one night with her. Hell, I don't even remember the details. But she's super hot and I wouldn't mind spending a second night with her."

"My, my, it must be love if you are looking for a second date."

Diana followed the ramp up to the top level and scanned the roof for Oscar. Nowhere to be found. Time to change the subject. "Mona Stewart. Did you know about her and her stepdad before the interview?"

Braxton patted her hand gently. "I suspected it. I just didn't know for sure."

"You've got to be fucking kidding me." Diana whirled her head around and gaped at Braxton. "You knew what that girl had been through and you didn't warn me? You sent me in there with no preparation?"

She was just plain ol' pissed off. There was a reason Diana had opted not to become a cop, leaving her younger sister to keep the family legacy alive. She couldn't stand to see hurt in victims' eyes. Just couldn't take it. She'd figured that out when she was a kid on a ride-along with her pop. He'd answered a domestic violence call in the eighties. They'd arrived after three other officers and the ambulance. No, not ambulance. Wagon. The word had felt good on her tongue, as if she was a cop just like her pop and his buddies.

Two medics had wheeled out a big gurney. They moved slowly,

no urgency. The red-stained sheet was pulled up over the head. Trailing behind them was a woman in a suit who was holding the hand of a little blond boy. His eyes were lifeless. He looked like a tiny, wounded bird and Diana had wanted to wrap him up and take him home. Her heart swelled and cracked when the woman loaded him into the backseat of her big Chevy. She was too young at the time to understand fully what had happened to him, but his vacant, lost look tore at her innocent acceptance that children were always loved and protected. Mona Stewart twisted her heart the same way.

"I said I *suspected* she was being abused." Braxton presented the case for keeping her in the dark. "If I'd told you everything you would have gone in there looking like you had an agenda."

"I feel like my guts have been put through a blender, just so I wouldn't appear to have an agenda?"

Braxton's hand soothed her shoulder, an attempt to calm her. Diana was not comforted. She recognized that she was dangerously close to crossing a line with her friend and she didn't give a damn. She pushed Braxton's hand away.

"Unfuckingbelievable." She shook her head. "No way."

"Get past it."

"Get past it? Braxton, you didn't push a young woman into inviting her monsters out into the light of day. You didn't sit and hold her while she cried like a child."

"No, I didn't." Braxton's voice was calm, like a doctor to an injured patient. "You also gave her more sympathy than she's ever gotten or ever will get from her own mother. You can be proud of that."

Diana took a deep, shuddering breath and climbed out of the car. The sticky air clung to her as she looked out over the city. She heard the passenger door open and close. Braxton folded her arms over the guardrail and stood next to her, silent and waiting. *This must be serious.* Braxton never wanted to be exposed to the humidity unless she was on her boat drinking Tanqueray and tonic.

"There was something else." Diana was embarrassed by her temper tantrum, and it was time to get this conversation back on track. "What was Charles Stewart's middle initial?"

Braxton cocked her head to the side. "Regis. Why?"

Charles Regis Stewart. Diana pictured Mona's rhythmic opening and closing of the cigarette lighter with the practiced flip of her wrist.

"Mona has his lighter and cigarette case. The initials *CRS* are engraved on the side."

Noise of city life grew beneath them. Traffic was building.

"You're asking yourself questions only Mona knows the answers to," Braxton said.

When they'd first started working together, Diana freaked the hell out when Braxton seemed to read her mind. Now she recognized Braxton was simply very good at reading body language. Her talent for observation was one reason she conducted successful interviews.

"Traci Stewart…she was something else." Diana had always known there were bad parents. But knowing that and being faced with the harsh reality were two different things. She couldn't reconcile the idea that someone like Traci could be called by the same title as her own mother.

"Not all women make good mamas." Braxton offered a simple truth.

"But she *defended* him. She ignored her daughter's pain and defended that bastard."

"I know."

Diana thought about the lighter once more. Only Mona knew why she had kept that memento of her hated stepfather. Perhaps she kept the physical reminder close at hand as a medal of sorts, the kind they gave survivors of war. Was it a marker of the power he no longer held over her? The battle was over and she'd survived. This seemed unlikely to Diana. When she and Angel split up, she'd shredded all their pictures, burned the emotional keepsakes—ticket stubs, love notes, programs to the opera they'd attended on their anniversary—and donated everything else to Goodwill. Why keep it? It all represented a lie.

Diana's stomach clenched when the second option occurred to her. Maybe it was a trophy. Not just a symbol of her survival, but of her triumph over him. She was alive, but more importantly, Charles Stewart was dead. Did Mona take the lighter as spoils for the victor? How much more could Diana had learned without the distracting presence of Traci Stewart? One thing was certain; she needed to talk with Mona again.

❖

The unmistakable growl of an elevator announced Oscar Knight's arrival at the top level of the parking garage across from the central precinct. Braxton turned as the doors slid open. "That's my cue to leave." She was in the car a few spaces over before Diana could respond.

Diana shook off the unsettled feeling and forced herself to focus on Oscar. Play nice or get down to business? "What do you have for me, Oscar?"

The detective chewed on an unlit cigar, his only comfort since he quit smoking two years ago, and gave the car a sideways glance. "You brought a friend."

He was not pleased. Diana knew he wouldn't be, but Braxton had insisted and it was damned near impossible to tell her no.

"You know Braxton." Diana waited for Oscar to acknowledge her statement. She wouldn't bring anyone to a meeting with him that would compromise his position. He needed to accept that. "She'll stay in the car."

When he finally spoke, he backtracked to the niceties Diana had skipped over. "How ya doin', Collins?"

Uncomfortable small talk. Great. "I'm doin'. How 'bout you?" That should be enough. God forbid he'd want to dig deep and say something meaningful. Diana reflexively reached for the medal of her patron saint, Michael the Archangel. It lay at her throat, framed perfectly in the open vee of her button-down collar. The prayer died on her lips under Oscar's scrutiny.

"My partner's kid called me today. I'm good."

Hell. He wanted to go deep. Diana's pop had retired six years ago. Before that he was Oscar's partner for twenty-odd years. Didn't matter how long he'd been off the job, Diana knew he would always be Oscar's partner in both their minds. Diana drew a long breath and jumped in. "Look, Oscar, I know it's been too long—"

"Forget it, kid." Oscar flicked his gaze over the skyline. "Just tell your old man I said hello."

Diana shifted her weight from one leg to the other. "I will." She was grateful for the reprieve but unsure how to direct the conversation to the topic she came for. Oscar was not one to be pushed.

"So, you have an interest in the untimely death of Charles Stewart?" he said.

"His wife filed a claim for a very expensive katana that went missing. I'm trying to cover all the angles in tracing it."

Oscar's normally guarded eyes revealed a flash of concern, then the practiced mask of cool reserve slid back into place. His face was a study of indifference when he spoke again. "I can't give you any paper on this guy. So you should take notes."

Diana pulled a digital recorder from her pocket and sat it on the guard rail. She pressed Record and said, "Okay." Diana wanted files. She wanted arrest reports. She wanted case notes. Instead she got editorial insight from one of Chicago's finest. That was worth something.

"As you know, he was the victim of murder." He waited for Diana to nod before he continued. "That katana you're searching for was the murder weapon. The FBI'll want it, so don't plan on keeping it if you find it."

"FBI?" Diana's head whipped up. "Why FBI?"

Oscar shrugged. "You know the drill. We call in the feds with serials. I've been assigned to the Violent Crimes Task Force for this case."

Serials. Serial killers. FBI. Diana took a moment to process what Oscar was telling her. "This was in the paper yesterday. Page three."

"That's right." A light summer breeze ruffled his thinning gray hair as he solemnly regarded her. "Media's not doing much with it yet."

"Okay, back up. Start from the beginning. Speak slowly. Pretend I'm three and small words are required, because I'm not connecting the dots."

"Twenty-three months ago Sergio Dominguez turns up dead in his living room. Carved up with an eighteen-inch hunting knife. Wife, Rosa, reports that a knife matching that description was missing." Oscar twirled his cigar between his thumb and forefinger. A nervous gesture. "You with me so far?"

"Dead guy. Big knife," Diana summarized. "Got it."

"Eighteen months ago same story, different guy. Mikhail Petrov. Smaller knife this time. Switchblade. Unlike Dominguez, he only had one wound. His neck was slit from ear to ear. Deep. I responded on that call. According to his son, Petrov had a switchblade that he liked to show off. To my knowledge, it's still missing."

Diana did the math in her head. "Five months apart. No apparent connection in MO. Except the missing blade."

"Right. There's more." Oscar paused, presumably to collect his thoughts. "Seven months ago it was Victor Delaney. Instead of the living room, the crime took place in the kitchen. Delaney was a chef. His set of knives cost more than the car I drive. Masamoto. Had his name engraved on them. Chef's knife was missing."

Diana blew her breath out in a long, low whistle.

"All those cases are still open. We didn't connect any of them until three days ago."

"Charles Stewart and his katana."

Oscar nodded. "Yep. Thing is, those other guys were at the bottom of the food chain. Delaney had expensive knives, but the sum value of everything else he owned didn't add up to half what they're worth."

"So the murders weren't initially a high priority." Diana chose her words carefully. She didn't want to challenge Oscar's integrity. Besides, she knew how it worked. Understaffed, overworked. There was always something else screaming for attention. Things got missed.

"We didn't know what we were dealing with. Now we're standing here with our dicks in our hands, looking like fools because we had a serial under our noses and didn't make the connections."

"Any other commonalities linking the first three victims with Charles Stewart? Besides being dead by sharp, pointy things."

"Not as of two days ago. You know how the feds are. They put a clamp on it as soon as they walk in the door. Look at you over the files like you're an idiot of the first order. *Joint* task force—yeah, right."

Diana didn't know what to say. She'd never had an investigation pulled from her. She didn't think she'd like it. She settled for a traditional expression of sympathy. "I'm sorry."

"Listen, I think you should leave this one alone," Oscar said. "Someone is doing some very bad things to these men. I don't want you to put yourself in front of it."

The sense of dread that had been nibbling at Diana's insides bit harder. With great effort, she ignored her unease. "I don't have a choice, Oscar. I have a job to do."

"I knew you'd say that."

Sounds of the city below them crept over the wall, filling the void in their conversation with the constant hum of car horns, revving engines, and construction in progress. A fire truck worked its way down the street several blocks over, announcing its presence with a screaming siren.

"One more question. Any suspects?"

"Not yet." The shake of his head was slower than usual, a sure sign he was tired. Oscar tried to dissuade her again. "You don't have to do this." He kept his eyes locked on the horizon, just to the right of Diana's head. "Really, you don't."

Diana sighed. "Yeah, I do."

It was the only answer she could offer and she knew he expected no less. She was, after all, her father's daughter. She had been given an insurance claim to investigate and her case had to be solved.

Thankfully, this request for help had gone better than the last time. For that investigation, the only name on her list had been a retired cop. Oscar, a veteran detective of twenty-eight years, refused to cross the thin blue line, and when Diana proved the man's knowing involvement in insurance fraud, their relationship had suffered. Oscar threw up a defensive wall of silence, refusing to accept calls from his old partner's daughter. Finally, Diana stopped calling, hoping he would cool off in time. A few months later, he'd left a message on her voice mail. "Hey, Collins, just checking in." Only a few words, but they meant the world to Diana.

This was the first time since their falling-out that she'd asked for his help with an investigation. She placed her hand gently on his arm, grateful that he was willing to mend fences.

"I appreciate the help, Oscar. Really, I do."

"It's good to see you, Collins." He lumbered off to the elevator. "Give Braxton a kiss and don't forget to say hi to your old man for me."

Diana gave a tight wave good-bye as she climbed back into her car. "Did you hear any of that?"

Braxton sat sideways in her seat, regarding Diana. "I heard him, shug, but don't even think about slipping me any tongue during that kiss he passed on."

Diana choked out a squeak that could have been called a laugh. The thought of kissing Braxton was not unpleasant, and if she ever got around to it, there'd definitely be some tongue involved. Today, however, she was feeling warm and fuzzy about waking up next to Cami. Soon as she had a moment alone, she wanted to make that phone call.

"He didn't really tell us anything new." Diana tried to steer her thoughts back on track along with the conversation.

"Sure he did." Braxton gestured for Diana to start the car and get moving. It was close to five and her husband would be waiting. "He gave us three other connected cases to look at. That's a lot."

"We're not even sure they're relevant." Diana knew they had to be if the feds were involved, but the thought made her queasy.

"You know they are."

Diana wound her way down the exit ramps and out into traffic. She thought about what it all meant. "We're not following a thief. We're hunting a serial killer."

The absolute deafening certainty of the statement filled the car and left no room for anything else. Not even air. Diana slapped the button to lower the window, inviting in the stale afternoon sun. The words "serial killer" were simply too big for her to grab on to. They didn't fit inside her mental grasp. She sucked in a lungful of life and prayed the spots behind her eyes would dissipate, rather than continuing to grow. They made their way back to the office in relative silence. Diana parked next to Braxton's car but left her engine running.

"Guess I know what I'll be doing this weekend."

"Well, we can start the research tomorrow," Braxton said. "Maybe we'll get lucky and you'll be able to relax this weekend."

"If not, I'll spend some quality time with Google and see what I can come up with." Diana's social calendar was drastically lacking of late. Granted, she had some very satisfying one-shot encounters, but Braxton was right. Two dates constituted a long-term commitment for her. She'd see if Cami was available Saturday night and she'd be at her parents' on Sunday, but that left a lot of time with nothing to do.

"Do you have plans?" she asked Braxton.

"Jakey and I are spending the weekend on the boat. There will be no research. Only drinks with little umbrellas in them and lots and lots of suntan lotion."

"That's it. I'm skipping out on my family and spending the weekend with you guys." Even as she said it, Diana knew she had no hope of escaping her commitments.

❖

The drive to her apartment after work was painfully long. She wanted to call Cami but couldn't afford that kind of distraction in traffic. Besides, she tended to be overly animated when driving. She didn't want Cami to hear her talking dirty under those circumstances.

Dirty talk. Diana's mouth went desert dry and a chill ran down her spine at the thought. Cami's half-whispered confirmation that she'd enjoyed their night together before Diana rushed out of her apartment that morning was enough to strip her of her common sense. Anything more and her brain would melt entirely. Definitely not advisable in the bumper-to-bumper afternoon commute.

She let herself in, kicked the front door shut, and dropped her bag on the floor. By the time she made it down the hall to her bedroom, her shirt was off and her pants were well on their way. The jeans and button-down were better than the suit she'd endured during the interview with Mona Stewart, but Diana preferred a comfy pair of sweats and a tank. She studied herself in the full-length mirror for a few minutes before slipping a black top over her head. It was definitely tighter than it was when she bought it. A few more early morning trips to the gym and a few less late nights with Jim, Jack, and Jose were on the horizon. Easier said than done. She was very fond of those three boys, even if they did kick her in the teeth every time they got together.

Diana tugged on the low-cut men's pajama bottoms she usually slept in and gave her reflection one last critical look. Maybe she should take up yoga. Mental clarity and super-lean, bendy bodies were supposedly the result. A winning combination by any standard. *Enough thinking about the gym.* She flipped off the light and headed to the kitchen. Online research or call Cami? Diana tapped the Enter key to wake up her laptop as she passed it on her way to the fridge.

The options for dinner ranged from not very appetizing to downright disgusting. She threw away a half-full take-out container of vegetable fried rice, passed on the leftover pizza, and settled for a bag of chips. The salsa she located next looked like it was ready to stage a full frontal assault on the nearest unsuspecting country. Diana contemplated sending it to join the rice in the trash, but was afraid it would crawl out and suffocate her in her sleep. She closed the fridge and retreated to a high-backed dining room chair, computer in front of her.

The empty inbox of her Gmail account blinked up at her. Diana was almost disappointed to not have thirty-six e-mails that guaranteed a longer, stronger erection or drastic weight loss in only two days. She reached for the phone on the kitchen counter, then hesitated. One-night stands were not uncommon for her. She liked their simplicity and was puzzled that she suddenly felt the urge to mess with the formula that had served her well for the past year. Her life was complicated enough without adding the drama of dating.

Leaving the phone sitting in its charger, she typed "Charles Stewart" into the search engine window. There were over seven million results, including a link to a Wikipedia entry. She refined her search by adding the middle initial *R* and lowered the field to just over four million. Fucking hell. That decided it.

Diana didn't need to check the slip of paper Cami had tucked into her pocket that morning. She had a hard time remembering her own birthday, but Cami's phone number was hers in a single glance. Instantly committed to memory. She grabbed the phone from its cradle, sank down onto the sofa in her living room, and dialed the number before she could change her mind again.

"Hello?" The soft, underlying laughter Diana remembered from that morning carried through the phone lines. She listened with a silly grin on her face, hoping Cami would speak again. She did. "Hello? Is anyone there?" This time she sounded annoyed.

Diana sucked in a deep breath and charged into the conversation. "Hi, Cami. It's Diana."

"Diana?"

Fuck. Maybe she forgot her name. Maybe she never knew the name. It was possible. "From this morning." Diana stammered, sounding every bit like a thirteen-year-old schoolboy. "I mean, last night."

Thankfully, Cami laughed. "I remember."

Warmth spread over Diana, like sunshine or an old blanket. Her reflection in the flat surface of her television showed that her smile bordered on ridiculous.

"Did you need something?"

The tone was innocent but Diana detected a hint of teasing just below the surface.

"I spent the day thinking about you." The sentence was out before she could stop it, so she plowed on full steam ahead. "And I'm hoping we can get together again."

Diana tried to picture Cami. This morning she'd been naked, an image that was hard to forget. She wondered what Cami was wearing now but decided not to ask. So far she'd been less than smooth in this conversation and she didn't want Cami to think she was a full-on, knuckle-dragging Neanderthal. If a beautiful mind went with those perfect tits, Diana didn't want to ruin all opportunity of enjoying both.

"Drinks?" Cami asked.

Drinks. That would be perfect. Diana couldn't wait to wake up with a twenty-pound load on her temple again. "We already tried that. How about dinner?" She wanted to remember their date this time.

"Wonderful." Cami's voice curled around Diana like a contented kitty, relaxed and at ease, but ready for action.

"Friday night?" Diana had intended to ask about Saturday, but she didn't want to wait that long. She hoped Cami was willing to forget all the rules about playing hard to get and not appearing too eager. At that moment, she didn't give a good goddamn about any of that. She wanted to spend time with Cami and she wanted it to start now. "This Friday, that is. Tomorrow." She really had to stop burbling.

"Tomorrow night," Cami echoed.

And with those two little words, Diana's brain raced off in a triple-x parade of naughty intentions. Mixed in with the flashes of sweat and groans, she glimpsed walks in the park, hand holding, and dinner with friends. She wanted to stay on the phone listening to that gentle voice until she picked Cami up tomorrow. She wanted to fall asleep to the sound of Cami's rhythmic breathing and wake up to her laughter filled with promise. Instead she wished Cami sweet dreams and closed the phone.

Twenty-four hours. That, and some polite small talk, was all that stood between tonight's humdrum normality and seeing Cami in all her naked glory again. Diana could hardly wait.

Chapter Six

The décor in the South Lake Domestic Violence Shelter was intended to be comforting, chosen specially to remind women of home. Ali found that ironic since the women who came here were fleeing their homes. She opened the intake form on her computer and took a deep breath. The first ten minutes at the shelter were the hardest. Ali just needed to get this new resident through tonight. Tomorrow they could start working toward being okay.

The woman cowered in an armchair, her arms hugged tight around her tummy. The bruises on her face were deep purple and still swelling. She flinched when Ali asked her name.

"Teresa." Her voice was hesitant. Defeated.

Ali knew that place well. She gripped the edge of her desk hard enough for her knuckles to turn white. It was the only way she knew to keep herself in her chair. She guessed Teresa to be in her early twenties, but her weary suspicion and pleading desperation made her seem twelve one moment and sixty the next. Ali wanted to comfort her, to promise it would all be okay, but experience told her the last thing Teresa wanted was the touch of a stranger.

"What's your last name?" Ali kept her voice low and smooth, infusing as much safety into the sentence as she could manage.

Teresa's automatic half-smile quickly turned into a grimace and she touched her tongue to her split and bleeding bottom lip. "Vasquez."

The blinking cursor on the electronic intake form marched along as Ali typed in the required data. Funding was a bitch and the shelter had to satisfy a litany of bureaucrats, so there was no way around the formalities. As much as she hated forcing these women to tell their story upon arrival, Ali hated what came next even more. "Teresa." She pulled the camera from her top desk drawer. "I need to take pictures."

She didn't want to see the wounds and pain firsthand, let alone in digital sharpness. The police, however, always wanted photographic evidence.

Teresa curled up into herself even tighter. "Please…no." Her eyes, desperate and caged, pleaded with Ali.

Ali sat the camera on the desk, the lens pointed away from Teresa. "I have to."

Teresa's bottom lip quivered as she stared at the camera. Distrust and fear on her face. Ali didn't hold back any longer. She moved to the couch where Teresa was sitting and eased down next to her. "I can help you, Teresa. You just have to let me."

Low, whimpering sobs shook Teresa as her rigid body crumpled into Ali's arms. Ali smoothed her hair and made shushing noises, similar to the way she would comfort a wounded animal. She held Teresa long after the desktop computer blinked into power save mode. Broken spirits should never be made to wait in favor of paperwork. Teresa's trembling breath evened out but Ali was reluctant to break the silence. She kept her voice low and soothing. "You're safe here. I promise."

❖

Jeter tapped lightly on the door frame of Braxton's office. "Please tell me you've got something good."

Diana looked up from her laptop. In the interests of effective communication, she'd moved to the small conference table in Braxton's office so they could easily compare notes. She preferred her oversized cherrywood desk to the ergonomically damned makeshift arrangements, but they had a lot to research and no time to waste repeating each other's efforts.

"We're just getting started, Jeter." Braxton pushed her reading glasses up into her hair, a move Diana usually found irresistibly sexy. Today she wondered why her colleague didn't visit the optometrist for some adjustments.

"The two of you have been in here all morning. What have you been doing? Having a pajama party?" Jeter's face flamed red the moment the words left his mouth.

Diana didn't know if it was because he realized how far over the line that statement landed or if it was because the image short-circuited his brain. Given the circumstances, either was a safe bet.

"Do you have any idea how many hits the name Charles Stewart generates on Google?" The question was purely rhetorical.

"Well…" Jeter cleared his throat. "I'll leave you two to it, then."

"Yeah, that's what I thought," Diana mumbled under her breath as she clicked out of yet another dead-end Web site.

She pushed her hands through her hair in frustration. As a general rule, Diana was the queen of research, but not today. They'd been at this since early morning with marginal results. Charles Stewart had been an active philanthropist. Site after site praised his kindness and generosity. If the Internet was to be believed, Charles had been an upstanding, civic-minded citizen. Nothing at all like the picture painted by Mona Stewart.

"This guy looks like a saint on paper," she said. "No wonder Mona couldn't get anyone to take her seriously."

"Did she try?" Braxton asked. Her quiet calm was the complete opposite of Diana's jangling emotions.

"I don't know." Diana skimmed a press release on the screen. Charles and Traci were at a gallery premiere. Charles had discovered the up-and-coming local artist shooting wedding films for a popular event coordinator. Disgusted, Diana remarked, "On top of everything else, he was a patron of the arts."

She clicked on the link to the artist's home page, adding his name to the list of Stewart acquaintances and associates. Someone in the art world could know the kind of people who might buy a costly collectible, no questions asked.

Diana scanned the page, an homage to an overinflated, self-indulgent ego. Groaning, she said, "Please tell me you're coming up with more than I am."

"So far nothing terribly interesting. Just last known addresses." Braxton was so frustrated with their progress she'd already given up on the Teflon-coated Charles Stewart, opting to track down information on the other three murder victims instead. Diana was tempted to do the same.

She stood and walked to the edge of Braxton's desk.

"What do we know?" she thought aloud. "Charles Stewart. Killed in his own home. The weapon used was a rare, expensive katana from his private collection, now missing. His stepdaughter has accused him of sexual abuse. His wife denies this ever occurred, and so far we have no evidence to corroborate Mona's allegations. Stewart was an active supporter of high-profile charities in Chicago. We have no leads for finding the sword. And the FBI believes a serial killer is probably responsible for the murder."

Braxton snapped her fingers to get Diana's attention. "Focus. Our job is to recover a valuable missing object that Carter and Lowe insured, not crucify a dead man or do the job of the police."

Diana didn't agree. "What about Mona Stewart? What if we can help her sleep through the night…" Diana let the sentence fade as the absurd thought behind her statement caught up with her mouth.

What could she possibly do to help Mona Stewart find peace of mind? Any settlement from Carter and Lowe would go to Traci, not Mona. Besides, it was her job to make sure that check never got issued. Still, she refused to give in to the suffocating weight of helplessness that assaulted her when she thought of Mona Stewart. She had to do something to help, she just had to.

"The man is dead," Braxton said flatly, without emotion. "If that doesn't help her sleep, nothing will."

Diana returned to her computer without responding. She bookmarked the artist's home page and was about to close out when she noticed a hidden link in the top right corner, a small black star next to the artist's name. Very easily overlooked. Hidden links always aroused her curiosity, just as they were meant to, along with every other gimmick intended to drive Internet traffic. Diana knew she was being gullible but she clicked anyway, and a new domain opened in a second browser window. She didn't expect results from following the link, but the investigator in her demanded that she follow every little lead, no matter how innocuous.

The screen faded to black. In the center of the page, about a third of the way down, "Siger Enterprises" was written in small, gold letters above a box for userid and password. That was all. No other links. No invitation for new guests to sign up. Nothing to click for a forgotten password.

"That's strange."

"Whatcha got?" Braxton circled around her desk and looked over Diana's shoulder at the black screen. "How'd you find this?" Her words were clipped.

Diana described her route and said, "Maybe it's nothing."

Braxton didn't respond right away. Finally she moved back to her own desk after squeezing Diana's shoulders. "Stuff like that is rarely nothing."

Only one way to find out. Diana went back to the artist's home page and clicked on the "Contact Me" button. Her message was brief. In the subject line she wrote "Siger Entertainment." In the body of the e-mail she wrote only one sentence: *I want access.* She left her personal e-mail address in the appropriate field and hit Send.

The state of Illinois maintained a database of all registered business owners. It was designed to help prospective business owners determine if the name they want to use was taken yet. Diana pulled up that database and typed in "Siger Enterprises."

"Fuck me."

"Okay, shug, but we should film it or something. Jakey's going to be pissed if he doesn't get to at least watch."

It took Diana a few seconds to realize what Braxton was saying. When the message hit home, she laughed that nervous "not sure what to do with that information" laugh. "Guess what I just found." She didn't wait for Braxton to respond. "Siger Enterprises is a corporation in good standing with the state of Illinois. Charles R. Stewart, president."

Braxton quirked one eyebrow, a sure sign of interest. "Anything else? Address? Type of business?"

"Listed as domestic. No address." That was normal. In Illinois, business descriptions were generally so broad they said absolutely nothing about a corporation's activities, and for some reason addresses were not included.

Diana picked up her cell and dialed Oscar's number.

"What can I do for you, Collins?" His smoke-strained voice greeted her.

"I've come up with another name. Hoping you can shed some light."

"Hit me."

Diana could hear sounds of traffic in the background. She pictured Oscar, his window open, driving down Michigan Avenue with his ever-present miniature notebook pressed against the edge of the steering wheel, a pencil poised to write in his other hand. She'd driven that way herself a time or two without incident. Still and all, she didn't like the thought of Oscar dividing his attention between writing down information and the bumper in front of him. Trying not to distract him for more than a few seconds, she gave him the business name and license number. He promised to get back to her soon and signed off with his customary gruffness.

Diana headed up a new sheet of her notepad with "Siger Enterprises" and jotted down what she'd discovered so far. *S I G E R.* The letters lifted and separated in her mind. When they settled back down in her mind, their order had reversed. *R E G I S.* Regis! "Siger is Regis spelled backward." Diana was intrigued. The name reversal was a vanity that smacked of male ego. In her limited experience, certain types of men liked to mark their territory, even subtly. "We have to find out what's on that site."

Diana wondered why Charles *Regis* Stewart's corporation had a hidden link on Kevin Pierce's homepage. Granted, it could be a discreet form of quid pro quo. According to Kevin's bio, he'd been filming weddings until he met Charles Stewart. Six months later, with the whiplash-inducing rise in popularity that the fickle art world was known for, his work was featured at the trendy Fifty50 gallery. Still, if he wanted to repay a debt to Stewart, why not do it openly, perhaps with a well-written thank-you in the acknowledgments section of his Web site?

Diana brought up Charles Stewart's Web site in another browser window. She'd been there several times already that morning, but this time she looked more closely, like a child on an Easter egg hunt. She scrutinized every page until she was satisfied that there was no link to Pierce or to Siger. Her curiosity was piqued. What could possibly be behind that login screen that Charles Stewart wanted to hide, yet Kevin Pierce wanted to advertise, even subtly?

Braxton glanced at the wall clock above Diana's head. "Shit. We're going to be late for the meeting with Bob and Jeter." She stood and straightened the tailored charcoal suit she was wearing.

Diana scooped up her files and followed Braxton out the door. They didn't have anything real to report during this daily briefing, but Jeter insisted they meet nonetheless. Her mind raced and she made another mental note: Find out if Mona ever told her story to anyone else.

Braxton was right. Their job was to recover the katana, but if Mona's abuse could be proved, then the value of the katana would mean something. Perhaps Mona could bring a damages claim against her stepfather's estate.

❖

Bob White offered his customary car salesman grin. "Diana, I was relieved to hear that disfiguring black eye didn't keep you from getting lucky Wednesday night. Looks better today. Swelling's gone down."

Diana glared at Braxton.

"Don't look at me. I didn't say a word."

"For Christ's sake, Collins, I'm an investigator." Bob's oily smirk was even more pronounced than usual. "It didn't take much to draw that conclusion."

One day Diana was going to give in to the urge to leap across the table and smack the shit out of him. Today, however, she chose the high road. "Trust me, Bob, if you woke up next to that woman, you would have missed the whole day."

Bob hooted and slapped the table, but said nothing more. Diana felt a twinge of guilt about reducing her experience with Cami to one crass comment, even if she didn't remember the important details. She would remedy that tonight. A repeat engagement was in order, only this time the menu would include a lot less tequila.

She turned away from Bob, blatantly ignoring him, and asked Jeter, "Did you guys start already?"

"No, we're just comparing notes." Jeter scanned the papers in front of him. "By the way, I, too, am glad you made it today."

Jesus Christ! Was anything sacred about her personal life? Did everybody know why she was late on the previous day? Fuck it all. Diana set her paperwork on the table, where several files were spread out along with photos of the missing katana. Trying for a warm smile, she said, "I'm sorry about my absence yesterday. I assure you, it won't happen again."

"Good." Jeter relaxed into the leather swivel chair at the head of the table. "Let's begin. Who wants to go first?"

For once, Bob remained silent and let someone else speak. Small miracle that. Or perhaps he actually had some respect for the senior member of the team. That concept was too foreign to Diana. Near as she could tell, he didn't respect anyone. When working with him, she tried to keep her communications brief and businesslike, hoping to avoid his tactless personal comments.

"We met with Diana's contact. He confirmed a few facts for us." Braxton opened the discussion. "He also gave us some new insights. Diana, want to elaborate?"

It was sweet of Braxton to let her explain the connection to the other murders. Big developments like this one reinforced her right to sit at the big table with the grown-ups. Savoring the moment, Diana said, "Apparently this isn't the first murder that fits the MO. Stewart is number four. Chicago PD believes we have a serial on our hands. The FBI has been brought in."

Bob gave a long, low whistle. "Damn."

"Have we followed up on this angle?" Jeter expected immediate results. He sometimes lost touch with the fact that investigations take time.

Braxton answered for Diana. "As you know, we spent the morning in my office doing research. We're planning to visit the other widows on Monday, see if they have anything insightful to share."

Jeter responded with a tight, controlled nod. He wanted more. Diana considered sharing what she'd learned about Siger Enterprises, but there wasn't really much to say until she heard back from Oscar or was given access to the site. She preferred to wait until she could reveal something that would impress her boss.

Jeter moved on to Bob while she was deliberating. "How 'bout you?"

"Spent today in court. Testifying in the Mercury case. Monday

I'm going to hit a few more fences. Not expecting to find much, but it's worth a shot."

Diana sneaked a sideways glance at Braxton, knowing she would be irritated. She'd ranted for a full ten minutes when Jeter hadn't assigned that task to her. She usually got to the fences before Bob could think about covering that angle. Braxton took great pleasure in *persuading* the unwilling to share their secrets. The clock on the wall indicated it was a little after five. "Let's wrap this up. I know some of us have plans for the weekend." Jeter nailed Braxton with a pointed look.

"One other thing." It was time for Diana to give voice to the questions that had been niggling at her brain since her interview with Mona. "This is more an observation than a question, but I'm hoping you all can provide some insight on this. Mona Stewart used a lighter with her stepfather's initials engraved on the outside."

"So?" Bob's expression clearly said, "Big fucking deal."

God, he was an ass.

"I doubt it's a trophy, if that's what you're thinking." Braxton patted Diana's arm. She didn't seem bothered that this was the second time the subject had come up between them.

"No. It just seemed odd to me. That's all."

Bob cleared his throat. "Keeping a memento like that is actually fairly common for victims of abuse. He was a constant in her life. As much as she hated him, he defined her reality in some regards and now she's not sure what to do without him." Bob didn't add a single inappropriate comment or gesture. His rare lapse into seriousness was greeted with silent awe.

A wave of cold realization rolled over Diana and landed in her gut. "So that's why they stay? Victims, I mean. Because they don't know what else to do?"

Braxton's hand moved to her shoulder. A comforting anchor.

"It's not that simple," Bob continued, "She was very young when the abuse started. She would have tried to make it stop, but the woman who should have protected her didn't do her job. That'll fuck with anyone. She's trying to find her way. That lighter is probably a reminder of where she's been."

Silence fell over the room once more, and Diana was grateful for that. She didn't want to make small talk just yet. She stared out the bank of windows across from where she was seated. She'd moved into the position of senior investigator months ago but hadn't really settled into her new job yet. Strange, considering how excited she'd been to get the promotion and move into the executive office, complete with one wall of windows. Her new workspace was a sign of status, a tangible symbol of the hierarchy at Carter and Lowe. Senior investigators, the moneymakers, were revered and afforded every luxury.

She'd worked hard, put in countless hours, to earn her place, yet she felt a bit like a little kid playing dress-up. The big office with the plush carpet and private bathroom, the deep cherry desk and inviting leather chair, the company car and expense account all hung a little too big on her, like a fine set of clothes a few sizes too large. Especially in the face of Mona Stewart's pain. She wasn't responsible for what had happened, but the truth weighed on her, clinging like a thick syrup, demanding something from her. Diana desperately wanted a shower.

Braxton slid her chair away from the table. "It's after five. Let's go, sugar." It was a silly comment, really. None of them left on time, certainly not on Friday.

Rather than arguing, Diana simply followed her out of the office with the foul residue of Mona Stewart's motivation balled in her stomach. She didn't care if Bob's explanation was right. She couldn't think of a reason good enough for Mona to hold on to a tainted reminder like her stepfather's lighter. As much as she wanted to recover the stolen katana, a small part of her cheered the killer who'd unwittingly avenged Mona Stewart.

Two days ago Diana had been battered but elated. She'd stopped a bad guy from doing bad things. That was a powerful feeling. Mona Stewart had stripped her of that victory, reminding her in glaring Technicolor that were much worse tragedies than a broke guy with a gun.

❖

Diana arrived ten minutes early at Cami's loft in the West Loop. The district of warehouses converted to edgy condominiums was close to Carter and Lowe's office building in the Loop and Diana's apartment in Wicker Park. She debated waiting until seven to ring the doorbell, but she didn't have that kind of patience. She took a deep breath and pushed the button. Nothing. No response. Mild panic rose up in her. Maybe she'd gotten the time wrong. Maybe Cami didn't really want to see her again. Maybe she had the wrong address. The maybes were endless and mind numbing. And out of character. Diana smoothed her hands over her hair and tried to reclaim a smidge of serenity.

When she raised her hand to knock, the door swung open and Cami stood there, slightly out of breath, shoes dangling from her hand and her hair battling its way out of its loose bun. Her skin had a light copper glow like the sun itself had reached down from the sky and blessed her.

Sunkissed. Oh, hell. One look at Cami in her light blue halter dress and the part of Diana's brain that filtered out clichés stopped working completely. Gauche compliments circled her mind like sharks gnawing at her usual wit. Dammit. They needed to leave soon or she'd drag Cami to the bedroom and make sure they both remembered the encounter this time.

"Diana. Come in." Cami gestured toward the living room with her head as she tried to slip on her pumps. Poised on one foot, she wobbled and lost her balance, tumbling forward into Diana's arms.

"Whoa, there. You all right?" Diana gripped Cami's waist low, where the swell of her hips just began.

They stumbled into the apartment and stood, clinging to one another. Diana kicked the door shut. Cami's eyes darkened and she worked her fingers up slowly into Diana's hair. Diana's heart stuttered to a stop, then slammed against her chest. She wanted skin. Hers and Cami's pressed together, sweaty and hot. At the same time, she wanted to run screaming from this woman. She didn't even know her and yet here she was, speechless and lost in the moment, hanging on to Cami like her life depended on it.

She closed her eyes and let her cheek rest whisper-close to Cami's. Lemon balm and mint swirled through her senses, leaving her lightheaded.

"God, you smell good," she whispered. Her brain was misfiring and sending out random bursts of prepubescent Don Juan. She wanted to be suave and sexy, but all she could manage was a series of non sequiturs. "Was it like this the first time?"

"Overwhelming and all consuming?" Cami turned so her mouth brushed Diana's ear.

The question hit her skin in a rush of soft, hot breath and sent shivers racing around her spine. Images assaulted her—Cami in a light summer dress sitting in her parents' backyard, children splashing in the pool behind her. The two of them curled up next to the fireplace in Diana's apartment, warm cups of cocoa in their hands.

Scared vertical by the thought, Diana released her grip on Cami and took a step back. "We have reservations."

The sexy half-grin dropped from Cami's face and her eyes faded from midnight to their normal sky blue. "Reservations. Right. Just let me get my shoes on."

Diana inched a little closer to Cami and reached out for her hands. "This is going to sound silly"—she linked their fingers and squeezed lightly—"but I don't want my only memory of tonight to be of you naked." She paused, a bad idea if the look on Cami's face was any indication. "Not that I wouldn't like that. I just want to get to know you."

She ended the speech with a nervous grin. It was ridiculous, really, this sudden shyness. She'd seen Cami naked, tasted the inside of her thighs. She didn't remember their night together, but that was incidental. It'd still happened. Yet something about Cami Michaelson turned her into a stammering teenager. And God help her, she liked it.

As they left the house, Diana tried to remember the last time she'd felt so undone. In the beginning, Angel Ramirez had taken her breath away. Diana wanted to know everything about her, from the inside out. She'd spent every hour they were apart plotting her way back into Angel's arms. The obsessive need to be with her ultimately killed their relationship.

On the day she was promoted to senior investigator, she'd left work early and rushed home. There was only one person she wanted to celebrate with—Angel. She found her in their bed smiling down at a stranger, that predatory, sexy look on her face. They moved together with the sensual ease of longtime lovers. Hell, to Diana's horror, they looked more comfortable than she and Angel ever had. When Angel saw her sagging against the bedroom door, she winked, her rhythmic thrusts never slowing. Months later, Diana realized Angel was inviting

Diana to join them. They had been sexually adventurous in the past and she probably thought this was one more stop on that journey. But Diana's dreams of happily ever after coalesced and shattered in that moment. The memory still made her raw.

"I hope you like Italian," she said, parking a few doors from Mario's.

Earlier that day, when she'd made the reservation, Diana had been pretty sure they'd never make it to the restaurant. Now that they were here, it seemed inordinately important that Cami approve.

Cami flashed a smile. "I love it."

Diana held the passenger door open. As they walked toward the restaurant, Cami pressed her hand into Diana's as though it belonged there. As far as Diana was concerned, it did. Public displays of affection were not high on her list of things to do, but this felt different, right somehow.

Warmth radiated from Cami's body and embraced Diana, chipping away her emotional resistance. Angel had been dark, full of reckless promise, and Diana craved her like a junkie chasing her next fix. The sharp edge of danger that defined her was nowhere to be found in Cami. She was sweetness and light. In her, Diana saw the safety of the late summer sun and she wanted to stretch out beneath her, inviting Cami's warmth to wash over and protect her.

She squeezed her hand in a silent promise to try. She hoped she would be strong enough to embrace whatever Cami was willing to offer, that she wouldn't allow the burden of Angel's transgressions to keep her from grabbing happiness with both hands. She looked up at the scripted red neon sign in the restaurant window. Diana had been eating here long enough that she knew both Mario and Maria, the brother/sister team that owned the place. As soon as she and Cami entered, Maria rushed over and air-kissed Diana's cheeks. Very continental.

After she left to secure a table for Diana and her "beautiful date"—a phrase that always sounded more romantic and less trite in Italian—Cami leaned over and whispered, "This is all very sweet, this getting to know each other thing, but you must know that I'm going to have you naked and begging before this night is over."

All Diana could manage was a gulp and a nod as they followed Maria to their secluded table in the corner. Romantic. She held the chair for Cami, something she'd never done for any other woman. The concept seemed outdated, foreign to Diana, but Cami's softness made Diana want to protect her. At the very least, make sure she was seated properly.

"Thank you." Cami smiled, small and secretive, like it was just between her and Diana. "I could get used to that."

"Me, too." Diana's chest swelled with ridiculous pride at Cami's comment. She wanted to make that smile appear again and often.

The tables at Mario's sported long, white linen tablecloths, the kind that reached all the way to the floor. Diana slid her foot out in front of her until she touched Cami's. She fought the urge to slip off her shoe and run her foot along the length of Cami's leg. If she gave in to that impulse, it would only be a matter of time before she found herself on her knees with her face buried between Cami's legs, all before they even ordered. Cami deserved to be courted, not groped beneath the table on their first official date.

Diana struggled with how to open the conversation. Small talk, something that normally came easily, escaped her completely. Usually she would begin with background information, but that would eventually lead to talk about her work. She didn't want Cami exposed to the mire that clung to every aspect of her search for the missing katana.

Cami flipped open the menu. "Tell me what's good." The teasing lilt of her voice hinted that she wasn't just talking about the dinner options.

"Everything." Diana didn't need to read over the list of entrées to know what she would order. "I'm getting the seafood Alfredo, but I've tried pretty much everything on the menu. I like all of it."

Cami nodded thoughtfully, but whatever response she had formulated was momentarily paused by the arrival of the waiter. She ordered the chicken linguini. "I love Alfredo, but this way I can try two different dishes."

"Thanks for coming to dinner with me." It was too early for declarations of gratitude, but Diana couldn't hold back. "I hope we can do it again."

Cami peered at Diana over her wineglass, her eyes teasing. She flicked her tongue over her bottom lip, collecting the drop of merlot that clung there. "We will definitely do this again."

Diana's mind echoed Cami's last word: and again, and again, and again. Her thoughts came to a jarring end when she felt Cami's foot slide up under the cuff of her pant leg.

Cami winked. "All we have to do is make it through dinner without one of us climbing under the table."

Diana was certain the meal would not end soon enough.

CHAPTER SEVEN

The once-cold beer stood neglected in the early afternoon sun, forgotten behind the screen of Diana's laptop. She rubbed her eyes and pushed her fingers through her long, chestnut hair. The words on the screen pulsed and slid out of focus. The late night with Cami had left her tired and able to think about precious little other than Cami's sweat-drenched skin and the arch of her back as she came.

"Put the work away, Di." Grace slid into the seat opposite and closed the laptop, clicking her manicured nails along the top to punctuate her message. "Time to focus on family business."

"Grace, I'm trying to solve a crime here." Diana tried to adopt a tone of righteous superiority. But her sister-in-law was right. She wasn't getting any work done, so there was no reason to hide herself away.

"We need to talk now, while the men are occupied." Grace tilted her head toward the family pool where they were playing water volleyball.

As if on cue, Rebecca, Diana's other sister-in-law, joined them at the patio table. Brigitte followed her carrying a handful of cold beers, ice dripping down the bottles. "Okay, we're here," she said as she set them in the middle of the table. "What's so urgent?"

"Anniversary. It's coming soon," Grace said.

Everyone clinked their bottles in a ritual toast.

"Yeah. Forty years." Rebecca let out a long, low whistle. "I love Cal, but damn. Forty years? That's just amazing."

Her gaze tracked to her husband. Calvin paused mid-serve and smiled at her. It was like they had some sort of internal beacon that drew his attention to Rebecca the moment she glanced his direction. He sent the volleyball over the net with a silly "I love my wife" grin on his face.

"I know what you mean," Brigitte said. After five years and two kids, the boundaries of love were stretched to the limit for her and her husband, Lucas. The tension between them was a common topic when Diana and Brigitte met at Bernie's for lunch.

"So, we should do something special." Grace brought them back on track. "Maxwell and I would like to send them on a cruise."

That was a bold statement for Grace. She usually waited for Diana to take the lead on issues involving money. Maxwell, her husband, worked as a financial advisor and Grace as an advertising executive. With two high incomes and no children, they took for granted a lifestyle the rest of the family didn't share. Grace was sensitive to this fact.

Brigitte's eyes clouded over. Diana knew her sister's budget was already stretched drum-tight. Between her salary as a city cop and Lucas's as an EMT, it was all they could do to afford daycare for their two small children. Diana followed her gaze across the backyard to the children playing tag. "A cruise," Brigitte said slowly. "That sounds expensive."

Diana placed a hand on her sister's arm. "I'm sure we can work it out."

Brigitte shook off the hand and pushed away from the table with a deafening scrape of chair legs against the deck surface. "No. I'm tired of working things out."

Before anyone could respond, she lurched to her feet and retreated through the sliding glass door into the house. Diana could see her brushing away tears as she rounded the corner that led to the bedrooms.

They sat, silent in the wake of Brigitte's outburst. After a few moments of stunned immobility, Diana recovered sufficiently to act. "I'll go after her. You two work out the cruise and the financial details. Count me in, and Brigitte, too."

Grace started to protest. "Are you sure? She didn't—"

"I'm sure. I'll take care of it."

Diana hated to see Brigitte so upset. She could take on a crazy man with a gun without hesitation, but her sister crying? That took real courage. Steeling herself against the emotional assault waiting in their old bedroom, she hurried to the end of the hall. Brigitte hadn't locked the door. If she'd really wanted to be alone, she would have.

Diana stuck her head in. "Bri? You in here?"

"Yeah. Where else would I be?" Brigitte sat, shoulders slumped, on the small twin bed that had been hers for eighteen years. "It's just so hard." She snuffled as Diana sat down next to her. "Why didn't anybody warn me?"

They sat together, not speaking, on the slightly lumpy twin bed. Diana wished she had some piece of wisdom to share with Brigitte. That was her job. She was the older sister. Instead of advice, she hugged her and kissed the top of her head.

"I love them. I really do." Brigitte cried into Diana's shoulder. "They just want so much. All the time. There's not even a moment of peace. You know what I deal with all day long. Then I come home to these two beautiful babies who just want their mama. Lucas is as tired and worn out as I am. We fight all the time." Brigitte's voice faded.

Diana had heard all of it before. She knew how much her younger sister struggled just to make it through the day-to-day burdens of being a cop and a wife and a mom. That was why she treasured the occasional lunch at Bernie's with Brigitte. During those few minutes, even if they were interrupted by guns and ex-girlfriends, Brigitte was more herself than at any other time.

"You know I can help."

Brigitte stiffened. "I can't ask you to do that."

"You're not asking."

"Di, we both work good jobs. We should be able to pay equally for our share of our parents' gift."

"Why? You have two children. I'm single. No kids."

Brigitte pulled a tissue out of a box on the bed side table. "Why should you have to subsidize for the choices I've made?"

"Because we're family and I love you. What's more important than that? Not money, that's for certain." Diana pushed a little harder. "Remember when you were pregnant with Emily? You were so scared. And I promised I would help."

Brigitte nodded slowly. "I remember."

"Let me keep that promise."

Brigitte sobbed and clung to her. "Okay." After several minutes, her tears subsided. "Will you tell Lucas?"

Diana furrowed her brow. That was another challenge. Lucas was just as proud as Brigitte. She couldn't just wrap him in a hug and promise everything would be all right. "That won't be fun."

Brigitte laughed. "No. It won't."

They returned to the backyard to find Rebecca in pursuit of Calvin. She and their three kids chased him across the lawn and she hit him with a full body tackle when he was within a few feet of the pool. They landed in the water with a thundering crash, followed by the children. Diana wondered if there would be any water left in the pool as the waves settled.

On the edge of the pool, Maxwell abandoned his lounger and stood dripping with water. The financial section of the *New York Times* hung limp in his hands. Something flashed across his face, a warring of emotions. Grace rose up from the chaise where she had been resting at Maxwell's side and gently removed the soggy paper from his hands, dropping it on the seat she'd just vacated.

"Looks like it's time for a swim, big guy." She planted a loud kiss on his lips before pushing him backward into the pool. Two seconds later, she jumped in on top of him. Maxwell surfaced in a sputtering fountain of water and dove for his wife.

Brigitte and Diana glanced at each other.

"Oh, yeah." Brigitte laughed.

They tore off across the lawn at high speed and leapt in unison into the deep end. Diana hadn't been in the pool all day and the first shock of cold hit her square in the gut, giving her a rush of nausea followed by exhilaration. She pushed her hair back as she broke the surface. That's when she realized she hadn't changed into her swimsuit.

"Dammit. I swore you guys wouldn't get me into the pool in my clothes this weekend."

Brigitte and Rebecca glared at her, and Rebecca scolded, "Language."

Maxwell laughed from the shallow end of the pool. "Nobody threw you in, Di. This was a purely voluntary swim on your part."

This was the way it always had been with her siblings. The laughter, roughhousing, and love. Diana knew from the moment

Rebecca tore across the yard after Calvin, they would all end up in the pool eventually. If it wasn't for the not-so-gentle encouragement from her family, Diana's life would be work, work, and more work. They forced her to relax and unwind. Sometimes she wished they would find a new form of recreation, one that didn't include the pool and being fully dressed.

"Everyone say cheese." Her dad waited for all twelve faces to look his direction before snapping the picture.

Diana eased over to Lucas and scooped the baby out of his arms. "They're doing it again." She nodded in the direction of their parents.

"Doing what?" Brigitte turned her face toward the back patio where their parents stood together, removing the burgers from the grill. They were talking quietly and looking pointedly at Diana. "Oh, that. They're just worried about you."

At twenty-nine, Diana was the only one of the four Collins kids who hadn't settled down. "There's nothing to worry about. I'm fine." Her voice was laced with defiance.

"Of course you are. But still, they want to see you happy, not fine." Brigitte swooped the baby out of Diana's arms and twirled him around, then returned the happy boy to his aunt. "They want you to love something other than your career."

Diana wrinkled her nose. "I date. It's not like I'm leading the life of a nun." Cami's tousled hair and teasing laughter echoed through her mind.

"Sure, but you haven't brought anyone home to meet them since Angel." Brigitte paused for a thoughtful moment. "How can they not worry?"

While her parents hadn't been very receptive when she first came out as a teenager, they'd at least been supportive. The support had segued into acceptance. Now they actively encouraged her to meet a nice girl and settle down. Like it was that easy.

"If there was anyone that special, I would bring her."

A distinctive ring tone sounded across the yard. Diana climbed out of the pool and motioned for her dad to toss her the phone, a calculated risk with the giant body of water behind her. It arced high and landed in her outstretched hand with a soft smack. She flipped it open without checking caller ID.

"Diana?" Cami's come-and-get-me smile reached through the

phone. Diana wished she were here. She'd love to see Cami in a two-piece swimsuit pushing up out of the pool, water streaming down her body.

"Hi." Diana sounded goofy and lovestruck, even to her own ears. As much as she wanted to talk to Cami, she needed to spend the day with her family. She only saw them once a week. "I can't talk right now. Can I call you back in a little while?"

She prepared herself for the inevitable interrogation as she said good-bye. All she got was a knowing smile from Brigitte and a pat on the shoulders from her pop.

As soon as their late lunch had been eaten and all evidence of the meal cleared from the table, Brigitte gathered her husband and children together. "We're taking off," she announced to the family at large. "I'm on patrol early tomorrow morning and it's a long drive back to the city."

Brigitte bent to kiss Diana on the cheek. "Thanks, Di. I don't know what I'd do without you."

"Back atcha."

No time like good-bye to deliver a difficult message. Diana delayed Lucas, with a hand on his forearm. She kept her voice low, just between the two of them. "We're sending Mom and Pop on a cruise for their fortieth. I'm covering Brigitte's share. Deal with it." Lucas tried to pull away but Diana held tight and refused to yield. He stiffened.

"I need to think."

"Nothing to think about. It's the right thing." She drew back far enough to look Lucas square in the eye. She wanted him to see her intentions, her resolve. "Don't make it more complicated than it really is."

Lucas dropped his arms but held Diana's gaze for several heartbeats. She didn't want to steal his pride. She simply wanted to help her sister. Finally, he gave his wife a wistful sideways glance, then dropped his head in a resigned nod. "Okay, Di. Okay."

Thirty minutes and a full round of kisses later, Brigitte and Lucas were finally able to get their two children loaded safely into the car. As soon as they made it out of the driveway, another round of good-byes started with Calvin and Rebecca.

Diana thought about how long it took for her family to part from one another. They would see each other again in a week, but still, they never skimped on the hugs and kisses.

"Don't forget, Auntie Di," her middle nephew, Russell, reminded her. "You promised to come to my school and talk about your job. Tuesday."

Diana mussed his hair. "I remember. Nine a.m. sharp. I'll be there."

"Sure you can afford the time away from work, sis?" The teasing tone from earlier was gone. As much as Calvin prodded her about relaxing on Sunday afternoon, Tuesday morning was all about work. "I know you're working on something big."

Russell's face fell with his father's question. Rather than answering Calvin, Diana held her nephew's gaze. "What could possibly be more important than a promise to talk to your class?"

The corners of Russell's mouth shot up in a megawatt smile that lit the whole yard. He threw his arms around Diana's neck in a fierce hug. "You're the best!"

They waved good-bye from the driveway, then made their way to the backyard. Her father rested his arm around Diana's shoulders and pulled her close. "I'm glad you're taking time for Russell, sweetheart."

"God only knows why he picked you," Calvin teased. "What's so fascinating about an insurance investigator anyway?"

"Must be the Columbo hats and long trench coats," Grace offered.

Diana rolled her eyes. "I don't wear fedoras or trench coats."

Her mother patted her shoulder consolingly. "Of course you don't, dear. Besides, Russell has no idea who Columbo is. He just loves his aunt."

"I need to get back to the city, too. I still have work to do before heading to the office tomorrow morning." She kissed her mom and dad good-bye and climbed into her car. She wished, not for the first time, that she had thought to carpool with one of her siblings. She hated the long drive back. This time, however, she had plenty to occupy her. She dialed Cami's number as she backed onto the street.

"Hello." Cami's soft voice came through the phone and caressed her.

"I miss you." It wasn't Diana's customary greeting, but it was the only thing her brain could come up with.

"I miss you, too." Loud cheers in the background almost eclipsed Cami's response.

"Where are you and what's all that?"

Cami laughed. "I'm at my sister's house watching the game."

"Ah." Bears versus the Patriots. That explained the noise. "Who are you rooting for?" It was a pointless question. Nobody in Chicago supported the Patriots.

"I'm not. I just showed up for the food."

"Not a football fan, huh?"

"I can tolerate it under the right circumstances." The pandemonium around Cami dropped to a manageable, seemingly muffled level, like she'd gone to another room.

"What are the right circumstances?" Diana forced herself to concentrate on the traffic around her. She knew better than to call Cami while driving, but just couldn't wait this time.

"The ideal game day for me?" Cami dropped her voice to a playful, yet intimate level. "Well, first of all, the right company makes all the difference."

Before Diana could think of a clever response, Cami continued, "And right now my sister's living room is full of twenty-two-year-old, beer-guzzling boys. Definitely not the right company."

Diana glanced in the rearview mirror. Christ. The sound of Cami's voice turned her into a smiling idiot, even when driving. "Who would you rather be with?" She tried to keep her voice light, allowing for the possibility that Cami would say her own friends.

"There's this woman I know." The playful edge was gone, replaced by low, sweaty sex. "She's got this amazing dark reddish brown hair that's so soft I want to curl up in it and get lost for days. And her skin is smooth, tanned perfection, but the muscles underneath are hard, unyielding. She'd have people believe that was accidental, like it just happened. But I'm not fooled. I'll bet she spends hours in the gym and lying in tanning beds. She tries hard but doesn't want me to know. And when she smiles… God. I love that smile."

Diana pulled over to the emergency lane and activated her flashers. No way could she stay on the road and listen to Cami's idealized vision of her. "She sounds like she might be special."

Cami's response didn't come immediately and Diana wondered if she'd lost reception. "Cami?"

"I…" Cami's voice faded. "I think she could be, but it's way too early for me to even *think* about saying that out loud."

Diana understood that. She wasn't ready to reveal the emotions that flooded in her when she thought about Cami. Even if she was ready, how would she describe what she felt? One minute she was overwhelmed, ready to run away. The next she was awed and humbled, wanting only to lie down with Cami and hold her tight. She saw flashes of possibility. Not the traditional white picket fence. Diana wasn't that kind of girl. But it would be nice to have Cami with her during the drive home from her parents' house, and she could see Cami moving comfortably through her loft as though she belonged there.

Her family would like her, Diana had no doubt. How could they not fall in love with her easy smile and ready laugh? Diana's heart surged against her chest at the thought of them all together, her parents, brothers, sisters, their spouses and children, and her and Cami. They provided her with much-needed balance, kept her from working seven days a week. It would be nice to take a little piece of that home with her at the end of the day on Sunday.

"Too soon? Maybe." Diana eased back into traffic. She needed to get home sooner rather than later. "Let me tell you about this woman I know." Diana sped down the freeway. If she was lucky, she'd make it home before the end of the game.

CHAPTER EIGHT

She'd promised, sworn on her mother's Bible while cowering under their bed, to protect Elena, to protect her from the men invading her parents' house like a plague. She'd wrapped her arms tight around her trembling sister.

"She's not as strong as you." Her father's words echoed through her mind. "Keep her safe."

That's when she first heard his voice, evil and enchanting, promising salvation, protection. "Poppets, don't hide from Ricardo. Come out and let me save you."

Elena had scrambled out from their hiding place, obedience to adults the only thing she knew. Ali snatched at Elena's hand, desperate to keep her from the man she knew was dangerous. She was gone before Ali could stop her.

"There you are, poppet. Is your sister back there, too?" The voice was soft, entreating. "You belong to me now. You must tell me the truth."

Ali crawled out. She watched as Elena's eyes grew saucer wide with fear. Ricardo Chavez wrapped his greedy hands around her three-year-old arms and squeezed. When Elena cried out, his hand whipped out, lightning fast, and slapped her hard enough to leave a mark. Her head and body flew back like a boneless doll's, but she was held firm in Ricardo's unrelenting grip. She slumped forward, tears streaming down her flame-red face, and a high-pitched keening, the hurt cry of a child, declared her pain and confusion.

Ricardo gripped her head, covering her mouth with one hand. "Listen close, poppet. I do not like crying. You must stop at once."

Elena's wails increased in volume and frequency.

"So be it." Ricardo held out his hand and one of his men obediently filled his palm with a long, thin blade, similar to the one Ali's papa used for shaving. With catlike speed he slid the knife across Elena's neck, cutting deep. Her hands flew to her throat, grasping at the fatal injury. Blood gurgled out of her open, soundless mouth and seeped between her small fingers. She turned to Ali, her eyes pleading, as she slid to the ground.

Life drained from Elena and stained everything around her crimson. Ali's heart transformed from broken coal to diamond as her sister's eyes faded to darkness.

Ricardo's disembodied laughter faded into a bored command. "Get rid of it." Venom and disdain infused his voice and gave purchase to Ali's rising bile.

At six years old she vowed all their suffering at the hands of this man would not go unpaid. Now, twenty years later, she was finally taking action.

Ali sipped her dark espresso, a reminder of her native Colombia. The rich flavor brought to life so many memories for her. Ricardo's cruelty and her escape to America played out first. By the end of her second cup, her past cycled back to the moment where her happiness had ended, the last desperate breaths of Elena's life.

In spite of the promise she'd made that day, she'd been helpless to avenge her sister's death. It wasn't until she'd found the women of South Lake that she found an outlet for her rage. She'd fallen on Sergio Dominguez, the first of her four surrogate Ricardos, by accident. But, God, it felt good to carve away his control. Knowing that Rosa would no longer suffer infused Ali with a sense of power. For the first time in her life, she could stop the pain.

Monday mornings were always the hardest. It was time to put away the watchful avenger and transition to the caregiver. The violence necessary to keep her women safe was best doled out on the weekends, and sparingly even then. Ali folded her dark hair into a long braid down the middle of her back. The motion was comforting, but she missed the feel of her mother's hands working through her hair. The small piece of her heart that still remembered her mother's love wouldn't let her change the style. To cut her hair would be to forever sever that connection, and she couldn't bring herself to do it.

Ali downed the last of her coffee and smoothed her hands over her ivory shell. She shrugged into her deep brown jacket and was ready to face another day as the director of the South Lake Domestic Violence Shelter for Women.

❖

Diana set a shiny apple in the middle of the reception desk. "Mornin', Fran," she said with a wink, never breaking stride on the way to her office.

At seven forty-five on Monday morning, the office was just beginning to see signs of life. All the real activity started closer to nine. Left alone with the shiny chrome and black leather, without the benefit of a human buffer, Diana felt the full impact the designer had intended. The office was meant to be imposing, even intimidating, although Diana forgot to see it that way during the normal course of business.

The laptop docking station was, in Diana's opinion, a brilliant invention. It saved her from an octopus jungle of cables and wires. She dropped her computer into place and fired it up. Three e-mails awaited her. Diana paused, her pointer wavering between them. The e-mail from Cami was labeled "getting to know you," and it made Diana's breath catch in her throat. However, she couldn't go through the day with a half-addled smile on her face, so she moved down the list.

The one from Siger would set her off on the business of the day, and she didn't want that undermining the high Cami's e-mail promised. So she opted to read Grace's e-mail first. It was filled with links to different cruise packages. Grace was leaning heavily toward a high-end option that would send the senior Collinses around Greece for two weeks. Diana loved the idea, but her parents wouldn't.

She hit reply and typed: *Grace, I'd love this cruise! You and I should go the next time I take vacation. Mom and Pop, however, would be happier with the Alaskan cruise. Think about it.*

Cami or Siger. Diana knew she should get going. They had a busy day ahead of them, but she couldn't stop herself from opening Cami's e-mail first. She wanted to get to know everything there was to know about her and then some. She double-clicked and leaned forward into the screen as if she would find Cami in there.

Di,

    We never talked about nicknames, so I hope it's okay if I call you Di. Cami is short for Camille. Yes, it's a family name.

    Friday night, standing in the door, pressed against you, all I could think about was the bedroom. Hell, I was ready to drop to my knees right there on the hardwood floor of the entryway. All I wanted was to listen to you come and feel you tremble in my arms, around my fingers.

Diana sat back and blinked. Damn. Barely eight in the morning and she was already wet and panting.

    But then you pulled away with that scared look on your face. I thought I'd lost you. But you took me by the hand and invited me into your life. It was sweet and unexpected and it touched me far deeper than a weak-kneed fuck against the wall ever could. Mario's was wonderful. I'd never been before. I think I told you that, but I can't remember for sure. My brain wasn't working quite right. I knew you looked amazing in those tailored slacks that hugged your hips and made your legs look nine feet long. And that button-down that was barely buttoned up... How'd you pull that off exactly? If I tried to dress like that, I'd look like a woman in drag. Not sexy. You, however, look ultra-fuckable and super femme.

Femme? Not a term she ever would have used to describe herself, but somehow it felt right to have Cami think of her that way.

    Maybe it was the candlelight against your skin or the soft shimmer of your hair. Did you know it rests perfectly against your breasts, dancing across them like they are the ideal stage for any play? Listen to me. I'm sounding like a trashy romance novel. I'm not the only one who noticed. Maria couldn't keep her eyes or her hands off you. I was struck by this overwhelming need to establish ownership. I wanted to crawl in your lap and tattoo my name on your tonsils. And I wanted her to watch. Who knew I had such a jealous streak?

That's what the evil glares Cami had aimed at Maria were all about. Diana laughed out loud. Cami, it appeared, was a hellcat in more ways than one. In the past, Diana had little tolerance for jealousy, but the thought of Cami staking her claim tugged at Diana's heart.

At any rate, we spent so much time smiling at one another that we never really talked. I want to get a little background information out of the way. First, I have no idea what you do for a living. Me? I'm a teacher. That makes summers free. I love to travel. How about you? Want to take a trip next summer? Europe? Mexico? Brazil? Thailand? You pick the place. It won't matter to me. I don't plan to let you out of bed long enough to see the sights, so the location really doesn't matter.

Wow! That was a little forward. Ha! Listen to me. I have no problem describing how much I want to fuck you and how I'm going to do it, but making plans for next summer, when this summer is barely ending, well, that just seems presumptuous. But I can't help it. That's what you do to me, Di. All my good judgment flies out the window, along with my reservations and any hesitation I would normally have.

I'm hitting send now, before I have a chance to think too long about what I just wrote. Don't hold out on me. You said you wanted to get to know me, so let's do it.

Diana hit Reply. She felt like a third grader passing notes in class, hoping to not get caught. Yet she couldn't keep the smile from her face. The thought of Cami in shorts and a loose pajama top, the cute tank kind, curled up in front of her computer sent Diana's brain into orbit. Did her fingers stumble over the keys or did she type straight from the heart? No delete, no backtrack, no hesitation. Just the forward movement of the cursor as she let her thoughts flow into the e-mail and straight to Diana's inbox.

I need to see you again, Diana typed. *Please say yes.*

The short note wasn't enough, but it was all she had time for. Braxton was waiting. Still, she felt guilty for not saying more. She hit Send and hoped Cami would forgive her brevity.

The e-mail from Siger Enterprises waited patiently while Diana collected herself. She didn't want to look at it. Even if its contents revealed nothing, she would be forced to think about work. She wasn't ready to expunge the languid sweetness Cami filled her with. Working on this case left a dark, nasty aftertaste.

The message was short and simple, with an underlying tone of accusation: *How did you learn about this site?*

That was it. No other instructions. It was a test. One that Diana didn't want to fail. She replied: *You know I can't answer that. Tell me what I need to do to get in.*

She pulled out her cell phone. For the first time since getting the damned thing, she needed access to her personal e-mail when she was away from her computer. She called up Kyle, who was thankfully at his desk, and he walked her through the setup. Then it was time to get Braxton and go.

The interstate crawled at a snail's pace, but, for once, Diana wasn't in a hurry to get where she was going. They hadn't called ahead to make sure Susan Delaney would be home. That tended to scare reluctant interviewees into missing interviews. They didn't want to take the chance that Susan fell into this category, so instead they gambled that she would be home when they arrived.

"Do anything interesting this weekend, sugar?" Braxton gripped the wheel lightly as she navigated across three lanes of traffic to make their exit. She approached driving with the solid nerves of a NASCAR driver. As long as she was in the driver's seat, everything was fine. Put her in the passenger seat and she turned into a timid child, afraid of the simplest maneuvers, like turning a corner.

"Define interesting." Diana knew exactly what Braxton was talking about, but she wasn't going to give it up without a fight. Just because Braxton was curious didn't mean Diana's sex life was available for public consumption.

"Interesting would be…what was her name? The one who made you smile like a fool? Cami?" Braxton dragged out the sentence, her eyes moving from the road to Diana and back again. "I knew it. You saw her this weekend."

Diana hated the smug presumptuousness that infused every word Braxton spoke, and she was reluctant, to say the least, to play along. Still, denial at this point was not an option. She was a miserable liar, and besides, she didn't want to tempt fate by denying her budding relationship with Cami. The concept of self-fulfilling prophecies scared the crap out of her.

"Yes." Her blunt reply didn't invite further comment, but that didn't stop Braxton.

"And? Tell me!" Just like that, Braxton turned into a curious teenage girl.

Her eager smile made Diana want to share. "We went to dinner at Mario's. It was nice."

"Nice?" The smile on Braxton's face spread to her voice. "I won't ask you to define nice."

Nice was Cami's thighs wrapped tight around her head, blocking out every sound but the heavy, panting groans of a woman on the edge of climax. The image came unbidden into Diana's head. Her face flushed and she cleared her throat. She couldn't think of a response to Braxton's backhanded question.

Braxton pulled up next to the apartment complex where Susan Delaney lived. "You going to see her again?"

"God, I hope so." Diana gave herself a mental knock on the head for blurting that out. She climbed out of the car before Braxton could comment further.

Top of the stairs, third door on the left, was where they found Susan Delaney. She made up for the lack of buzzer on the front entrance by having seven dead bolts and a chain on the door to her apartment. It took all of Braxton's persuasion to talk their way through these cautionary barriers.

Diana smiled her best smile and extended her hand. "Mrs. Delaney, it's nice to meet you." She managed not to cringe when Susan's tobacco stained hand grasped hers. The whole apartment was veiled in a haze of Benson & Hedges.

"Not Delaney anymore. I went back to Hansen when that asshole bit it." Susan's voice was whiskey-soaked and held an edge of perpetual exhaustion. She tugged her worn, Pepto pink housecoat tightly around her waist. "How can I help you girls?" She couldn't have shown less interest in an answer.

"Ms. Hansen," Braxton changed the name with a conciliatory smile, "we have a few questions about your former husband, Victor Delaney." AKA, the asshole who bit it.

Susan lit a new cigarette, mindless of the one already in the ashtray trailing smoke up to the ceiling. "What do you want to know about him?" Steel tempered her voice. This was not a comfortable topic.

Diana explained their involvement and stressed that they weren't with the police or the FBI. Susan's expression didn't change when Diana mentioned the serial killer theory and their interest in the weapon used to kill the late Mr. Delaney.

"I already told this to the police, and the FBI." She drew out the letters of FBI, adding an extra syllable to each. "I don't know who killed my husband, the bastard."

"You don't seem like you were very fond of him." Diana stated the obvious.

"What's to like? He was an asshole." Susan tapped out another cigarette.

The longer they were in the apartment, the more Diana questioned Susan's motivation for unlocking the door in the first place. Diana stared longingly at the painted-shut windows. No fresh air getting into this place.

"Why'd you marry him?" That was typical Braxton style. Don't waste time. Ask the questions that matter.

"He asked." It was desperate simplicity at is best. "He didn't start hitting me until after we'd been married a couple of years."

Diana's stomach churned. "How long were you together?"

"Eight years. I finally get up the nerve to leave, then the asshole got himself killed."

A dim mental light went on in the smoke-induced haze of Diana's mind. "You left him? Where'd you go?"

"South Lake."

"How long before he died did you leave?" Braxton's voice told Diana that she was done. She was just asking questions to be polite. They'd be out the door soon.

"Two weeks. Give or take." Susan looked around Braxton to the muted TV against the wall.

Braxton smiled and stood. "We won't take up any more of your time."

Diana offered one of her business cards, along with an entreaty to call if she thought of anything else. She couldn't get out of the suffocating room soon enough. The stench of ancient, stale smoke clung to her suit like black sludge in a gutter—not really there, but not letting go either. They navigated the stairs quickly.

"Why'd you cut it short?" Diana wanted to learn something now that she was able to breathe. The air was still oppressive with humidity, but getting through it didn't require utensils.

"She wasn't even living there when it happened. She didn't see anything. No wonder the police didn't push harder." Braxton unlocked the car and they both climbed in.

The similarities between Mona and Susan dug at Diana. They'd both left shortly before the murders and, more frightening, they both lived in tiny, smoke-filled prisons of their own creation. The thought raised bumps on her arms. "Think Mona will end up like this? Broken, hard, and alone?"

Braxton started the car and let the engine idle. She answered without looking at Diana. "It's possible. If she finds help from the right people she might be okay."

Diana sucked in a steadying breath of clean, fresh air. She needed her head back in this game. "She's not the only one. There are thousands of young women just like her."

The irony of the situation didn't escape her. She'd intentionally chosen a career that would insulate her against that kind of suffering. She didn't know how Brigitte faced human tragedies every day.

"Not thousands. Probably more like millions."

Millions. "After this is done, I'm going on vacation."

A sun-drenched image came to mind—Cami lying on a white sandy beach, face down, bikini top undone, while Diana applied lotion to her back. The thought made her feel a little better, a little more leveled out. A sense of hopeful possibility washed over her. She could see herself on that shore, far from ugly realities, part of something beautiful. Diana stared out the windscreen, disconcerted by her lapse into romantic fantasy. Normally, her idea of escapism was a few stiff drinks followed by sex with a woman she didn't care about. Right now, however, if the opportunity presented itself she knew she would walk away, uninterested.

"I'm losing it," she said.

"You're obsessing over a woman," Braxton replied with discouraging conviction.

"No, I don't think so."

Diana willed her thoughts and feelings to unscramble. She felt jumpy and tense, just as she had that afternoon in Bernie's Fish Shack. Stepping outside herself, she realized an internal landslide was gathering momentum. The person she counted on being and the perspective she took for granted were eroding right in front of her, and she was powerless to stop the process. Worse still, she wasn't even sure if she wanted to.

Who was the familiar Diana Collins anyway? A week ago Diana would have answered that question quickly and without reservation. Since then her reactions to Cami had forced her to reevaluate. They'd spent precious little time together, not nearly enough to warrant deep self-assessment. That another person could have such an extreme impact on her so quickly filled Diana with dread and excitement. She could only compare her feelings to the thrill of rappelling. The first time she made a descent, she'd wanted to run away out of fear. At the same time, she wanted to jump off that cliff just to prove she could. All the safety lessons, the explanations about her gear and how the instructor on belay would not let her fall—none of it calmed the ring of fear that gripped her heart. Still, she refused to give in, to allow her frailty of emotion to keep her from conquering the task. It was an act of pure faith when she leaned back on her heels until she was perpendicular to the cliff face. The rush of exhilaration she felt, suspended between earth and sky, far surpassed any risk.

Cami scared and inspired her in the same way. Was it time to shed her fear and step off the cliff again?

❖

Ali pulled up short of Susan Hansen's block. Her lungs pounded and her thighs twitched. This part of her run was always the hardest. The halfway mark, when she hit the wall. She always stopped, rested on the bench at the bus stop and watched over Susan for a few minutes while she caught her breath. Then, without going any closer, she'd turn around and head back to South Lake.

Susan had been free of her husband's clutches for only a few months and Ali felt a need to stay close to her, checking up on her without intruding. Somehow, knowing she was safe kept Ali's pain at bay. She'd been too weak, too little to stop Ricardo Chavez from hurting her sister, but Victor Delaney had fallen easily under his own blade and would never hurt a woman again.

Today she lingered on the bench longer than usual, thinking about her life's purpose. Sometimes she felt desperate. So many women needed help, and there was just one of her. What could she possibly achieve? For every brutal creep she removed, thousands more just like him went about their daily lives without facing justice or consequences. Still, she couldn't bear witness to the pain visited upon these women and remain impassive. Keeping them safe was her job and she had to do it for as long as she was able.

Ali watched the black Mercedes back out of its parking spot on the opposite side of the street. She'd recognized the two women in the car as they exited Susan's building, the same women she saw at Mona's place last week. That was more than a coincidence. It was a threat. Red seeped in and colored the edges of her vision. This would not do. She waited until they drove away, then stood and stared at the building, tempted to find a reason to knock on Susan's door. But that would be a mistake. She wanted to know if the women were detectives, but she would have to find out another way. Asking Susan would draw attention to herself.

She started jogging back the way she came. She'd been gone too long. The women at the shelter would worry if she didn't return soon. Resolved calm enveloped her, comforted her. She increased her pace.

❖

"I'm beginning to think we're chasing our tails." Diana let her pent-up frustration show as Braxton pulled away from Lora Petrov's house. They'd found the wife of the second victim at home, high on prescription painkillers, in another house filled with smoke and gloom.

"Now, now. We learned something."

"That all these women think tobacco is a food group?" The

city rolled by at a good clip. It would take no time at all to find Rosa Dominguez's address in the pre–rush hour traffic.

Braxton laughed, the free, throaty laughter of a woman who loved life. "We learned that both women checked into the South Lake Domestic Violence Shelter shortly before their husbands were murdered. Connect Rosa and we'll have a trifecta."

The depth of what they were doing hitting home. Find the murderer, find the murder weapon. Diana stuffed that thought away, somewhere deep. She didn't want to think about the ramifications, like what exactly they would do if they discovered the killer's identity and tipped off the police only to lose the katana. The killer had probably shifted it by now, if he wasn't keeping it as a trophy. If he'd hidden it, he would never tell the police where it was. Murderers preferred not to hand over prima facie evidence.

"I think that's it." Braxton pointed to a small, white house.

The lawn was overgrown, more weeds than grass. Even the driveway had tall dandelions springing up through the cracks. The house appeared vacant and forgotten. Diana climbed out of the car, eager to get the next conversation over with.

Braxton knocked on the door and called out, "Mrs. Dominguez?"

No one answered from inside.

"You're wasting your time." An ancient Latina woman sitting on the front porch of the house next door greeted them. She spoke with a strange rhythm that matched the steady up and down of her rocking chair.

"Really?" Braxton made her way over, followed closely by Diana. "Why's that."

"They're dead." The woman's frank tone made Diana stop walking. People usually found a tactful way around the unpleasant truth. This woman brandished it like a banner.

After introducing them, Braxton asked, "What happened?"

"Tragic, really. That poor woman. He hit her, you know. Heard her crying out all times of day and night. Then, one day, she up and left his sorry ass. I cheered for her. I really did. That man was no good. But I guess he got his." The woman ended with a self-satisfied nod of her head.

"What do you mean?" Braxton encouraged her to continue. Diana was happy to let Braxton take the lead.

"Well, he was murdered. Chopped right up with a hunting knife. Deserved it, too. You shoulda seen what he did to her. She was forever coming up with some new bruise or another. She'd just duck her head and walk away, quick like. But I knew. Can't get nothin' past ol' Bertie. No sirree."

Sergio's abuse of his wife and subsequent murder was known information. Oscar had shared that with her during his abbreviated report on Charles Stewart. Where Rosa Dominguez went when she left her husband and how she died was news.

"Where'd Mrs. Dominguez go?"

"She came back, shortly after he was killed. Tol' me she'd been at a shelter. You know, one of those places for women whose men don't treat 'em right. It was good she went, too. He was fixin' to kill her. Every day it got worse for her."

Bingo. Three for three went to a shelter. Thank goodness every neighborhood had a resident busybody. "Do you know which shelter she went to?" Diana asked.

Bertie stopped rocking and scrunched up her face. "Well, let me see. I reckon she told me. Something about a lake. I just don't rightly remember for sure."

"Could it have been South Lake Domestic Violence Shelter?" Braxton's voice was level, unassuming. Diana could sense the underlying currents of excitement, but a casual observer would think the answer was of no consequence to her.

"Why, yes. It was."

"Just one more question." Braxton tapped her pen against the side of her little notebook. "What happened to Rosa?"

"Hung herself. Poor thing. Two days after she moved back here. They laid her out real nice at Mortenson's and put her in the ground over at Calvary." She examined Diana. "You look like a nice Catholic girl. You know Calvary?"

Every Catholic in Chicago knew Calvary. It'd been there since before Christ died. "Yes, ma'am," Diana answered in her best Sunday school voice. "I know Calvary."

"Good. You should go see her. Pay your respects."

"Yes, ma'am. I'll do that." It wasn't such an odd request. Diana could picture her grandmother making the same demand of any other young Catholic she met for the first time. When people died, Catholics showed up in droves. One detail niggled. "I'm sorry, ma'am, but you said she killed herself?"

"Oh, she did all right. But her priest convinced the diocese that even though he was already dead, she really died at the hands of that man Sergio."

Diana crossed herself. "She must have been well loved."

❖

Braxton pulled out into traffic. The first hint of evening showed on the western skyline, foreshadowing the shorter days and longer nights to come. The conversation with Rosa's neighbor had left Diana feeling unsettled, but her colleague seemed unaffected.

"So, what do you think?" Diana asked.

"I think we caught a lucky break."

Diana agreed. "What's our next move? South Lake or revisit Mona?"

"South Lake." Braxton didn't hesitate. Apparently she'd already decided. "First thing in the morning."

"Actually, it'll have to be second thing in the morning for me."

Braxton arched an eyebrow with cultivated precision, a move Diana knew well from interviews she'd observed. "And what will you be doing first thing?"

"Show-and-tell." Diana grinned, doing her best to look mischievous.

The lines of Braxton's face shifted between annoyance and envy. No doubt she was trying to decide whether to lecture her on responsibility or grill her about who she'd be doing the showing and telling to.

Responsibility won out. "Jeter's not going to like you missing another meeting because you can't keep it in your pants."

Diana laughed. "No, not like that. You remember my nephew Russell? I'm going to his school. He wants to show off his Auntie Di."

Braxton's frown relaxed into a smile. "Okay, you go entertain the kiddies and I'll spend a little more time online doing research. Then we can pay a visit to South Lake."

"Sounds like a plan." Diana felt the heavy weight of their case battle for emotional supremacy with the memory of last night with

Cami. She gave herself up to the stop-and-crawl pace of the traffic and forced her thoughts to the happy side. Vacation in Cancun. Or wherever else Cami wanted to go. That would be her reward when this was all over.

Chapter Nine

The internal labyrinth of Our Lady of the Sacred Heart Elementary School was exactly the way it was when Diana had attended long ago. She kept her eyes focused straight ahead in an attempt to keep scary penguin nuns out of her line of sight. Once they got into a person's head, it took decades to get them to leave. She still had a recurring nightmare about Sister Mary George towering over her, demanding math homework she knew nothing about. At twenty-nine, she didn't need another nun nightmare.

She made her way to Russell's classroom and paused outside the door, unsure if she should knock first or simply enter without invitation. The specter of a hostile nun rapping a ruler on the edge of her desk loomed before her. Reminding herself that she was an adult who had taken down a robber, she knocked assertively and entered the classroom like she had every right to be there. A room full of smiling six-year-olds and a radiant teacher with wild blond curls seemed to agree. Diana stared in astonishment. Cami? What in the name of all that was holy was she doing here?

Her e-mail had said she was a teacher, but did not mention Sacred Heart or kindergarten. Diana's feet seemed cemented to the floor. Her ability to formulate a sentence had disappeared along with her ability to move. After a few false starts, she muttered, "Oh, hell."

Giggles erupted and someone yelled, "She said a bad word."

"Auntie Di, you can't say that here!" Russell ran to her side and wrapped his arms around her middle.

Cami's mouth curved into a picture-perfect smile, revealing

sparkling white teeth. "No, she can't." She crossed the distance between them, her hand outstretched in greeting. "*You're* Russell's aunt?" Disbelief rang through loud and clear in her voice.

Diana's mind was filled with the memory of Cami, naked and golden, stretched out across her bed. Heat flushed up her chest and flamed over her face and all she could manage was a lame nod of her head. Cami lifted her hand a little higher, reminding Diana that she was supposed to respond to the customary greeting. Christ. This woman made her forget how to shake hands. Her ability to articulate was still on hiatus, too. Very smooth.

She jerked her hand up to grasp Cami's, and a rush of excitement tingled over her skin and settled in her belly with a thud. "Come sit by me, Auntie Di." Russell tugged on her other hand, dragging her toward his small desk in the middle of the room. "Look, I have a chair set up for you and everything."

Diana kept her eyes on Cami as she walked to the front of the room. It was a nice walk. Well worth watching. Her fingers tingled where Cami's had slid across them.

"Auntie Di, sit down." Russell's voice was impatient.

He pointed to a chair that might as well have been doll furniture for all the good it was going to do her. He had already reclaimed his seat and Diana realized that every child in the room was staring, waiting for her to stop ogling their teacher and get with the program.

"Sorry." Finally! Her speech returned. She lowered herself onto the munchkin-sized chair. It sagged under her weight and she prayed it wouldn't collapse beneath her.

As Cami resumed her lesson, Diana wished she'd thought to bring her laptop in with her. Not that Cami's teaching was boring, but at least Diana could have pretended to work. Instead she was stuck with playing out every hot-for-teacher fantasy she'd ever dreamed up. On the rare occasions when Cami's eyes met hers, Diana knew she wasn't hiding her lustful thoughts very well. But she let herself off the hook. With such a distraction right in front of her, who could blame her for a little self-indulgent visualization?

"Russell." Cami's voice startled Diana into focus. "Why don't you introduce your aunt to the class?"

"Come on." Russell's eyes sparkled with excitement as he led

Diana by the hand to the front of the room. He placed his hands on her hips and turned her to face the class. "This is my Aunt Diana."

"Russell, tell us about your aunt." Conspiratorial laughter edged Cami's words.

"She's a 'vestigator." Russell's voice was heavy with meaning. "Her job is very important." He looked up at Diana with big, serious brown eyes.

"Diana, why don't you tell us what that means?" Cami retreated to the far corner of the room, near the window.

"Well, Russell is correct. I'm an investigator. My job is to find things that have been misplaced." Diana kept her explanation simple. Six-year-olds would never understand the finer points of insurance fraud or property recovery.

A girl with big round glasses raised her hand. "What kind of stuff?"

"Well, anything of value." Diana reached into the inside breast pocket of her blazer. "I brought some pictures to show all of you." She handed a few to the students sitting in the front row, starting with the girl who asked the question.

"I've found things as small as a postage stamp and as big as a marble statue. My favorite, hands down, was a collection of vintage toys. There was a cap gun made more than a hundred years ago, and one of the first Barbie dolls ever made."

She left out the part about the toy collection being worth over four million dollars. The owner had moved the toys to a storage unit, then reported them stolen. He needed money and had hoped to collect insurance instead of having to sell his precious toys. Diana found them in a unit with no weatherproofing or climate control, secured with a generic padlock, the kind for sale at any hardware store for $6.99.

"What happened to the toys?" a ruddy-faced boy asked.

"That man ended up having to sell his toys to pay a fine for hiding them and then lying about it. And the really sad part is, because he didn't take care of his toys properly, they weren't worth as much as he thought."

When Diana's time was up, she collected her pictures from the students and Russell ran up and slipped his hand into hers.

"You were great, Auntie Di. Will you stay for recess?"

The pleading look in his eyes was almost enough to convince her, but the case pressed on her mind. She needed to get to South Lake or Braxton would do the interview without her. "No, sweetie, I've got to go back to work. But I'll see you on Sunday, okay?"

She bent down to eye level and he gave her a big kiss on the cheek. "Okay. You're the best aunt ever."

He raced out the door with his classmates, leaving Diana alone with Cami. Fighting the urge to bury her face in Cami's neck, Diana asked, "Walk me to my car?"

"Yes, but I only have fifteen minutes." They allowed silence to settle between them as they made their way to the main entrance. When they stepped through the big metal doors that separated inside from outside, Cami said, "Thanks for coming in today. I enjoyed your presentation a great deal."

Diana was caught off guard by Cami's offhand, casual formality. She wanted more. She wanted Cami to confirm that something was building between them. Rather than grabbing Cami by the shoulders and kissing her hard until she had no choice but to acknowledge their connection, Diana simply said, "My pleasure. I wish I could spend more time with Russell."

Awkward silence accompanied them, along with the morning sun, as they descended the steps to the visitor lot. The faint hum of a lawn mower could be heard in the distance.

"Yes, he's a special young man." Cami turned and caught Diana's eyes. "With an extraordinary aunt."

They stopped in front of Diana's car. Ever the smooth talker, Diana fumbled for a comeback as she pulled her keys out of her pocket.

"Please tell me you're not a nun." The question came bursting out of her before she realized what she was implying.

Her mind refused to wrap her memories of Cami's body in thick black cloth and a habit. A wave of nausea washed over her as the voice of Sister Mary George condemned her to the deepest level of hell for her transgressions.

Laughter bubbled out of Cami. "No, definitely not."

"Thank God for that. There aren't enough Our Fathers and Hail Marys in the world to keep me from going to hell for thinking naughty thoughts about a nun."

Cami took a half-step closer. "You did a lot more than think about it."

"And I want to do it again." Diana hesitated, then jumped in with both feet. "And again. As many times as you'll let me."

It's not like she was promising forever or mentioning the L-word. She was pragmatic. She didn't believe in love at first sight, but she wanted to give some room to the feelings she had. Cami wasn't like everyone else and Diana had to know what that meant. She stared at Cami intently, seeking a clue.

Cami returned her regard with one of the small, secret smiles that Diana learned to crave during their dinner at Mario's. "Good. I'm glad."

Her hand brushed over Diana's knuckles and she took the key ring from her unresisting fingers. The simple, unintentional intimacy stole away Diana's grasp of reason and logic. She didn't care that they were standing in front of her old elementary school. If she didn't move, and quickly, she was going to kiss Cami until her clothes fell off her.

Diana took a step back. She tried to think of something playful and meaningless to say, but every sentence that jumped to mind was just like her last one and she didn't want to sound obsessed.

Cami unlocked the driver's side door. With a gentle smile, she asked, "What are you doing later?"

"Having dinner with you?" A full dose of anticipation worked itself into Diana's voice, turning what would normally be a statement into a question. Thankfully, Cami seemed to find Diana charming as an uncertain thirteen-year-old. "At my place?"

Cami tilted her head to the side. "Can you cook?"

"No, but I can order takeout like nobody's business."

"Okay." Cami ran a finger along the inside edge of Diana's lapel, stopping when she reached the top button. "Your place tonight, but next time I'll cook."

The thought of Cami in her kitchen wearing a knee-length skirt and apron gave life to a naughty housewife fantasy. Rather than playing itself out, the image froze with Diana pressed up against Cami from behind, her arms encircling her waist. Slowly it rewound until Diana saw herself arriving home from work, sun dropping in the sky. She parked in the driveway of a perfect suburban home, four bedrooms, two-car garage, and perfectly manicured lawn. Cami waited in the door, a smile on her face.

A bell rang inside the school and Cami knitted her brows together. "I need to get back inside."

Diana gave her hand a squeeze. "My place at seven?" Diana wasn't ready to let her go, but managed to not throw Cami into the backseat of the car and convince her to stay.

Cami started across the parking lot. "I'll call for directions," she said over her shoulder.

Diana mentally ran through the menu for her favorite Thai restaurant as she climbed into the driver's seat. She tried to scowl at the smiling fool in her rearview mirror, but she just couldn't do it. Tonight takeout, but next time Cami wanted to cook for her. Even the traffic on her way to the office couldn't pull the semidazed grin off her face. She didn't allow herself time to think about what her daydream of domestic bliss really meant. She was just happy to have a dinner date with her beautiful kindergarten teacher.

❖

South Lake was a haven. The dark purple evidence of violence shadowed the bodies of the inhabitants, but Ali felt safe inside this building. In time, most of the women here would feel the same way. Danger lurked outside, back in the real world, but never crossed the shelter's threshold, that narrow edge between safety and pain, light and dark.

Ali's favorite room was the meal prep area. Despite the stainless steel sterility of an industrial kitchen, it was infused with the love and energy of every woman who had passed through the facility. Ali relaxed in its reassuring warmth as she chopped celery into manageable sticks.

A plump Latina woman joined the group already assembled, greeting a couple of the residents she knew.

"Hi, Teresa," Ali welcomed her with a warm smile. "Come to help?"

Deeply etched fear still haunted the corners of Teresa's eyes, but the enthusiasm seemed genuine. "Absolutely. What can I do?"

Ali pointed Teresa toward the woman in charge of coordinating meal prep. As part of the requirement for staying at the shelter, each woman had to participate in the household and general upkeep duties. Organizing a meal was no small task. If done properly, everyone got fed at approximately the same time.

The disembodied voice of the receptionist on the overhead paging system called Ali to the front of the building. She dried her hand on a towel and turned over the large chef's knife to Teresa. "Careful. It's sharp."

The intake area was surprisingly quiet. A few office employees were on the phone and one was taking in a donation. Ali entered expecting to find a frightened woman in need of her help and protection. Instead, the two women she'd seen outside Susan's apartment yesterday looked up at her expectantly. Ali had planned to track these women down, determine the nature of their interest in Mona and Susan, and assess how much of a threat they were. It certainly simplified matters to have them show up at her place of work. The impossibility of coincidence filled Ali with a sense of unease. She forced a smile and she hoped the women would take it as a friendly greeting.

The older of the two stood and stretched out her hand. "I'm Braxton Rinaldi. This is my business associate, Diana Collins."

Ali appraised Braxton with the cool indifference of a seasoned hunter, but Diana's greeting caught her off guard.

"Ms. Sandoval, the work you do here..." She seemed to be searching for the right words, clearly at a loss. "It's so valuable. Thank you for being here to protect these women."

Ali had been thanked many times over the two years since she'd been at the shelter, generally at fund-raisers or by grateful family members. The compassion and gratitude in Diana's words wrapped around her heart, clouding her red-tinged clarity. She spoke with the familiarity of someone who'd been there, someone who could relate. Ali wondered if she'd made use of a similar facility at some point in her life. If she'd checked in here since Ali was on the staff, she'd remember.

Diana carried herself with confident authority and Ali decided it was unlikely that she'd ever been, or ever would be, a victim of domestic abuse. Her high cheekbones, the firm set of her jaw, said she was a woman who would fight back. Sharp intelligence colored her blue eyes and there was a layer of fuck-you attitude barely contained beneath the surface of her perfectly tanned skin. Ali wished she could bottle up this apparent mental strength and issue it to every woman who checked into South Lake.

"How can I help you?" She held Diana's eyes longer than necessary, searching for an unspoken answer to her questions. When Diana blinked, breaking the eye contact, Ali turned to include Braxton in the conversation.

"We're insurance investigators for Carter and Lowe," Braxton said. "We're investigating the loss of a valuable katana." She produced a photograph of the sword Ali had held in her hand as blood dripped silently down the blade.

They weren't with law enforcement, which minimized the immediate threat they presented. Ali would have relaxed if not for the danger of her situation. If a pair of insurance investigators had found this place, the police could not be far behind.

Cagily, she said, "I don't understand."

Braxton nodded, her face thoughtful. "A man named Charles Stewart owned the sword. We believe his stepdaughter, Mona Stewart, might have stayed here in the weeks before it was stolen."

Ali watched Braxton closely, listening to what she was saying and searching for clues as to what she wasn't. Braxton's expression was contemplative, a look that was meant to make Ali feel comfortable, relaxed. It had the opposite effect. Ali felt her body coiling tight with tension. She forced herself to relax and leaned casually against the edge of the nearest desk.

"Not sure how I can help."

"Can you confirm that Mona stayed here?" Braxton looked hopeful.

There had to be more to this. Knowing that Mona lived at South Lake for a short time would only be useful if Braxton believed the katana's disappearance was somehow linked to the shelter. Ali shook her head, masking her anxiety with what she hoped was the right blend of professionalism and remorse. "You know I can't. That's confidential."

Diana gave Braxton a sideways glance. "Of course it is."

"Can I ask you a question?" Ali waited for Braxton to nod. "How would that information help your investigation?" She worded her question carefully. Her brain was a raging maelstrom. It was difficult to pick out one thread and follow the thought.

Braxton shrugged. "I'm not sure that it would. We're simply

trying to recreate the family's activities during the weeks leading up the theft."

The noise in Ali's head picked up in volume to five-alarm loud. Perspiration glued her clothing to her beneath her arms and at her waist. That was Braxton's second reference to the missing sword, but she'd made no mention of the murder. She definitely knew about it or she wouldn't have referred to Charles Stewart in past tense.

Ali forced a smile. "Perhaps you should ask the woman in question, Mona Stewart."

"Perhaps." Braxton echoed her sentiment, her eyes narrowed ever so slightly.

Ali let the silence grow between them.

Diana looked at her colleague, tension showing in the corners of her eyes. "We understand." She pulled out a business card. "Call me if you think of anything you can share." She paused for a moment. "Or if you need a volunteer to help with anything here."

It was a common offer, made impulsively when visitors felt helpless and wanted to do something. Most could not follow through. Ali understood why. Very few people could cope with daily exposure to damaged women and children. They weren't tough enough emotionally.

"Thank you, I'll keep your card. We always welcome donations, too, of course. We take Visa."

Diana nodded eagerly. "I could probably come for a couple of nights each week, after work."

"Then I'll add your name to our list, and when we train our next volunteers we'll be in touch."

Ali knew she would never invite this woman into the sanctity of the shelter. She would see things Ali couldn't afford for her to see. Diana wasn't a threat to these women, but she could be a threat to Ali's ability to protect them, and that would have to be monitored.

"You've done a great job with the décor." Diana looked around. "It's not institutional at all. The place has such a positive feel."

"It does," Braxton said. "So it's important that we don't disrupt the atmosphere. I would hate, for example, to discuss our suspicions with the police." Diana seemed startled by her colleague's remark, but Braxton continued, regardless. "Those guys just don't know how to tread carefully."

"Your suspicions?" Ali allowed a trace of anger to enter her voice.

"We don't suspect the shelter of anything," Diana said quickly.

"And that will continue," Braxton said. "So long as no one acts suspiciously."

Diana whispered something terse in her ear.

Braxton's expression was long-suffering. "I'm not accusing anyone of anything."

"They're not hiding the damn sword here," Diana replied, not bothering to whisper this time.

Ali tried for an incredulous laugh. "We keep no weapons on the premises, I can assure you."

"We simply have to follow up every avenue," Diana said apologetically. "If Ms. Stewart lived here, as we believe, it's possible that she could have concealed the sword somewhere if it was in her possession."

"I wish I could help, but the women here count on us. I would lose my job if I breached confidentiality."

"And that's how it should be." Diana gave Braxton a sideways glare. "We'll get the information we need another way."

"Do you think Ms. Stewart has the sword?" Ali asked innocently. "Is there a scam or something?"

"We don't think so." Diana hesitated. "But we have to be sure. It's our job to find it, no matter who has it."

"I see." Ali hoped she sounded like anyone else placed in the position of answering questions when they didn't know what had really happened. "The insurance company doesn't want to pay the money?"

"They never do without proof," Diana said. "So our job is to find the insured item or verify that it can't be found. Then the claim can proceed."

"In other words, we have paperwork to complete." Braxton sounded weary. "If I leave anything out, the claim goes nowhere, and it sure looks to me like Ms. Stewart could use the money."

Braxton shrugged her well-defined shoulders. Ali was surprised by the pale pink suit she wore, but she'd learned a long time ago not to be fooled by external appearances. Braxton might look harmless, but Ali could tell she was far from it. Underestimating this woman could be her undoing. Ali thought quickly. Braxton made reference to Ms.

Stewart needing the money, but Mrs. Stewart, Mona's mother, did not. Any settlement that was paid out would surely be issued to the widow, not the stepdaughter. Braxton was baiting Ali. Insurance companies were vast bureaucracies, and she could see that Braxton was the kind of woman who didn't appreciate having incomplete paperwork returned. Too bad. She would just have to make something up.

But she'd made an important point. Ali suspected Charles Stewart had left his useless wife well provided for, but Mona would probably get nothing. The katana was worth a lot of money. When she gave the sword to Mona, she'd intended it to be a symbol of her victory over Charles Stewart, a sign that she had survived and he had not. Now, she saw it in a whole new light. Mona could sell it or return it for a finder's fee. Money was the great equalizer. Ali could add the idealistic vision of a modern-day Robin Hood to her self-image.

She wondered how much time she had before the police found their way to the shelter. Days? Weeks? Hoping to buy some time, she said, "I see why this is important. Please leave the matter in my hands and I'll see what I can do."

The visitors exchanged a satisfied look.

"Thank you, we really appreciate your help." Diana hesitated as though weighing her words. "And something else… If the police come around asking the same questions, could you avoid helping them?"

Ali could not hide her surprise completely. "I don't understand."

Braxton also seemed puzzled. She frowned uneasily at Diana.

"The thing is, if they find the sword first, it will be treated as evidence and that will hold everything up."

"Evidence," Ali echoed.

"I'm good with the idea of a little biblical justice for men who harm women," Diana said in a joking tone. "But it's bad luck that this katana was probably used to kill Ms. Stewart's stepfather. That's why the cops want it."

Ali felt the veneer over her emotions slip. Diana announced the murder with such casualness, but Ali knew it was a calculated lob. They were watching to see how she would react to that bit of news. She didn't know how to react. Should she ask what Diana was talking about? How shocked should she look? She wrestled her mask back in place.

"Well, unless they have a warrant, they can't search our records." She kept her tone light, hoping to match Diana's casual manner.

"That's helpful to know." Diana leaned in a little closer. "They're usually a good week or two behind us in investigation anyway, so we have plenty of time to wrap this case up before they even show up here."

Ali showed the investigators out, her thoughts racing. A week, maybe two. That was how long she had to come up with a game plan. She retreated to her office and let her mind wander without restraint. First she needed to check on Mona Stewart, assess her mental state. Would Mona protect her prize, the katana Ali had left on her doorstep the morning she'd first seen Braxton and Diana? Or would she turn it over to them, unwittingly leading them closer to Ali? Would they even continue their investigation if the sword was recovered? Ali needed to find some answers and quick.

Chapter Ten

Diana held her breath as Braxton forced her car into a nonexistent break in traffic. The driver of the SUV behind them honked and gestured obscenely. Still, she couldn't help but feel pleased with their visit to South Lake. "That was fruitful."

Braxton nodded in agreement. "Do you think she realizes how much she actually shared by not saying anything at all?"

"Possibly."

Most people didn't think about how much their silence conveyed. Ali's stark refusal to confirm whether Mona Stewart had lived at the shelter was to be expected. But she'd dropped a big hint by offering to follow up on their request. That offer alone told them all they needed to know. If no record existed, Ali would not have suggested she could look into bending the rules. Diana wondered about her motives and how much she knew.

"Did you see the way she looked at us when we arrived?" Braxton's voice was low, contemplative. "We were being sized up."

Diana had definitely noticed. The woman's searing appraisal had felt predatory, like a jungle cat moving in for the kill. It was out of sync with the role she carried out in the community as caretaker for battered women. "Yeah, I noticed. She mellowed once we started talking, though."

"Still, her demeanor was disconcerting."

"Maybe she's just naturally suspicious, what with her work at South Lake."

"I guess." Braxton still sounded skeptical.

"Think we should tell Oscar?" Diana asked.

Braxton pursed her lips. "Let's wait until we have something concrete to share with him."

That made sense. Everything they had now was simple speculation, but they were close to crossing a line and she had no doubt Braxton knew it, too. Right now, they could argue that they were just doing their jobs, following the trail that would lead them to the missing katana. But obstruction of justice was a serious matter. As soon as they confirmed a few more facts, they would have to share what they knew with the police.

"So, what do you say, ready for another visit to Mona Stewart?" Diana didn't want to tear the scab off the girl's wound yet again, but they had no choice. She was one of four women whose victimizers had been murdered in crimes the police and FBI thought were linked. The shelter was a common factor, which could mean all four women had come into contact with the killer. Or even if they hadn't, someone from the shelter might have. Anything was possible.

Diana considered various scenarios. *A shelter worker upset by what she sees confides in a friend who just happens to be a vigilante. A worker at the shelter takes her duties a little too seriously and eliminates extreme threats by killing the abuser. Perhaps a protective brother acts out in an exaggerated sense of duty and can't stop with only one.* Or maybe it was coincidental that all the women stayed at the shelter. What if there was another connection she was missing completely? Diana wished, not for the first time, for a copy of the police files.

"I'm in court tomorrow and I need to prep," Braxton said. "But we have to move on this. Think you can talk to Mona by yourself?"

"Sure, I'll head over there now."

Braxton patted Diana's leg, the reassuring touch of a concerned friend. "I know last time was rough. If you want to wait, we can do this when I'm free."

"No, I'll go insane if I have to look at another Internet search."

As much as she didn't want to talk to Mona alone, there were too many coincidences and unanswered questions. A thought jumped into her mind. What if the killer heard about their visit to the shelter? Ali Sandoval wasn't the only person who'd seen them there, and she intended to see if she could help them. That meant she would talk to people. Word would get around that questions were being asked about

Mona Stewart. Could they have placed Mona in danger? Surely not. The killer targeted men. Abusive men. Was that intentional, or did he have another motive entirely?

Braxton was chatting about her court case, but Diana didn't hear a word she said. Between her dinner plans with Cami and worry for Mona Stewart, there wasn't room in Diana's thoughts for tomorrow.

❖

Diana took it as a good sign that Traci's Jag wasn't parked in front of Mona's apartment this time. If the last visit was any indication, Mona would be more comfortable without her mom there. This time Diana wasn't surprised when Mona buzzed her in without using the intercom. The very concept of a walk-up apartment baffled Diana. She cursed every stair on the way up to Mona's apartment. Goddamned missing elevator.

"Didn't think I'd see you again." Mona stood in the open doorway. A Gitanes Brunes dangled from her fingers.

"I have a couple of things I want to go over with you," Diana said. "Do you mind?"

Mona made a motion with her head that wasn't exactly a nod and retreated back into the apartment, leaving the door open. Diana followed her in to the kitchen. The counter was littered with pizza boxes and Chinese take-out containers. Mona pulled a glass out of a sink overflowing with dishes. She rinsed it out and poured herself a generous amount of Bacardi. "You want any?"

Diana preferred her rum blended up in a fruity drink with a little paper umbrella. "No, thanks."

They moved to the kitchen table and Mona moved a pile of mail, clearing a place for Diana to sit. "How can I help you?"

Diana debated which question to ask first. Odds were Mona knew very little, if anything, about her stepfather's company, Siger Enterprises. Might as well save it for the end and start with South Lake. "Where did you stay before you moved into this apartment?"

"My mom's house."

Glaring omission of the shelter. Intentional or oversight? "Nowhere else in between?"

Mona dropped her cigarette into an empty beer bottle. "I spent about a week, maybe two, at this shelter. South Lake. It's a place for battered women." She pushed out the word "battered," like it didn't taste right in her mouth.

"I know the place." Diana wanted more information. She wanted Mona to talk, hopefully without the tears. Weeping made things awkward. "Why did you go there?"

Mona swirled her drink in her glass, staring hard at the liquid. "I had to go somewhere. I couldn't stay in his house anymore."

"Did something happen?" Fuck it. Of course something happened. Diana rushed to clarify. "Something different than usual?"

Mona shrank into her chair and gulped down the remainder of her drink. She pulled another cigarette out of the silver case and lit it with the matching lighter. After taking several long drags, she said, "It was always bad. The things he did. I wanted to move out so many times, but I'm a student." The words came with quiet precision, like they'd been formulating in her mind for a long time, waiting for a willing audience. "Mom insisted that I live at home or they wouldn't pay for tuition."

She fell silent for a while, her expression introspective as though she was searching for an answer that was good enough to justify her choices. "I'd lived with it for so long. I believed him. Ya know? He said I belonged to him." Suddenly she looked up at Diana, like she'd remembered she wasn't alone. "You hear something enough times, it becomes real."

"I can see that."

Diana couldn't see that at all. She'd never been in a place where her head had been fucked with so severely that she believed she deserved the things Mona assumed were inevitable. Even when her relationship with Angel disintegrated and Diana wanted to put her fist through everything she saw, she never thought she deserved to be cheated on, let alone sexually assaulted on a routine basis. She wished the mind was like a mental dry erase board. Then Mona could just clean it off and start over. Instead it was more like recycled paper with permanent marker. The edges were never clear, bleeding out and touching everything around it.

"He never really hit me. He burned me with his cigarette, more than once." Mona rubbed her thumb over the monogrammed letters on the lighter, making them shine. "And he cut me. He said he liked the blood…watching it pool up and bubble over. I cried once. He locked me in the attic for three days. My mom was out of town. I never cried after that." She stood abruptly. "I need a refill. Sure I can't get you anything?"

If Mona got any more detailed with her descriptions, Diana would be willing to mainline the rum. No wonder Mona drank so much of it. "But you finally made the decision to leave," she prompted softly.

Mona paced back and forth across the kitchen. "Yes. Looking back it seems almost silly compared to everything else. One day I notice the books on my shelf were a little off, so I tried to straighten them. I found a tiny camera on the underside of one of the shelves. I don't know how long it had been there."

Compared to all the things Mona had endured up to that point, this seemed like a pretty small thing. "Why did that bother you so much?"

"Don't you see? He wanted to save those moments, the ones I most wanted to forget. He wanted them to be permanent. What if he showed the video to someone?"

It all boiled down to denial. As long as Mona could pretend the abuse wasn't real to other people, then it was okay. The possibility of someone else knowing sent her running. Diana pulled a cigarette from Mona's case. One of them needed to smoke after this kind of confession. If Mona didn't want to, Diana was just about willing to take up the habit on her behalf. She lit the cigarette and took the smoke into her mouth. She held it there, not willing to inhale the toxic fumes. No smoking allowed. She passed the cigarette to Mona and blew out the mouthful of smoke. "But you talk about it now."

"Not to anyone else. Just you and my therapist. That's part of my healing process, according to Dr. Rosenburg. I have to talk through it with someone other than her."

"Why me?" The responsibility of being the only other person to hear Mona's confession made Diana slightly nauseous. So far all this investigation had brought her was a list of dead men and a smoke-filled view of broken women. No sword.

"You're the first person to ask. And you're a dyke." Mona tensed, her eyes betraying her desire to take the comment back as soon as the words left her mouth. "You are, aren't you?"

Not a question Diana preferred to answer during an interview, but there wasn't a graceful way out of it. "Yes," she said, then directed them back on topic. "Why South Lake?"

"Luck of the draw. I checked the Yellow Pages the day I found the camera. I left before he came home from work."

"Did you tell anyone where you were going?"

"No." Mona downed another gulp of rum.

Diana debated ending the interview. There wasn't much Bacardi left in the bottle. She didn't want to know if there was another one in the cupboard waiting to be opened. A couple more questions, then she'd wrap up. "You didn't stay at the shelter very long. Why is that?"

"He was killed." Mona's voice was flat. "The bogeyman was dead, so there was no reason to hide anymore. Why would I stay?"

Why indeed? But learning how to not be a victim took time, much longer than two weeks. Still, she had a therapist and shelters did not have unlimited accommodation. Mona's circumstances had changed. "Did you make any friends while you were there?"

"Friends? Not really." Mona took a long drag. "There was one woman. Ali. The director of the shelter. She helped me a lot."

"What did she do?"

"She just…" Mona paused. "Listened. It was like she truly understood. She didn't judge me. I felt protected when she was around. I haven't felt like that since. I try to think of reasons to go visit her, but then I don't get around to it. I guess I don't want to go back there."

So Mona hadn't just talked to her therapist. She'd also confided in Ali Sandoval. Wondering how much she'd revealed, Diana asked, "Did you tell her what had happened to you?"

"Yes. Not everything. But I told her about the camera and some of the things he did to me. She was pretty angry with him." Mona clenched her jaw, slowly grinding her teeth in the pause between her thoughts. "It felt good to hear someone talk about him like he wasn't a saint."

Diana winced, thinking about Traci's deluded defense of her late husband. "He was human scum, Mona."

Mona stared hard at her. "You actually mean it. Thank you."

The thought that anyone would hear Mona's story and not agree made Diana mentally shudder. She asked, "Was there anyone else you talked to there? Another employee? A resident? Anybody?"

"No, just Ali."

"I have to ask you this again, I'm sorry. Do you know where that missing sword is?"

An emotion that Diana couldn't read flashed over Mona's face. "If

I had it, I'd frame it and put it on the wall." The bitterness in her tone chilled Diana.

"There's just one last question. Charles owned a corporation called Siger Enterprises. Is that name familiar to you?"

Mona's face relaxed. "If you want to know about his business interests, you should ask my mom. She knows about that stuff."

Diana wasn't convinced that Mona was being truthful about the sword, but it would take the police and a search warrant to find out if it was in this apartment. She was satisfied, however, that Mona didn't know any details about Siger. Diana thanked her and left her to her bottle and seemingly endless stream of French cigarettes. She couldn't wait to shake the smoke out of her clothes and talk to Braxton.

As they pulled into the bright daylight of the roof level of the parking garage, Diana saw Oscar waiting for her near the elevator. Braxton pulled into a space on the opposite end of the garage, giving Oscar plenty of room. Diana would have preferred to meet him alone, but Braxton had finished getting her paperwork ready for the court case and insisted on joining her.

She placed a strong hand on Diana's leg, stopping her as she was climbing out of the car. "You know, shug, I'd be happy to talk to Oscar for you if you just want to rest for a few minutes."

Diana scratched her temple and tried to look contemplative. Braxton had been trying to work her way into Oscar's circle for a long time. He was a valuable resource and it killed her that he clammed up around anyone other than Diana.

"We could do that," Diana said. "But I'm assuming you actually want to learn something about Siger." With that she stepped out into the light and crossed the roof.

Oscar seemed happy, yet reluctant to see her. He smoothed his hand over his graying hair, then pulled at his tie. The knot loosened, hanging open to the right. That movement, more than anything, worried Diana. Oscar was generally careful with his appearance. He kept his clothing simple and professional. White dress shirt, solid-colored tie— this one was dark blue—blazer, black slacks, and solid black shoes. His wardrobe had remained constant throughout Diana's life, and it was a comfort. If it were any other person, a slightly askew tie wouldn't be cause for alarm. With Oscar, it made Diana hesitate.

"You sure you want to play in this sandbox?" he asked.

So, Oscar had learned something about Siger. Diana mentally pumped her fist in victory. "No. I'm not sure at all. But I have no other choice." In deference to Oscar's serious mood, Diana tried to keep the glee out of her voice. She loved it when new information came to light.

"Not sure I can tell you anything you don't already know." Oscar stuffed his hands deep in his trouser pockets, his worn trench coat bunched around his wrists. The pause was long enough to make Diana wonder if the conversation was going to continue. "Siger Enterprises, Charles Regis Stewart listed as president and CEO. He was the primary shareholder, but not the only one. His interests in the company went to his wife, Traci. It's listed as an entertainment company. No further description other than *specialty*."

No new information here. "Anything else?" Diana hoped her disappointment didn't show. She hated to appear ungrateful.

"I pumped the feds but found myself on the receiving end of an interrogation. They are very interested in learning more. Not interested in sharing."

"Typical." Diana forced a grim smile. Oscar was probably used to banging his head against the famous federal wall of silence, but she was grateful he'd done so on her behalf.

"There are several FCC investigations pending," he said.

"Interesting. Any idea of the basis?"

The Federal Communications Commission regulated the information airways: television, radio, phones, and the Internet. Enforcing regulations for Internet violations was difficult at best. Often infractions were easy to find but extremely difficult to trace to the source. As a result, the FCC focused its efforts on Internet service providers, acting in the capacity of antitrust regulation more than anything else.

"You know they only investigate extreme cases. And if that isn't enough to chew on, they're working in cooperation with the FBI."

"Christ." The implications knocked Diana off kilter emotionally. The list of things that would generate that kind of attention was very short. "What do you think? Drugs, terrorists, or money laundering?"

"You forgot one." Oscar paused, looked out over the skyline. "Kiddie porn."

Diana's guts clenched. Everything about Charles Stewart and his damned katana was covered with poison. "You think that's what it is?"

"Hard to say for sure."

Wind blew over the rooftop garage, stirring up bits of discarded paper before dropping them down onto the street below. Diana rubbed her hands over her eyes. This was all more than she wanted to think about, but still, she owed Oscar for his help. Seemed only right to give him something to take back, even if she hadn't moved much further than guesswork. "I have some information for you."

Oscar's face brightened. "I like when the two-way street is part of the deal."

Diana smiled. She also liked it when she was able to pass information to Oscar instead of the other way around. "Your crowd probably has this figured out already, but all of the murder victims sent a battered woman into the South Lake Domestic Violence Shelter for Women. It's the only common link I can find."

Oscar rocked back on his heels. "You're saying all the wives ended up there?"

"The three wives, and one stepdaughter." That was an interesting point. They weren't connected by the type of relationship they shared with the dead men. "Charles Stewart's favorite victim was his wife's daughter from her first marriage."

"How do you know?"

"We talked to all of them." Before he could articulate the annoyance that creased his face, she said, "I know we were reaching, but we thought if we could get a lead on the sword if we figured out a link between them."

"Don't tell me you've been snooping around that shelter, too."

Diana nodded, embarrassed.

"Jesus, thanks for giving the guy a heads-up if that place is the common factor."

"I don't think any guys work there," Diana said softly.

The thought gave her pause. She'd simply assumed the killer was male. Most serial killers were, and the crimes were so violent they didn't seem like a woman's work. Charles Stewart was a big man. She couldn't imagine how a woman could have subdued him physically, but that was sexist. She and Braxton together could take down a man, no problem. What if the killer was a woman, or two women?

She pictured Mona with one of the battered wives from the refuge. That could explain her brief stay. Had she found someone there who could help her in a quest for revenge? Diana frowned, trying to piece together a theory that made sense. Charles Stewart was the fourth victim, so Mona couldn't be part of a team that had carried out all the killings. She'd had no connection with South Lake when the other men were murdered.

Oscar had shared her silence, also seemingly lost in thought. "I guess they get these women talking. Group therapy, and all."

"Yes, they support each other. It's a nice environment. A place where women can start to build a new life."

"You gotta wonder if someone put ideas in their heads," he said. "A ringleader."

"You think the women killed their abusers?"

"Maybe not their own husbands, but they could've been recruited into some kind of killing club. Revenge and such."

Only a man could come up with a notion like that. "Are you serious?" Diana tried not to sound patronizing. "The women who end up there are shell-shocked. Beaten down. They're not sitting around planning whose husband they can kill. They're trying to figure out where to go and what to do to stay safe."

"I'm a detective, Collins. We don't take theories off the table till we can disprove them. You got something better?"

"No," she admitted.

"I'll pass the information along," he said, obviously gratified.

Diana hated to think what the FBI's next move would be. If they all thought like Oscar, they would probably want to chase down every woman who'd been in the shelter for the past few years looking for this "ringleader."

"Just do all those women a favor and tread carefully," she said.

"You got it."

"And if I learn anything else about Siger, I'll turn it over to you so you can make your FBI friends look like slackers."

Oscar smiled. It broke up the serious lines and grooves of his face, giving him a comical evil clown look. Diana knew he was thinking about making the bust just to toss it back in the faces of the feds. No city cop liked the dressing down Bureau drones felt entitled to give.

"You do that, Collins," he said, and ambled back to the elevator.

Diana returned to the car and sank down into the passenger seat with a sigh. "It kills me that all our information today is essentially noninformation."

Braxton started the car but didn't shift it into gear. "Still no reply from Siger?"

"Nothing. Maybe Bob's come up with the goods. I thought I'd give him a few days before I hound him."

Braxton backed out of the parking space. "Sugar, don't you ever check your e-mail?"

Of course she did. That was all she'd been doing since sending the request to Siger, but that correspondence was in her personal account. She sighed. "I haven't had a chance to get into my work account since yesterday. What did I miss?"

"Bob's been reassigned." Braxton joined the slow crawl of traffic back to the office.

Diana pulled out her cell phone. It was one of those complicated numbers that took pictures, stored her calendar, did e-mail, even surfed the Net. Mostly she used it for phone calls. She logged into her e-mail and scrolled through the tangle of messages in her inbox. Sure enough, there was a notice from Jeter informing her that Bob had other duties now.

"I need to get an assistant," Diana said.

Senior investigators, along with the many perks of the position, were generally assigned one or two junior staff members to assist them. The policy gave juniors exposure to bigger cases and provided seniors with support that helped them close investigations faster. Diana had worked with Braxton in that capacity for years. When she got her big promotion, they'd kept the dynamic the same. It was time to rethink their approach.

Braxton patted her on the leg. "I think we both should, after we finish this case."

A wave of anticipation and trepidation rolled through Diana. As much as she wanted to recover the katana, she wasn't sure how she felt about accessing the Siger Web site. For some reason, whatever lay beyond the password-protected gate made her uneasy. She had discovered so little about the company that she could only assume it was some kind of shell operation. Maybe Charles Stewart had done what thousands of businessmen did, setting up a bogus legal identity to conceal assets from his wife, or the IRS, or business associates. He could easily have put Traci's name on the legal documents. Men did that all the time without their wives' knowledge.

"So, plans with your new girlfriend tonight?" Braxton's voice held an edge of uneasy teasing that hardened on the word "girlfriend."

The extra emphasis made Diana's heart melt as her muscles tensed. "She's not my girlfriend." She left "yet" off the sentence, but she was thinking the word loud enough that Braxton should have been able to hear it.

"You didn't answer the question." Braxton spoke softer, without the judgment coloring her words.

Diana considered asking Braxton what was behind the frosty attitude toward Cami. They'd never even met, so it couldn't be based in anything real. There was no point in posing the question because Braxton would likely deny it. She'd talk to Diana about it when she was good and ready.

"We're having dinner together at my place."

Braxton looked shocked. "You don't cook."

Diana smiled, sure that it was a goofy "I'm crazy about this girl" kind of smile. "Takeout."

They traveled in silence the rest of the way back to the office. Diana was content to leave Braxton to her thoughts as she was rather preoccupied herself. The very mention of Cami sent her heart rate through the roof and her stomach through the floor. No wonder Cami felt the need to correspond through e-mail. Diana turned into a blushing, stammering girl when they were together. Hopefully she'd have lots of time to get over that reaction so she could show Cami how charming she could be when all her faculties were in full functioning order.

CHAPTER ELEVEN

Diana waited just inside her front door, eager for Cami's arrival. She almost wished she'd decided to cook instead of picking up Thai food. At least then she'd have something to do besides wearing down the finish of her hardwood floor. Of course, Diana's culinary stylings were unreliable at best, and she didn't want to send Cami running for the door after the first bite.

She'd spent the week tense with anticipation, knowing that eventually they'd track down the missing katana but dreading the bits of nastiness that popped up along the way. Tonight, listening carefully for the sound of Cami's footsteps in the hall, she was filled with a different kind of anticipation. The edges were laced with excitement, nervousness, lust, and emerging hope. Diana turned the knob at the first hint of Cami knocking, a half-fulfilled rapping cut short by Diana's impatience.

Cami's expression flashed from surprised to pleased to determined as she stepped across the threshold, inviting Diana closer with a smoldering look. She kicked the door shut behind her as she wrapped her arms around Diana's waist.

"I've got to get you a key so you don't waste so much time knocking."

The last half of the sentence was lost in the crush of their bodies as Cami pulled her in for a tight hug. Key? The implication left Diana light-headed and dizzy. It wasn't a planned announcement, but the sentiment tasted good hanging in the air between them.

Cami clung to her and whispered, "I missed you."

Logic dictated that she hadn't known Cami long enough to have anything other than an overwhelming case of lust. Logic didn't stop her heart from pounding out of her chest at the thought of coming home to Cami. The tedious chores she abhorred, like laundry and dishes, sounded enchanting so long as Cami was going to be there. She had it bad.

"God, I missed you, too." Diana ran her fingers through the long, blond curls framing Cami's face.

She trailed her hand down Cami's body, reveling in the trembling flesh beneath her touch. A voice in the back of her head screamed doubt at her, freaked that Cami affected her so much. But she tuned it out, refusing to shut herself off from her burgeoning feelings just because she had a few irrational insecurities. All that mattered was this moment with Cami wrapped up in her arms, trembling, ready, and trusting.

Diana released herself to Cami's embrace, waiting for the urgent edge to fade. Cami's fingers slid down Diana's back, coming to a stop at the brief strip of skin between her low-slung jeans and black tank. Her touch held the confidence of familiarity with an underlying sweetness that made Diana weak. The desperate need to possess that had driven their previous encounters was fast giving way to a deeper need to know more than just the contours of flesh.

She released her hold on Cami, lingering long enough to brush her lips over the smooth skin of Cami's neck and cheek. The spicy scent of basil, onion, and yellow curry filled Diana's apartment, an aromatic reminder that dinner was ready and waiting. But Diana had other priorities.

"Come on." She drew Cami into her home and passed by the dining room without a second glance.

She led Cami up the stairs to her open loft bedroom and paused when the reached the edge of her bed. Cami stood perfectly still, the mattress against the back of her knees, her eyes searching Diana's face.

"Is this okay?" Diana's voice came out low, a rough whisper.

She ran her knuckles along Cami's cheek and around to cradle her head. Her fingers tangled in the loose hair at the base of Cami's neck, her thumb working slowly down her ear. She was asking for so much more than permission to get naked and sweaty. She wanted to go slow, get lost, and find their way back together. She wanted to show

Cami that the building connection was real, that it extended beyond base instinct. She wanted to hold Cami, dinner forgotten on the table, and promise the future in the press of their skin. She wanted to convey everything she was afraid to say out loud.

Diana waited for an answer, her attention focused on the brilliant blue irises giving way as Cami's pupils expanded. She retraced the path along Cami's ear until her head dropped to the side.

Pushing into Diana's touch, Cami said, "Yes."

That one word granted Diana the permission she'd been waiting for, the acknowledgment that this would be more than just a hot fuck. Still, she held herself back, forced herself to go impossibly slow. She wasn't ready to give voice to the wave of emotions that threatened to overwhelm her, but she needed to know that Cami was there with her, drowning in the same relentless tide.

Cami wore a light summer dress, no buttons or zippers, just a simple long shell that strained around her breasts and hips. Diana rested her hands on the curve of Cami's waist with gentle curiosity. She'd rained hot kisses over Cami's body, but she'd never invested the time to learn its plains and valleys. She stretched her fingers down and inched the cotton skirt up by degrees, just a minute bit of fabric, until it was bunched together in her hands. Cami's body tensed and tightened, bumps rising on her exposed skin, and Diana resisted the urge to drop to her knees and worship. She held Cami's gaze as she tugged the dress over her head, leaving her in her white lace bra and panties.

She'd seen Cami naked, spread wide, panting, begging, dripping, but she'd never seen her this vulnerable. Diana stepped back, sweeping Cami's body hungrily, trying to memorize the details. The tattoo dipping into the top edge of lace at her hipbone was familiar, but she'd never noticed the dark mole on her torso or the white line just above her left knee, a scar from an adventure Diana knew nothing about. There was so much to learn about her, and Diana wanted to take it all in.

Before she could make the return trip to Cami's face, Cami guided Diana's hand to her panties, silently asking for them to be removed. Diana drew them down, gliding her hands over Cami's legs as she went.

Cami's scent reached out to her, eclipsing the almost forgotten curry waiting downstairs. It was hot and full of need and Diana wanted to rush forward, push Cami onto the bed, and bury her tongue in the essence of her desire. She held herself back, trembling with the effort. Tonight, she promised herself, was about more than carnal relief. Cami deserved to be treasured. She forced herself up until she was standing again, much closer to Cami than she'd been moments before.

The sun dropped below the horizon and the only light in the room was the dim illumination cast from the street lamp below. It was enough to see the hunger, hope, and tenderness in Cami's eyes. Diana wished she'd thought to light some candles. As far as romantic gestures went, she was falling way short. If she regarded Cami with enough reverence, perhaps she would forgive her lack of preparation.

"I'm scared." Her voice was small, a step above timid.

Cami rested her forehead against Diana's and closed her eyes. "Me, too."

"I don't want to stop."

Silence stretched between them as Cami opened her eyes to meet Diana's steady gaze. "Neither do I."

Diana felt Cami's fingers at her fly, coaxing the buttons open. Before her jeans settled around her ankles, Cami jerked the tank over Diana's head. Her movements held none of the slow reservation of Diana's. They'd acknowledged that this was more than sex and agreed stopping wasn't an option. The look of determination on her face filled Diana with aching anticipation. She wasn't wearing a bra or panties, and Cami's sudden burst of aggression left her naked and dizzy with the change of pace.

As she adjusted to the idea of moving a little faster, Cami flipped open the clasp on her own bra with one hand. She shook it off her shoulders and fell back against the bed, pulling Diana with her. Just as quickly, she rolled until she was on top, her hair hanging in a fine curtain around Diana's head. In only a few seconds, Diana had gone from being fully clothed and vertical to naked and on her back. She reached out for Cami, her fingers itching with desire.

"No." Cami pulled away. Her voice was filled with steely determination as though she were fighting to put their relationship back into terms she was comfortable with. "Just let me touch you."

She curled her fingers into Diana, filling her with the sharpness of her words. Diana whimpered when Cami withdrew, then entered again, quick and hard. The abruptness of it left her weak and she wanted to pull back, slow Cami down, return to their previously sweet pace, but she couldn't. Diana rolled her head to the side and arched her back, drawing Cami in deeper. If this was what Cami needed, this rushed, harsh edge in the middle of making love, Diana would ride the wave with her. With each stroke, Cami stretched over Diana, panting, her eyes begging for control, for the return to the familiar, urgent burn of lust without complications.

Diana focused on the flow of Cami's fingers inside her, gathering her tighter and tighter until she shattered. Release crashed over her and she collapsed against the bed, grasping Cami to her chest. The room solidified around her, one pinpoint of light at a time. She wrapped Cami in her arms as the timpani in her ears settled to a manageable hum. That was when she noticed the spreading moisture against her chest, the tense line of Cami's body.

With a practiced move, she reversed their positions so Cami was on her back. Poised over her, Diana watched the tears well in Cami's eyes and tumble down the side of her face.

"Shh." She wiped the wet streaks away with the tips of her fingers. "It's okay." She held Cami, trying to convey with a look, a touch, that Cami was safe and loved.

"I'm sorry." Cami drew her down into a lingering kiss. "I wanted…" She hesitated, her voice fading. "I wanted to be tender and loving and it was just so damn intense. I panicked."

Diana could understand that. She was scared out of her mind, too. She tightened her grip, determined to convince Cami that her fear was understandable and, more importantly, they would get past it, together.

"You panicked?" She kept her voice light. "Well, I hope I'm around every time you freak out, because I don't want you to do that with anyone else."

Cami half laughed, half sobbed. "Okay."

As gently as she could, Diana kissed Cami. She retreated slightly and held her mouth a breath away from Cami's. She let the moment build, then flicked her tongue against Cami's bottom lip, an invitation for more. Diana deepened the kiss, sliding into the warm, wet tangle of soft muscle and sharp teeth. It was a preliminary invasion and she cherished Cami's surrender, her trust that Diana would protect her on this leg of their journey.

Diana held herself rigidly over Cami as she kissed her. Her body was close enough to feel the charge between them, but not close enough to touch. It was maddening and tantalizingly sweet torture. She worked her way over Cami's skin, letting her mouth lead the way. There was no pattern, no design, no ultimate target, just the gentle arch of Cami's back, her urging hands drawing Diana down, her soft voice whispering encouragement and reverence. For every rushed, impatient thrust Cami had punished her with earlier, Diana countered with ten gentle, imploring kisses full of promise and gratitude.

In the moment before Cami's shuddering release, watching her damp skin glow in the dim light, Diana surrendered to the perfection of their rhythmic dance. She'd found the place where she belonged, hovering over Cami, buried deep inside her, unable to tell where one ended and the other began.

❖

Anyone else would have missed the article. Ali seldom read the business section, but she'd been drawn to it today and allowed her instincts to guide her. Three-quarters of the way down, tucked between a notice of an upscale hotel opening and news of a local real estate developer indicted for fraud, was a name that made her heart clamor against her rib cage at breakneck speed.

Ricardo Chavez, respected Colombian businessman, was coming to Chicago to attend business meetings and seek medical treatment for an unknown condition.

Ricardo Chavez. The name sent tendrils of fear streaking down Ali's back. The edges of her vision blurred. She gripped the table and blinked with deliberation, desperate to erase the name from the newspaper in front of her. But it was etched on the page, bold as day. There was no wishing it away. She'd spent fourteen years begging for mercy from that man. Her escape from Colombia to the U.S. had taken a full year, a year she'd tried unsuccessfully to blot from her memory.

Even now, everywhere she went, she felt his evil reaching for her across the miles. He'd always promised she would be punished for her disobedience. He would drag her back to his estate by her hair, the same way he'd taken her there when she was a small girl. He would teach her the need for loyalty by carving it into her skin.

Ali crunched the evening newspaper into a tight ball and hurled it at the wall. She stood with jerky urgency, flinging the chair back onto the floor. Strains of disharmony filtered through the thin walls, evidence of her neighbors' nightly battle. The dull hum of the ancient refrigerator roared in her ears, clouding her brain with white noise.

Hot, salty tears streaked down her face and she cocked back her fist. Anger surged through her, propelling her fist toward the wall. Before the punch landed, fear sapped her momentum and her palm connected flat against the wall in silence. With no outlet for her rage, she slid down to the floor and hugged her knees tight to her chest, rocking her body in search of comfort.

Ali stayed in a crumpled heap, playing his name over and over in her mind until the sun crept closer to the horizon and a sharp ringing ripped through the room. Ali reached for the handset, answering out of long-ingrained habit. The only calls she ever received at home were from the shelter with some minor crisis or another. Her greeting sounded rough and dry. "Hello."

The unknown voice held the false cheeriness of a person looking to make a sale. "I'm calling on behalf of…" The words faded and melted away.

"I'm not interested." Ali dropped the handset back into place without waiting for a response. The call wasn't what she expected, but the interruption jarred her out of the self-pitying spiral of fear she'd fallen into.

She retrieved the paper from the floor and smoothed the crumpled surface. The promise of revenge churned in her stomach, gaining strength as it traveled the length of her body. She squared her shoulders against the demons of her past as a ghost of a smile played on her lips. Ricardo Chavez was coming to town. She would make him pay.

❖

Diana stared at the blank wall across from her desk. She hadn't been able to shake the image of Mona Stewart's pain, and it clung to her like a thick syrup. She desperately wanted a shower. Last night with Cami she'd been able to push the case to the back of her mind. Today, faced with sifting through the sordid facts again, she wanted to curl her body around Cami and hold on tight.

The writing on the computer screen blurred. Electronic alphabet soup.

Charles Stewart
Victor Delaney
Mikhail Petrov
Sergio Dominguez

After a long, frustrating day, she'd been unable to find any common link between the four men, save South Lake. They'd each sent a surviving female relative through those doors in search of refuge. Shortly afterward, they'd ended up dead. Something significant had to break soon.

Diana clicked over to the minimized browser window that was open to her e-mail. Still nothing. She'd checked it compulsively every two minutes all day long. The official reason she couldn't stop checking was Siger. She needed to hear something from them soon. The real reason was Cami. Not that she needed to open another e-mail from her at work. The naughty things she said would eventually pop up on an alert for IT. The information technology department kept close tabs on the type of data that filtered through the firewall the company had in place for Internet traffic. Certain words and key phrases automatically generated a flag. The last thing she needed was to explain to Jeter why a kindergarten teacher wanted to suck her off and leave her begging. Sweet Jesus.

"Any luck, shug?"

"Nothing yet."

Diana met Braxton's eyes. Her brows were knitted together, a sure sign that she shared Diana's frustration. In an uncharacteristic move, Braxton wasn't wearing a suit jacket, and the sleeves of her tailored shirt were rolled up to the elbows. She stood with one hand on her hip as the other worked its way through her hair, pulling her shirt tight across her chest. Diana was mesmerized. No doubt about it. Braxton had a droolworthy body.

"One of these days I'm going to take you up on that offer," Braxton said.

Diana jerked her eyes back up to Braxton's face. She had one manicured brow raised and her mouth curved in a cocky half-smile. Diana couldn't help but match the smile. It was an old game of innuendo and teasing, and God help her, she liked it. A lot.

"What offer?"

Braxton regarded her in silence for a moment, then said, "You have plans tonight?"

"Nope."

"Really? No Cami?" Braxton's voice held a mixture of surprise, disbelief, and relief. That was odd.

It was a legitimate question. The mere mention of Cami's name sent a troupe of freaked-out butterflies cavorting through Diana's body. She felt elated and nauseous at the same time. The feelings were scary as hell.

Late last night Diana had awakened to find Cami looking down on her, that unreadable half-smile on her face. She ran her fingers lightly over Diana's skin, circling ever closer to her straining nipple, but never quite touching it. Diana didn't move, didn't speak. She held herself there, open to Cami, silently encouraging her to explore and take what she wanted. When her hand reached the juncture at the top of Diana's legs, she braced herself, ready to be invaded forcefully as she had been earlier. Cami had kept her touch light, teasing Diana over the edge with achingly delicate strokes. Diana didn't know if she had ever felt so naked in her life. Every carefully constructed wall crumbled under Cami's loving touch and in the moment between build up and sweet, shattering release, Cami looked into her soul and really saw her.

After the intensity of last night, she wanted to give Cami the time and space she needed to grow comfortable with where their relationship was going. Truth be told, she needed the distance just as much as Cami did. At this point, Diana would normally be moving on, looking for a new playmate. Instead she kept diving deeper into Cami. As good as it felt to be in Cami's arms, could she really trust her with her love? She was still scraping the pieces back together from her heartbreak over Angel Ramirez.

"She's busy tonight." Diana kept her voice even.

"You've been spending a lot of time with her."

Diana didn't like where this was going. Braxton didn't make casual observations about Diana's life. There was always a point. "Yes, I have." She heard the hint of apprehension in her response and she cringed inwardly.

"How well do you really know her?"

Diana didn't answer. How could she? In reality, she didn't know

Cami well at all. She knew that she ached to see her again, but not much more than that.

Braxton tilted her head to the side, her face drawn in concentration. Diana braced herself for what Braxton would say next.

"How well did you know Angel?"

The question hit her like a blow to the chest. She'd thought she knew Angel well enough to trust her. Obviously she was wrong. Her heart couldn't afford that kind of mistake again.

"Ouch." Diana allowed the hurt to show on her face. "Cami's nothing like Angel." She hoped.

"Good." Braxton turned to leave, finishing the conversation over her shoulder in that come-and-get-me way that Diana loved. "Let's get a drink."

Chapter Twelve

Smokers crowded around the entrance to the Closet, a neighborhood bar that catered mostly to lesbians. In the past, Diana had gone with Braxton to local straight bars. This time, however, she didn't have the energy to ward off overly friendly men who fell prey to the alcohol-inspired belief that they were God's gift. She'd given up pointing out that she was a lesbian. That just upped the stakes. Men thought they could change her mind if she just gave them the chance.

Diana watched Braxton take in the room, trying to see the scene through her eyes. A room too small for the number of women packed inside, even on a Wednesday night. Loud monitors playing never-ending music videos. A cramped dance floor adjoining a lounge area with too many tables and not enough space. Any hope of intimacy was lost in the din. And there were women. Lots and lots of women. Sitting together, holding hands, leaning close, pressed together on the dance floor, leaning over to offer a fresh drink.

A mischievous smile worked its way onto Braxton's face and Diana relaxed. They found an empty corner table. The low light obscured the view, making it an isolated haven that, mercifully, was not directly beneath a speaker.

As soon as they were settled in their green-upholstered bench seats, Diana said, "No table service. What can I get you—bourbon rocks?"

The drink Braxton ordered depended greatly on the day she was having. Normally it was vodka martinis. Dirty. Diana suspected she chose that drink as an excuse to say "dirty," not because she was crazy about martinis. It worked out fine for Diana because she liked the way the word sounded wrapped in Braxton's sexy New Orleans drawl. Days like today, however, called for something stronger.

Braxton spread her arms over the back of the booth, relaxed and confident. "Works for me."

Diana returned with their drinks to find Braxton being chatted up by a wallet-on-a-chain, super-butch dyke. She looked bored, disengaged. Time to rescue the straight friend from the big bad lesbian. A bar fight was not on Diana's agenda for the night, but she couldn't resist bumping her hip into the woman as she slid into the booth on Braxton's side. Amber liquid sloshed up to the rim, but not over the edge when Diana set Braxton's drink on the table. She leaned in close and kissed Braxton on the lips, lingering long enough to send a clear "back the hell off" message to the stranger. As she began to pull away, Braxton wrapped her hand around Diana's neck, weaving her fingers into the fine hairs at the base of her head, and pulled her in for a second kiss. Diana relaxed and went with it. Kissing Braxton was nice, like a cold beer on a hot day. Comfortable. Not exciting.

"Mmm." She licked her lips when the kiss ended. "Miss me?"

Braxton ran a finger along the line of Diana's cheekbone. "I did."

With a wink Diana turned back toward the woman still standing near their table. She looked her up and down. Not flirty. Not challenging. Simply taking stock.

"Thanks for keeping her company while I was getting our drinks." She smiled a sugary-sweet fake smile and topped the look with a proprietary "I'll kick your ass" glare.

At that, the woman mumbled something polite and shuffled off into the crowd.

Diana returned to the other side of the table. As much fun as it was to flirt with Braxton, sitting this close, with the minty taste of her gum still in her mouth, it wasn't right. Braxton was married. And straight.

"Tell me what you learned today."

"About the merry widows?"

Diana cringed at Braxton's callous nickname for Susan Hansen, formerly Delaney, and Lora Petrov. Their husbands, at least on the surface, were real bastards. Their lives should be better without them. Still, that characterization was a little harsh.

"Both women had an experience similar to Mona's," Braxton said.

"Nothing memorable, no special friends, only at the shelter for two weeks. They both mentioned how caring Ali Sandoval was, how safe they felt in her care."

Diana ran her nail under the Widmir label on her cold bottle of brew. Oscar would need to know this little detail as well. She took a long drink. "Why does it feel more and more like we're chasing a killer, not a sword?"

"You know the rules. Follow the lead, no matter where it takes you."

Every investigator knew the score. Diana was no exception. Still, the lead was taking her to a place she didn't want to follow, down a dark road filled with pain. And what about Ali Sandoval? The woman obviously did her job well, and demonstrated compassion and caring toward the traumatized women she helped. Before long, she would fall under the scrutiny of the combined task force. Maybe Diana could wait to tell Oscar the next time she saw him. Frankly, she didn't know why they were working so hard to catch this killer. He, or she, was doing the world a favor by eliminating men like Charles Stewart.

"What do you think about Ali?"

"I think—" Braxton paused mid-sentence, her drink suspended halfway between the table and her mouth. "I think she's headed this way."

Diana turned in her seat and saw Ali moving through the crowd toward their table. The black tank and black Levi's hugged her body perfectly, moving in uniform grace with her muscles. Her eyes, her take-no-prisoners attitude, her gunslinger walk, all conveyed a greedy confidence. Diana wanted to know this woman better.

Ali slid into the seat next to her without waiting for an invitation. "Ladies." She glanced at Braxton but let her eyes linger on Diana. The predatory gleam evident at the shelter was back. "Can I buy you a drink?"

It was an old line, but Diana's beer was surprisingly low. As were her inhibitions. Ali's eyes left her feeling vulnerable and unable to escape. And there was an underlying desire to climb inside and stay awhile, get to know her. It was a disconcerting combination, to be simultaneously drawn in, yet desperate to run away. "Yes, please."

Ali left to get their drinks. Diana watched her walk away, the tight curve of her ass begging to be touched.

"I wonder what she's doing here," Braxton said. Her voice was muted, fading away as the sentence progressed.

"I have no idea. I don't think she's a regular."

Diana was certain she would have remembered seeing her here before. She was exactly the type of woman she would invite home for the night. Sexy, hot, and oozing danger. That was her type. Until Cami, the golden-maned kindergarten teacher. The flirtatious "you know you want it" smile that Cami flashed last night, right before running her tongue along Diana's clit, filled Diana's mind. A shiver ran the length of her spine and she gulped down the rest of her beer.

They'd agreed not to see each other tonight, but now, sitting at the bar, surrounded by the pulse of sweat and alcohol, Diana wanted nothing more than to be with Cami. Even the thought of lying on the couch watching DVDs with her appealed to Diana. She pulled out her cell phone and sent Cami a text message. *I want to come over.*

Before she heard the comforting blip of a reply, Ali placed their drinks on the table. Two beers and one bourbon.

The overcrowded lesbian bar was not a typical hangout for Ali. She'd trailed the two women here from their office building, and when they entered the Closet she hadn't realized what kind of establishment it was. It only took a few moments inside the doors to figure out what she'd stumbled into. One, if not both, of these women was a lesbian. Her money was on Diana.

The song changed from the heavy club beat that had dominated the night to a strong Latin rhythm. Ali's body responded and she held out her hand to Diana.

"Dance with me."

Diana cocked her head to the side. "Braxton, do you mind?"

Braxton started on her second drink and waved them away. Apparently she didn't mind at all.

Ali led Diana to the dance floor, her body moving in sensual time to the beat, and pulled her close. The tune wasn't formal enough for a standard salsa, but a modified version would work. If Diana could keep up. Ali surrendered to the music, letting it float over her, around her, through her. Taking it in and welcoming it. To dance was to express gratitude to the music. And surprise, surprise, Diana could keep up.

The press of bodies around them on the tiny dance floor limited movement, but their hips moved in time, flowing and swaying together. Ali moved her hand lower down Diana's body, stopping just shy of her back pockets. Music calmed her like nothing else. When she danced, the anger and blackness of Ricardo's world was temporarily muted.

"This wasn't what I had in mind when I saw you here," Ali said.

Diana dropped her hands to Ali's waist. "What did you have in mind?" Her voice held a hint of promise.

"I wanted to get to know you better."

"I haven't seen you here before," Diana said.

Ali searched her face, looking for a clue to Diana's intentions. Who was she talking to right now? Diana the investigator or Diana the club girl looking for a good time for the night? Diana's face remained impassive, giving Ali nothing to base her response on. She erred on the side of caution. "No, you haven't. This is a first for me. I had dinner across the street and saw you come in here. I couldn't resist."

Diana's face relaxed into a genuine smile, full and radiating confidence. "Couldn't resist? Hmm." Her hands slid lower, cupping Ali's butt. She drew Ali forward and rotated her hips in a slow grind.

Ali, on the other hand, danced with clinical precision, applying pressure in the right places. She didn't understand how women allowed themselves to be overcome by desire during a dance. Dancing was about creation, life, and release. Sex, on the other hand, was never about fun in her world. It was simply a means to an end. She released herself to the rhythm, grateful that Diana was willing to accept her explanation without further probing.

The music faded into the next song and she pulled away from Diana. "Let's go back." She needed to get Diana to the table where they could all talk and Ali could learn what these two women knew, if anything.

They were almost back to the table when Diana took her cell phone from her pocket. She flipped it open and read the screen. "Text message," she said.

Her smile reminded Ali of children at Christmas. Not real children, of course. In her experience at the shelter, children were not that happy, Christmas or otherwise. Diana's expression was movie-Christmas happy. She sat next to Braxton, leaving Ali the opposite side to herself.

"So, was that good news?" Braxton asked.

"Very good." Diana kissed her on the cheek. "I know you're going to hate me for this, but I need to go."

"Cami?" Braxton played with the swizzle stick in her drink.

"Yeah." Diana's face flushed red. "She's waiting. Is it okay, Braxton?"

"It's time for me to leave, too." She drained the rest of her bourbon. "Thanks for the drink, Ali. It was nice seeing you."

Diana said her good-byes and they were gone. Ali was left alone, with two beers and a room full of lesbians, but no idea how much these women actually knew. She left the full bottles on the table and sliced her way easily through the crowd. She'd try a different method next time, maybe invite Diana to lunch.

Two weeks. Possibly less. That was the amount of time Diana estimated before the police caught up with her investigation and showed up at the shelter. It seemed such a short amount of time to sever her ties to Chicago, but in reality it was far too long. Since she'd emigrated from Colombia, Ali kept her life simple, ready to relocate at a moment's notice. When the time came, she'd grab the already packed bag from beneath her bed, throw in her scrapbook and the pictures of her family, clear out the safe she'd installed in the floor, and disappear into the night. The waiting, unsure of what the police knew balanced against the eminent arrival of Ricardo, was testing her patience. She needed more information and Diana was the bridge to the police.

Ali only needed a few more days, long enough for Ricardo to check into the hospital where he would be at his most vulnerable. Then she would strike, carving away his hold over her once and for all.

❖

What a strange night. So far she'd had her tongue in Braxton's mouth and her hands on Ali Sandoval's ass. Both fell short of the knee-trembling state Cami left her in.

Her thoughts drifted back to the dance she shared with Ali. Latin music was a libido-driving, sexual carnival of fun for Diana. The groove made her pulse pound and her skin sweat. It made her want to grind against the nearest tight body. Tonight had been different. Ali, though her body moved in all the right ways, felt distant and removed from the beat. Their salsa was teenage-dance awkward until she pictured Cami's smile, the flow of her hair, the line of her body. She got lost in that image and surrendered to it. That was when she'd grabbed Ali's butt.

With a pang of guilt, Diana parked against the curb and stared up at the darkened windows of Cami's bedroom. She'd spent three years with Angel building a relationship, a future. They'd talked about buying a house, having children, and growing old together. Those dreams had been built on shifting sands and constructed out of false promises. Angel had unintentionally taught her to look beyond words, to listen to the nagging voice of doubt that urged her to stop and think rather than plowing forward.

She still believed in love and commitment, but she doubted it would ever be real for her. Cami made her hope for it again, with a deep, throbbing intensity that couldn't be ignored.

Hell, Cami made her forget about her ever-present lust for Braxton. Before meeting Cami, Diana would have pounced all over the opportunity Braxton presented tonight. She was sexy as hell, Diana's own private Mrs. Robinson, and tonight she had been willing beyond the playful banter of the past. All Diana could think about in the face of Braxton's desire to switch teams, if only for the night, was Cami. They'd agreed not to see each other, deciding it was for the best, but Diana couldn't hold herself back.

Her thoughts were still raging as she climbed the steps to Cami's apartment. The ancient elevator might have been faster, but it also might have stranded her between floors, giving her hours to think herself in circles about Cami.

She waited on the wrong side of Cami's locked front door and knocked again. "Cami?" She lifted her voice just a little. She didn't want to disturb the neighbors this late at night.

The door swung open and Cami stood to the side to let her in. "Come on in."

She dropped an easy kiss on Cami's lips, not demanding, just glad to be in her presence. "You look great."

Cami was wearing a thick, pink robe that spoke of snuggling

and comfort. She slipped her hand into Diana's, weaving their fingers together, and laughed. "You got it bad if you think I look great in this."

Diana regarded Cami seriously. "No doubt, I got it bad."

They made their way into the kitchen where a kettle of water was just starting to steam on the stove. "I'm making tea. You want a cup?"

Diana didn't drink tea. Or coffee. Or hot chocolate. Pretty much any hot thing in a cup and she was a pass. To wake up in the morning, she went for a run. To relax, she'd have a beer. To unwind, tequila. "I'd love some."

The teakettle whistled and Cami turned off the stove. "Have you eaten?"

If the bag of chips from the vending machine around two counted, then yes, she'd eaten. "Not yet."

Cami selected a brown bag from the cupboard and emptied the contents onto a plate. "They're from the bakery down the street." She set the croissants on the island that divided the kitchen from the dining room and pointed to the bar stools skirting the counter.

Diana positioned herself atop one of the stools so she could watch Cami move about the kitchen. The comforting feeling of domesticity settled around her like a warm blanket. She and Angel had lived together for two and a half years, but the day-to-day tasks always held an underlying tension, unlike the relaxed, openness of this moment with Cami.

Framed photos lined the walls of the dining room. Some obviously family portraits: Cami, her parents, and the younger sister she'd mentioned on Sunday. There were also snapshots—Cami on a donkey, a sombrero on her head; Cami and her sister with backpacks slung over their shoulders, the Roman Colosseum looming in the background; Cami in the front seat of a roller coaster, a scream painted on her face.

"Tell me about your sister." If Cami felt anything close to the instinctive protectiveness Diana felt for Brigitte, then she had to be all right.

Cami set a mug in front of Diana, her own cupped between her palms. "Lisa?" Cami's voice held a reflective pride and her smile lit the room. "She's a complete pain in my ass. She's finishing her last year at UIC."

University of Illinois at Chicago was Diana's alma mater. "What's her major?"

"Chemistry. She plans to be a pharmacist."

There were so many other things they could be talking about, like where their relationship was going, but Diana wanted to know about Cami's family, learn if they were as important to Cami as Diana's was to her. Besides, nestled together in Cami's kitchen, Diana couldn't bring herself to worry about what she was feeling, if she was setting herself up for inevitable pain. She relaxed into the conversation, simply enjoying Cami's company.

"Chemistry?" Diana wrinkled her nose. "There goes any thought of comparing notes when I meet her."

Cami tore off a piece of croissant and popped it in Diana's mouth. "You went there?"

The pastry was buttery sweet and melted on Diana's tongue. She stretched over the counter and kissed Cami. She wanted to taste the smile on her lips. The croissant paled in comparison. "Yes. And you?"

"University of Florida." Cami's eyes took on a dreamy quality. "I wanted to live in the sun."

Florida sun? Tension flooded Diana. She was sure she could adapt to the weather if that's what Cami required, but she couldn't live that far from her family. "Why'd you come back?"

"Simple." Cami offered a wry smile. "My family is here. Florida's hurricanes just don't compete."

"If it's sun you want, we'll get a summer home in the Caribbean." The sentence slipped out before Diana could catch it. She felt her face flush and she sipped her tea, waiting to see how Cami would respond.

She set her cup carefully on the counter, her smile softened around the edges and extended to her eyes. "I've always been a bit partial to the Caymans."

Diana'd never been there. "Me, too."

The conversation flowed easily as they finished their tea and croissants. When the cups were empty, Cami slipped off her stool and reached for Diana's hand. "Spend the night?"

It was far too late already. If Diana wanted to get any sleep at all, she really should head home. Cami tugged on her hand, leading her to the bedroom, and Diana followed, unable to deny Cami.

The bedside table was conspicuously empty. "I owe you an alarm clock."

Cami laughed. "Do you always assault your alarm clock when you wake up?"

"Only when my brain feels like it's going to explode." Diana picked up a book that was lying open on the bed, marking the page with her finger as she read the cover. "*Silas Marner?*" The nineteenth-century novel had been required reading for her freshman literature class. It was not a story she would choose for light reading.

"Eliot was brilliant." Cami hung her robe on a hook in the bathroom and smiled. "Come to bed and I'll show you."

Diana watched Cami climb beneath the covers, an invitation in her eyes. She handed Cami the book and removed her jeans but kept her panties and tank on. Cami was inviting her to spend the night in her arms, get used to the feel of each other, without the demands of sex. Diana's body tingled as she slid into the bed and tucked herself into the crook of Cami's arm, her head resting on Cami's shoulder.

Warmth spread through Diana as Cami pulled her close and smoothed her hand over her hair in a rhythmic cadence. She began to read, her voice giving life to the words written on the page. Diana developed a newfound appreciation for the depth of George Eliot's writing as she hovered between awake and asleep, wrapped in Cami's embrace, her voice filling Diana up to overflowing. She was semiaware of Cami closing the book and sliding down in the bed, never releasing her hold on Diana. She felt Cami's breath on her skin in the moment before their lips touched and she swelled at the simple beauty of the connection. Despite any nagging doubt or lingering insecurities, the bond between them was real and it grew stronger in the absence of sex, not weaker.

Diana's last thought as sleep overtook her was of Cami, how she didn't need any more time or space to sort out her feelings. She only hoped she'd be brave enough to talk to Cami about everything that was in her heart and her willingness to take whatever Cami was able to offer.

CHAPTER THIRTEEN

Diana awoke to the sound of running water. A shower. She stretched and peered around the room. A slow smile crept onto her face. She was at Cami's.

"You're awake." Cami leaned against the bathroom door frame, a towel dangling in one hand. Drops of water clung to her body and Diana wanted to lick every last one from her gleaming skin.

"Morning." She got to her knees and crawled over the twist of blankets covering the bed until she reached the end, her eyes locked on Cami's. She would be late to work this morning and every other for just a taste of what Cami offered.

Cami wrapped the towel around her body and held up a hand. "No. I have to get ready for work."

The playful rebuke didn't stop Diana's progression as she slid off the bed and moved across the floor to stand in front of Cami. She placed her hands on Cami's hips and pulled on the towel. It slid easily down the curves of Cami's body and gathered at her feet. Diana traced the line of Cami's jaw with her tongue, stopping just below Cami's ear. She kept her voice low, exhaling the words into the soft skin. "I'll be quick."

Diana backed Cami up against the wall, pinning her with a hard, penetrating kiss. After all the tenderness of the past two nights, Diana wanted to show Cami she was still capable of raw and demanding. She moved her hands over Cami's body, squeezing, pressing, smoothing, grabbing, but always headed south.

The taste of Cami's mouthwash, a sharp unforgiving mint, pushed

Diana to go faster, reminding her of their other obligations. She didn't fall on Cami's breasts like a starving man at a banquet, bypassing them altogether with a promise to spend hours making up for it next time. With her left arm wrapped low around Cami's back for support, she massaged Cami's clit with the fingers on her right. So wet. So ready.

Cami moaned. "Please."

Her head rolled back and Diana latched on to the pulse point at the base of Cami's neck, sucking hard as she pushed deep inside her. The silky, slick pull on Diana's fingers made her hungry for more and she urged Cami to open her legs wider. Cami's face was a canvas of passion and need as she dug her nails into Diana's back, pleading. Diana could feel Cami gathering, her muscles tightening until she cried out, collapsing against Diana.

Diana brushed kisses over Cami's eyes, her cheeks, her nose, everywhere her lips could reach. "I've got you. It's okay."

Slowly, Cami collected enough strength to lift herself away from Diana. "Wow. I love the way you say good morning."

She said it lightly and Diana knew it was meant as a tension breaker, nothing more, but she chose not to let the comment pass.

"There are a lot of things I'm coming to love about our relationship. Saying good morning is definitely on the list." The comment wasn't everything Diana wanted to share with Cami, not by a long shot. She was unable to continue, her voice cracking at the end.

Cami started to speak, then stopped, her face a battlefield of emotions. Finally, she said, "Di, this is all so new to me. I feel like I'm falling down a deep well and I'm not sure what's waiting at the bottom. Even so, I can't stop myself. I don't want to. When I relax and just hold you, not thinking about what it all means, I'm fine. When I try to come to terms with my feelings, I get overwhelmed and freaked out and think crazy thoughts about needing time away from you to sort it all out."

Diana tightened her grip. "So don't think about it. Just be with me."

"I'm trying." Cami rested her head against Diana's shoulder. "God knows, I'm trying."

Later that morning, with her clothes on and her arms empty, a million responses came into her mind. Any one of them would have been better than the silence she'd let grow between them as she comforted

Cami. Diana gripped the steering wheel and tried to focus on the traffic around her. Finally she pulled over, unable to think beyond the need to send a message to Cami. As cars crawled angrily past her, Diana tapped the keys on her cell phone. She didn't pause before hitting Send, afraid she'd push Delete if she gave herself half a chance. Her plea went out to Cami, unfettered by insecurity. It simply said, *Please, trust me...trust us.*

At a few minutes past eight, Diana made it to her office. The taint of her investigation waited for her, but the night with Cami clung to her and kept her grounded.

"Look what the cat dragged in." Braxton knocked as she entered Diana's office. "Ready to get to work?"

Not by a long shot, but she wouldn't tell Braxton that. All she wanted was to return to the heat and glory of Cami's arms. Instead she'd spend another day mucking through the emotional battlefield left behind by Carter and Lowe's former client, Charles Stewart. "Let me get a cup of caffeine, then I'll be ready."

"Long night?"

Diana felt heat creeping over her face. "I was up late."

Braxton's mouth curved in a knowing smile, her sarcastic thoughts evident as they walked down the hall to the break room. Diana poured herself a cup from the aromatic brew in the pot and sniffed it suspiciously. Heavy and sharp. She added sugar and tasted the results. Nasty. It would do.

"Can we work now?" Braxton's tone was teasing, not impatient.

"Let me check my e-mail first, then we'll head out." Diana took another sip as they made their way back to her office. "I'll let you rough up some fences." Even though the angle had been covered by Bob, Diana wanted to revisit a few of the businesses in the area that were known to traffic in stolen goods. The effort would likely be fruitless, but it was better than staring at her computer screen all morning.

"Finally." Braxton issued an exaggerated sigh of relief. At least Diana hoped it was exaggerated.

At times, Braxton could be a little too enthusiastic with her *interviewing* techniques. She wore tailored suits, chose beauty over comfort when buying shoes, and kept her weekly manicure appointment no matter what. In spite of presenting a girly outward impression,

Braxton loved a good brawl. Nothing thrilled her more than charming a bad guy into a false sense of security before kicking the crap out of him when his defenses were down. It was slightly sadistic and Diana loved her for it. With this case, however, there was too much riding on their investigation for either of them to stray too far off track. Indulging the urge to bully the fences for too long would be detrimental.

The computer had booted up and drifted to the screen saver during their short trip down the hall. Diana tapped the keys to wake it up and logged into her personal e-mail account. She was checking for a message from Siger but hoping for one from Cami. She was only half disappointed. Siger Enterprises had replied. She held her breath as she brought it up in the view window. It said:

A password costs five grand. Follow the link, make the payment and you're in.

Blood pounded in her temples. What could be worth five thousand dollars just to look at? Nothing legal, that was for certain.

Reading over her shoulder, Braxton let out a low whistle. "Damn."

"I need to call Oscar." Diana dialed the number for the central precinct. She wanted this conversation very much on the record.

After several minutes, Oscar came on the line. His greeting was rough, solicitous, and annoyed at the same time.

"It's Diana. I have news."

"Collins?" Oscar sounded confused. She never called him at the station. "What can I do for you?"

"I heard from Siger. They want five thousand dollars for a password."

She could almost hear Oscar's wheels turning in the long pause before he spoke. "Diana, don't do anything until you hear back from me." He disconnected without saying good-bye.

"What did he say?" Braxton asked.

"He called me Diana." As soon as she'd finished college and started working, Oscar had moved away from the name he'd used all during her childhood and addressed her only by her last name, his sign of her acceptance into the adult world. "He's worried."

When the phone rang again almost immediately, Diana snatched it up. "The feds want to be there when you log in. You okay with that?"

Oscar worded it as a question, but Diana knew refusal wasn't really an option.

"Should I come to you or are we going to do it here?"

"We're already on our way."

Holy crap. Oscar was leading the feds to her building. She'd better not get arrested over this.

Thirty minutes later, four men and one super-hot woman, all in perfectly pressed suits and dark sunglasses, crowded around Diana's desk. Oscar stood next to Braxton on the opposite wall. That was good. She needed the friendly faces to focus on while the feds zeroed in on her laptop.

"Let me get this straight." Braxton's voice was formal, bordering on icy. "You want her to put up the five grand that will break your case open for you? And, if she's lucky, you won't arrest her?"

One of the suits pulled off his sunglasses and said, "Ma'am, this is a federal issue, I'm going to have to ask you—"

Braxton cut him off, the look on her face telling him he could choke on the rest of his sentence for all she cared. "Listen, this is a federal matter because we invited you to our party. Not the other way around. You fellas need to back the hell off, and quick, or I'll have security escort you out of the building. The next time you talk to us will be through our lawyer. Got it?"

Diana loved it when Braxton went all killer instinct. She liked it even more when she did it to protect her. Braxton was a good friend. The suits remained impassive, their faces the perfect mix of attentive boredom. Diana wasn't sure it was a good idea to provoke them, but she trusted Braxton.

"All right." Suit number one spoke in that perfectly modulated voice of a federal officer. "The federal government will provide funding for this venture and Ms. Collins will not be taken into custody."

The more they haggled, the less Diana wanted to go anywhere near that Web site. She doubted it contained anything that would lead them to the katana, but she was suspicious that the content would give her nightmares. Five FBI agents wouldn't drop what they were working on and rush over to her office unless they expected a big payoff. Given what she knew about Charles Stewart from his daughter, entering the site would be the equivalent of opening a cyber Pandora's box, unleashing God only knows what kind of nastiness with the click of the button.

"I have a better idea. How about I just give you the information and you investigate the site somewhere other than here."

"No can do." The suit closest to Diana placed a hand on her shoulder. Strangely, the touch felt reassuring, not aggressive.

She looked up at a beautifully androgynous woman. In the middle of the federal machismo and the threat of jail was a kindred spirit, a family member gently offering to guide her through safely. She met and held Diana's gaze.

"We'd much rather do this at the federal building, but the operators of this site are good. We've been investigating Siger for some time now and we've been close before. They always slip away."

"Who are they?" Diana asked. She'd kept herself from speculating too deeply about Siger. She knew anything that secretive wasn't likely to be innocuous. People didn't hide hobbies like baking brownies or stamp collecting. In spite of the gnawing suspicion, she wasn't ready to make assumptions about what would be on the other side of the password.

"It's a pornography investigation," the special agent replied carefully. "They have filters set up. They'll know if the account is activated from any computer other than this one and they'll know if the money doesn't come from your account. Either of those things happen, they deny access and we start looking for a way in again." She knelt down next to Diana's chair. "We have to do this."

"About the money," suit number one began again.

Diana waved her hand dismissively. She didn't care about the money. Her bonus when they recovered the katana would be five times that amount. The expense was a worthwhile investment if the password led them closer to the sword. "I can cover it."

"We *will* reimburse you."

Braxton leaned over the desk, concerned. "You okay with this, shug?"

Funny. Last night she'd been all over her, a faux lesbian seductress. Today she was all mama bear protective.

"I'm good."

Diana pulled her personal credit card out of her wallet. No company expense account for this purchase. The cursor blinked, ready for her to enter the magic sixteen digits. She took a deep breath and typed them in. She hit the Enter key and the pressure in the room intensified. The screen evaporated pixel by pixel and morphed into an all-black screen, save gold scripted lettering. *Welcome to Siger Enterprises.* She clicked on the logo, bracing herself for what came next.

Shots of children with much older men covered the screen. Diana squeezed her eyes shut, but not before she noticed the picture of a much younger Mona with fear in her eyes. A man, no doubt Charles Stewart, stood behind her, one hand on her hip, the other wrapped tight in her hair. He seemed oblivious to her helplessness and the tear carving a path down her cheek.

Diana forced her way through the suits at a dead run for her bathroom, bile choking the back of her throat. Before she could kneel down at the toilet, everything she'd eaten for the past week came charging back up her esophagus and out her mouth. Her hands trembled as she wiped away a tendril of spit.

Remorse for Mona's suffering gave way to the sharp taste of irreconcilable anger. She'd typed in her account number with a healthy shield of denial guarding her. One simple keystroke had stripped that hope away, leaving her with the hard truth. She'd known, deep inside, what would be waiting, but that didn't make seeing it any easier. One thing was certain. If she ever found out who killed Charles Stewart, she'd send that person a thank-you card.

❖

"Shug, are you sure you're up for this?" Braxton asked the question for the fifth time since leaving the office.

"I'm positive, Braxton. Can you please drop it?" Diana knew Braxton was just worried. Hell, so was she. But she needed a distraction, something to help her put her focus back where it belonged. On finding the missing katana. Visiting the known fences in the area was a perfect way to do that.

"Bob already did this," Braxton said. "We're going to come up empty."

Diana took in Braxton's too-relaxed posture. She knew the calm façade was forced, manufactured, and she could see concern in the soft lines of Braxton's face. She *never* passed up an opportunity to get in these guys' faces, but was willing to if that was what Diana needed.

"Braxton, I need to work off some energy. It's either this or another round in the gym."

"Since you put it that way, it better be this because your eye is finally healed."

Diana ran her fingers over the still tender but no longer purple and swollen flesh around her eye. It'd been over a week since the incident at Bernie's. She jerked the door open and said, "Let's get this over with."

Dave, the proprietor of Dave's Pawn and Loan, met them at the door. "Ladies, how can I be of service today?" Dave was used-car salesman slick.

Diana declined the offer to shake his hand. She'd had enough unpleasantness for one day, thank you very much.

"We're looking for a very special item." Braxton greeted him with professional courtesy. It was an act, Diana knew. Beneath the surface, she was coiled tight and looking for an excuse to let loose.

"Right over here I have some beautiful jewelry."

Diana didn't even glance that direction. No doubt he had some very nice jewelry. And every piece with a broken dream to go with it. She didn't want that kind of legacy anywhere near her skin.

"No, not jewelry," Braxton corrected him. "We're looking for a sword. A gold katana."

"What is it with that thing? First Bob comes in here ready to bust heads, then Chicago's finest, then the feds, now you two." Dave shook his head in frustration. "At least you're nice to look at," he mumbled as he walked back behind the counter. "I don't have that sword. Nobody does. I checked around. Anything causing such an uproar is worth some research, don't you think?"

Diana left Braxton to hash it out with Dave. This conversation was going nowhere. She leaned against the back of the car while she waited. Under normal circumstances, she did not encounter federal agents. The deeper she got into the search for the katana, the more they popped up. They'd made the rounds of the local fences, too. That was to be expected. It was a murder weapon used by a serial killer. But why were they so interested in Siger?

Diana thought back to the words of the female agent. *We've been close before.* She'd spoken with the frustration of a woman denied many times over. The team of agents in her office that morning couldn't be linked to the hunt for the killer. They'd only started their search a week ago, not enough time for them to have found Siger and been rejected often enough to learn the electronic safeguards protecting it.

Diana pulled the female agent's business card out of her breast pocket. Special Agent Amber Faherly. Before she could think better of it, Diana dialed the numbers and waited. The response was brisk and official, a "state your business" greeting only a fed could pull off with such a sense of entitlement.

"This is Diana Collins." In case the special agent had forgotten her, she added, "From this morning."

"I know who you are, Ms. Collins. How can I help you?"

"Tell me what you're looking for."

"I don't understand." Amber Faherly sounded confused.

"You're not looking for the serial killer, are you?" Diana knew the answer without any confirmation, but she wanted it.

There was a long pause, then the agent's voice came through the line, hesitant. "Not exactly. We've been tracking this kiddie-porn ring for well over three years. Today was a big break for us. The information our techs pull off your computer could provide the missing piece we've been waiting for."

Diana was not pleased with the reminder that they'd confiscated her laptop. Everything of importance was on the network server or backed up on a jump drive, but it still didn't feel good to know all her electronic communications were going to be dissected by a team of computer geeks.

"I'm never going to see that computer again, am I?"

Faherly chuckled. "Never say never, Diana. But I wouldn't count on it."

"I won't. Thank you, Agent Faherly." Great. Five thousand dollars and a computer. How much more could this case cost her?

Chapter Fourteen

Ali's legs pumped, propelling her body along the street at a relentless pace. No matter how hard she ran, the dark ghosts from her past kept pace. She rounded the corner that marked the halfway point of her daily run. Rather than stopping for a moment to observe Susan Hansen's house, Ali pushed herself harder. Sweat trailed down her back and pooled in the waistband of her running shorts. She could feel Ricardo's hot breath on the back of her neck, his voice whispering across the miles that she'd never be free. Not while he lived.

Everything that had been good in her life turned to black dust the day he entered it. Her parents, dead. Elena, dead. All at his hands. It would feel good to avenge them, to quiet their clamoring for justice. She'd been unable to do it before, when she fled Colombia. She'd been young, timid, and weak. She wouldn't make the same mistakes this time.

The shelter came into view and Ali slowed her pace to a brisk walk. She forced the haunting echo of Ricardo's voice into the farthest recesses of her mind. In South Lake, she was trusted to keep the occupants safe from harm, something no one was able to do for her. She couldn't allow herself to be distracted by the past.

When she entered the shelter, a quiet calm overtook the rampaging emotions that had propelled her down the street. According to the clock on the wall, she'd completed her run fourteen minutes faster than most days. Taking away the time she usually spent watching Susan's apartment, that was still four minutes faster than normal, give or take.

As was her ritual, she stripped down in the anteroom of the

community shower. It was deserted this time of day. The cool water rinsed the sweat from her skin, taking the mental noise from her run with it. By the time she fastened the last of the little pearl buttons on her silk shirt and tucked it into her knee-length, camel-colored pencil skirt, she was ready to be the protector that these women expected, that they deserved.

❖

Diana sat in her car outside the shelter for a full ten minutes. Mentally she ran through the list of reasons why going in would be bad. Top on the list, Ali was frightening in a feline predator sort of way. Also, she wasn't likely to have a change of heart and give Diana the confirmation she needed. Ali was holding on tight to that information. If the killer was connected to the shelter, possibly working there at that very moment, going in again could spook that person. Oscar would be mad as hell if they tracked their suspect to South Lake only to discover Diana had scared him away.

Then she reviewed all the reasons why she should go in. The top item on that list was almost the same. Ali was intriguing. In a feline predator sort of way. No matter how many excuses she made to justify the visit, or how many reasons she had to leave without going in, it all came down to the simple matter of her wanting to see Ali again.

She needed to do something beyond just sitting in the parking lot. She was bound to attract the attention of security at some point. Assuming this facility had security. *That's a question to ask. Does a facility designed to shelter and protect battered women employ big, burly male security guards?* Would anything else work as a deterrent if a pissed-off husband came calling?

Enough debate. Diana slid out of her car and approached the front door. She hoped her walk conveyed confidence. After the events of the day so far, she wasn't sure she felt even remotely confident.

She identified herself to a faceless voice over a speaker box and the front door popped open. Ali was waiting for her just inside, her hair slightly damp. Diana wondered if she'd been working out.

"Ali, good to see you. I hope you'll forgive the unannounced intrusion."

She was surprised when Ali shook her hand warmly. The calculated precision from last night was no longer present in her motions.

"Of course, Diana. How can I help you today?"

No wonder these women felt safe with her. She exuded discipline, control, and self-assurance. She carried herself like a woman who knew the score and it fell in her favor. They made their way back to Ali's office.

The first day they'd met, she had felt simultaneously warned and welcomed. Then at the bar Ali had been making all the right moves for a successful seduction, but they were emotionless. Everything was flat, no excitement, no tension. Just a woman working through a well-rehearsed routine. The experience had been disconcerting.

"I was hoping we could talk more about Mona Stewart. Braxton can come on a little strong and I thought you might be more comfortable speaking with me alone."

She didn't expect her offer to be accepted and was surprised when Ali seemed to consider it.

"No." She shook her head with a sad smile. "Unfortunately it does not change what I'm allowed to disclose."

"Oh." Diana didn't know why that disappointed her so much. What did she expect? That she would forge this great bond with Ali and she'd lead her to the killer with a helpful smile? Not on this plane of existence. "That's too bad."

"I really am sorry, Diana." She reached a hand over and squeezed Diana's knee. "If I could help, I would."

Diana marveled at the tender remorse in Ali's voice and touch. Suddenly she felt bad for leaving her at the bar so abruptly. "I really should apologize about last night. It was rude of me to leave like that. I just had a bad day and really needed to see my…" Diana paused. What exactly was her relationship with Cami? "Girlfriend." Next time she saw Cami she'd have to clarify that point, figure out if that was really what she was to Diana.

"I understand." The hard edge in Ali's eyes softened and yielded to a warmth generally shared between old friends. "I'll let you make it up to me. Dinner? Tonight?"

❖

Her phone rang, without fail, every time she lathered shampoo into her hair. "Fuck it all."

One of the requirements Carter and Lowe placed on their investigators was that they answer the phone, no matter what. Diana slid open the shower door and took her phone from the tile countertop.

"Collins." Her voice came out sharper than she intended, but considering the shampoo that had just run into her eye, the tone was fairly mild.

"Can I come over?" The slight edge of desperation in Brigitte's voice caught Diana off guard. She wished she could say yes.

"I have a dinner date in an hour. Come over after?"

"A date?" Brigitte was momentarily distracted from whatever crisis had compelled her to call Diana.

"Not a *date* date," Diana explained. "I'm following up on a lead. We're meeting at Mother Hubbard at seven." Mother Hubbard was a well-known vegetarian restaurant. Diana had been surprised yet pleased when Ali suggested that location. "I should be home by nine, nine thirty, tops."

"Diana, are you in the shower?" Brigitte laughed. "I'm sorry I interrupted you."

"It's okay. Are you going to be okay until I get home?"

"I'll have to be."

"I love you, Bri. We'll work it out." Diana knew that whatever "it" was, Lucas and money were involved. Since the birth of their second child, the couple were at constant odds with one another with money at the center of most of their disagreements.

Brigitte ended the call with only a hint of the desperate pleading her voice had contained when she'd greeted Diana. Diana had debated inviting Brigitte along. After all, dinner with Ali wasn't a date. Ultimately she'd decided against it. She still wanted Ali to open up, share what she knew about the internal workings of the shelter. She'd never do that with another person at the table.

Diana hurried through the rest of her shower and getting dressed. She chose her outfit carefully. Seduction was not on her agenda and she wanted to send that message loud and clear. Comfortable, but not tight, blue jeans and a white, blousy button-down. She left the top two buttons open. It was just enough to see a hint of the black tank underneath. To finish the look she slipped into her worn leather motorcycle boots.

They were a classic style, three-quarter height with a harness around the ankle, and fit her feet perfectly. The sleek, black Mean Streak had only left her garage a couple of times this summer. Maybe Cami would want to take a fall foliage tour from the back of her bike. The thought of her nestled against her ass, legs spread wide, fingers splayed over her stomach, left Diana breathless, her gut twisting.

A few passes through her hair with a brush, then she walked out the door. Dinner, and hopefully an overdue break in this case, were waiting.

CHAPTER FIFTEEN

The line at Mother Hubbard was long, but the wait was short. The staff here turned tables with awe-inspiring speed. Ten seconds after the last group left, the table was cleared and reset and a new party seated. It was amazing to watch. Diana wondered how they went about teaching that level of precision, dedication, and urgent execution. Fortune 500 companies struggled to operate at this level, yet this privately owned, small family business had it down.

Diana and Ali settled into the cozy two-person booth. The low light and soft music implied intimacy. If Cami had been sitting opposite her, it would have been downright romantic. "I love this place. Thanks for suggesting it."

"I don't come here very often, but always enjoy it when I do." Ali's accent was stronger tonight than it was during the day. Perhaps she was more relaxed.

The waiter brought them tall glasses of iced water and asked for their drink order. Diana opted to stick with water. As much as she loved a good beer, she felt the need to stay sharp around Ali. Surprisingly, Ali ordered a Cuba Libre—a rum and Coke with lime juice. For some reason, Diana had expected her to be a bit more conservative.

Diana fished the lemon out of her water and sucked on it. If only she had a little salt and a tequila shot. "I don't know why you invited me to dinner. Why are we here?" It wasn't the most polite approach, but the question had been nagging at Diana all afternoon. It was time to clear the air.

Ali smiled softly, a hint of mystery at the edges. "I know why you are here, Diana. You want me to reveal something about my work, about those women. But I won't."

Diana didn't think her motivations were so transparent. Obviously, she was wrong. Denial seemed pointless, but there was no need to confirm. "Why are *you* here?"

"That's simple." Ali paused while the waiter set her drink down.

"Are you ladies ready to order?"

The question wasn't unexpected, but Diana hadn't even cracked the menu. She'd eaten here enough times to fake it if necessary. "Ali?"

Ali didn't hesitate. "I'll have the tabouli wrap."

Yum. Diana hadn't considered that. Still, she preferred her old standby. When the waiter turned to her, she ordered the cornmeal tempeh plate. She wasn't entirely sure what was in it, but it made her taste buds sing.

"Where was I?" Ali took a slow sip of her drink. "Oh, yes. Why am I here?" She waited for Diana to acknowledge the question. "I just want to get to know you, Diana. That's all." She said it simply, like there was no room for any other answer.

Perhaps she had misread Ali, been unclear about what she had to offer. "Ali, I'm flattered, but I'm really not available right now."

Oh, hell. Did she really just say that? Ali was smoking hot, but her cold, perfunctory approach at the Closet didn't appeal to Diana. She wanted passion and fire. Preferably in the form of an equally smoking hot blond kindergarten teacher.

Ali laughed. Not the uncomfortable laught of someone who had just been rejected and was trying to pretend like it didn't matter, but the comfortable, deep laugh of someone who just heard the funniest thing. "That's not what I meant. Although I'm sure it would be…interesting, I'm not looking for anything romantic. I got the message loud and clear last night when you left to meet your girlfriend."

"That's right. I did mention Cami last night, didn't I?" Diana blushed. She'd run out of the bar like a woman possessed. She couldn't wait to wrap herself around Cami, to get inside her. Her thoughts needed a rapid redirect or she'd end this meeting with Ali the same way.

The waiter arrived with their dinner and the usual warning about hot plates. Diana turned the conversation back toward the shelter, her purpose for being here. "I spoke with Mona Stewart again. She confirmed staying at the shelter."

Ali tensed, her jaw muscle twitching slightly. She took a bite of her dinner without responding.

"She's very fond of you. Had nice things to say."

"And who else have you been visiting with?" Ali sat her fork down with the same cold precision she'd used the night before.

"Lora Petrov and Susan Hansen. They're all linked through South Lake." Diana scooped up a bite of food. "And the gruesome deaths of their abusers."

"This is what your partner was talking about, correct?" The warmth from earlier leached out of Ali's voice. "You're searching for a serial killer?"

Diana shook her head and swallowed her food. "No. I'm not interested in finding the killer at all. Far as I'm concerned, whoever killed those men did the world a favor." The image of Mona Stewart with her stepfather sent a shudder through Diana. "All I'm looking for is a sword."

Ali visibly relaxed. "The one used to kill Charles Stewart, right?"

Diana nodded. "I know you can't confirm anything, but *if* you know Mona Stewart and *if* you care about her at all, please, go see her. Convince her to get back into some classes. She's not doing well at all and she needs to learn how to cope with everything that has happened to her. I don't want to see her wind up like Rosa Dominguez."

Diana sent a mental apology out into the night for not visiting the grave of the dead Catholic woman like she'd promised. Her grandmother, God rest her soul, would've been disappointed.

"Rosa." Ali spoke softly, almost a whisper. "That was tragic. So sad."

The background noise in the restaurant sharpened, then faded away. All Diana could hear was the pain in Ali's voice. She didn't know what to say, what to do. She took another bite of tempeh and chewed in silence.

Before either woman could recover, Diana spotted Brigitte in the crowd of people in the lobby waiting to be seated. She rushed over to Diana, her face contrite and relieved at the same time. "I'm so glad I found you. I know you said to wait until later, Di, but I'm just wrecked.

I had to talk to you." Without pausing she held her hand out to Ali. "Hi, I'm Brigitte, Diana's sister."

The waiter quietly slid a third chair up to the table and asked, "Will you be enjoying dinner here this evening?"

"Oh, no, I couldn't. I just need to see my sister." Brigitte's expression was a combination of embarrassment and panic.

"Don't be ridiculous." Ali smiled with her whole body. It took Diana's breath away. "Join us."

Brigitte perched on the edge of the chair, like she was ready to bolt at a moment's notice. She looked at Diana's plate and took her fork. "Thank God. I'm starving."

Diana watched Brigitte devour her dinner with disbelief. "Brigitte, what are you doing here?"

"Di, I'm sorry. We're getting hammered at work ever since the press ran away with the whole serial killer thing. Lucas is bent over money and our lack of it. The kids won't stop pulling on me. I just had to get away from there. I couldn't wait. Not one minute longer." Her bottom lip trembled. "I didn't know where else to go."

"Shh, it's okay." Diana smoothed her hand over Brigitte's cheek and pressed her lips to her forehead. It was awkward holding her with the corner of the table between them, but Diana didn't let go. It broke her heart to see Brigitte cry and Diana knew she was on the verge of a meltdown. "It'll be okay. I promise." She made nonsense noises of comfort until she felt her sister relax and the tremble in her body ease.

Brigitte pulled away and wiped her eyes with Diana's napkin. "Oh, God, I got makeup all over your shirt."

Sure enough, Diana's once white shirt was smudged with tears and black mascara. "It's okay, Bri. It'll wash out." Diana doubted it would. Black mascara on a white shirt would likely leave a stain. "Even if it doesn't, so what? I have lots of other shirts." She kept her voice small, private, just between them. "Now eat." She slid her plate over to Brigitte.

Brigitte smiled, then seemed to remember they weren't alone at the table. "So, Ali, how do you know my sister?"

"She's looking for something and she thinks I can help her find it."

"How goes the search for the missing sword, anyway? Think you'll get to it before the FBI?" There was playful challenge in Brigitte's voice. She liked to push Diana.

"Of course I will. They're all caught up in catching a killer. All I want is a pointy sword." Diana hoped she sounded more confident than she felt. So far she was just chasing her tail.

Brigitte nodded. "I bet you will. And you," she turned to Ali, "what are you doing to help her?"

Ali dabbed the corner of her mouth with the white linen napkin. "Very little, I'm afraid."

The conversation relaxed into easy banter between the three of them and Diana watched as the stress and tension Brigitte carried into the restaurant with her fell away. Not many women would be as gracious about Brigitte's unexpected arrival as Ali was. Diana wondered if Ali had a younger sister of her own.

❖

"Tell me about your family, Ali." Diana asked the question out of genuine interest, not a desire to be cruel. Ali was certain of that. Still, the question sliced through her.

"I'm afraid I have no one." She purposely kept her answer vague.

Watching Diana and Brigitte together stirred up unsafe emotions in Ali. Diana was so protective of her younger sister, so caring. Ali tried to imagine her life if Ricardo hadn't charged into their home all those years ago. Would she and Elena have shared a relationship like the one she was witnessing? The image fractured and splintered every time it got close to solidifying in her mind. Her vision filtered red and she fought for control. Ricardo had tainted everything in her life. She didn't want him to touch this moment. She pushed the thought, along with the memories, down deep. She'd take them out later and examine them when she was alone.

"Really?" Diana had a look of disbelief. "What about your parents? Brothers? Sisters?"

"My parents were killed when I was very young. As was my sister. I am all that remains of my family." Ali willed her voice to stay even, unbroken.

Brigitte covered Ali's hand with her own. "Tell us about it." It was a simple request, no pressure or expectation.

Ali gulped her drink and felt the burn in her stomach. She wished they'd put more rum into it, instead of all Coke. She was used to people closing down, shying away when she shared just the cursory details about her family. Never before had someone asked to know what really happened. She looked from Brigitte to Diana. Nothing but gentle encouragement.

"I grew up in Colombia. The first six years were wonderful. I lived with my mother and father and my younger sister, Elena." Her voice began to shake and she signaled the waiter for another drink.

"You don't have to tell us. It's okay." Diana regarded her across the table. No judgment.

Diana said they owed a debt of gratitude to the person responsible for killing Charles Stewart, Victor Delaney, Mikhail Petrov, and Sergio Dominguez. Would she feel that way if she knew the person responsible was sitting across from her, taking comfort in the warmth of her eyes and the touch of her sister's hand? Diana was worried about Mona Stewart, moved by the death of Rosa Dominguez. Ali wanted to share her past with this woman, invite her to dinner with her personal demons. Staring into those shimmering brown eyes, Ali wanted to trust her.

She took a deep breath and began to speak. This time she would not stop until she was finished. "My uncle owed a great debt to a very powerful man named Ricardo Chavez. He was unable to pay, so he fled the country. Ricardo is not the type of man who allows debts to go uncollected. He came to our house and killed my mother and father. It was a message, a show of strength, that he was untouchable and no one could get away from him. My sister and I hid under the bed. She was three. When he commanded us to show ourselves, she did. She was a baby. She only knew to obey adults. She was crying and he told her to stop. Of course she couldn't. I crawled out as he slit her throat from ear to ear."

It was the first time Ali had given voice to the events of that night. Her voice sounded hollow and raw to her own ears. If she were Diana, she would dismiss it out of hand. *Things like that don't happen in this country.*

Brigitte tightened her grip on Ali's hand. "What happened to you?"

"I spent the next twelve years as his personal plaything. Like all pieces of property, I was shared at his discretion." Ali shut herself off from the flood of emotions. She couldn't unleash her fury here. "It was hell."

Silence. Diana and Brigitte didn't so much as swallow.

"But now I live here. Land of the free, home of the brave." Ali changed the subject. "So, how about the two of you? What was your childhood like?"

Diana laughed and some of the tension at the table dissipated. "Typical stuff. Two parents, four kids, not enough bathrooms."

The rest of the evening was spent on relative small talk. Ali didn't mention her childhood again. For their part, Diana and Brigitte didn't ask any further questions.

❖

Ali stood outside in the cool morning air, staring hard at the building across the street. University of Chicago Medical Center. The man who destroyed everything good and right in her life had stretched his evil taint across two continents and was lurking inside that building. Ricardo Chavez. The name shot tendrils of panic and rage coursing through Ali. She could hear his voice, seductive and sinister, reaching across the years to caress her fears to life.

He'd died so easily the first time. Only it wasn't him. When the haze had lifted, the dead body at her feet was Sergio Dominguez, not Ricardo. All for nothing. When Rosa took her own life a few days later, it left Ali's need for vengeance unfulfilled. Sergio had been a red-tinted, rage-driven masterpiece. Then it was stolen from her, like a balloon with no air. The framework was there, but it lacked importance, depth. It left her feeling hollow and used.

Ali lifted her Marlboro to her lips with trembling hands and took one last, long drag. The nicotine coursed through her body and she felt a surge of calm. She crushed the dwindling cigarette beneath her heel and walked across the street. She'd never been to this hospital before, but the information desk just inside the door was occupied by two elderly volunteers.

"Pardon me. I'm looking for my uncle's room. Can you help me find it?" With her voice steady and calm, she sounded like a concerned relative, not a bloodthirsty enforcer of justice.

"If you tell me his name, I can tell you how to get to him." There was a playful glint in the woman's eye that made Ali think that the blue tint to her curly white-gray hair might be intentional.

A few keystrokes on their computer revealed that Ricardo was assigned to room 3112. "That's on the third floor, honey. Want me to show you the way?"

"That's sweet, but I'm sure I'll manage." She didn't want witnesses for this visit.

Ali didn't wait for the elevator, opting for the deserted stairwell instead. She took the steps two at a time, remembering the death of Mikhail Petrov, husband to Lora. He died without dignity, laughing, cursing, crying, and begging all at once, his bravado at war with the smell of his own death. She saw the whole scene, perfectly orchestrated and executed with precision, like an observer from far away. Three hours later, still covered in blood and struggling to open her front door with the red-slicked key, what she'd done penetrated her consciousness. It was beautiful. She stood under the pounding spray of water, watching the crimson evidence of her victory swirl down the drain, and knew she would kill again.

The first night after his death, Lora cried and Ali held her, comforted her. Ali watched as Lora's fear of her home fell away with each tear and she felt powerful. All the power in the world was hers for the taking in room 3112. She just had to confront Ricardo, and with him her darkest fears, and claim it.

Resolute determination carried her to Ricardo's door. She stood with her hand on the knob, unable to move. She forced her breath in and out, fighting the black dots that blurred her vision.

"Where the hell am I?" Ricardo's voice sounded thin and weak, barely reaching Ali. The underlying sense of entitlement, ownership, still dominated his tone.

The past six years of hard-won freedom slipped away from Ali. One sentence from Ricardo tore away the veneer of strength and left her stripped and vulnerable, close enough for him to reach. The need for vengeance liquefied and pooled on her skin in a fine layer of sweat. She was left with an overwhelming need to flee, to run hard and fast away from the man who would own her. She did the only thing her screaming mind would let her. She ran.

Chapter Sixteen

In the tradition of Bernie's, the service at Namaste left a lot to be desired. The great Indian food more than compensated. Diana didn't know what it was that attracted her to restaurants with an abundance of fuck-you attitude among the staff, but she gravitated to them nonetheless.

"If the server doesn't come soon, we could always try somewhere else." Cami didn't sound irritated, just matter-of-fact.

"If you want. I'm more interested in the company than I am in where we eat."

It was true. Simply sitting at the table with Cami covered Diana with a blanket of calm that had eluded her since dinner at Mother Hubbard. Ali's revelation about her life wouldn't let go of Diana. It grabbed on to her guts and made them churn like the tide.

Cami tipped back her bottle of beer and swallowed the last of her India pale ale. Diana followed her gaze to their server who was busy filling salt shakers three tables over. For a change, Diana wasn't drinking beer. She wasn't crazy about IPA and since it wasn't actually brewed in India, as the name implied, it seemed disingenuous to drink it with her curry. If her curry ever arrived. Still, Cami looked like she wanted another.

Diana stood and picked up Cami's empty bottle. "I'll be right back."

The waitress didn't look up from her task when Diana cleared her throat to get her attention. Diana glanced over her shoulder at Cami and shrugged. She didn't like being ignored, but more importantly, she didn't want Cami to be hungry *and* thirsty. All she needed was sitting in the drink station, not two feet away. Diana opened the door of the small refrigerator and pulled out an IPA. She was almost back to the table when the waitress intercepted her.

"What are you doing with that?" The tone went beyond accusatory to insultingly judgmental and acidic.

Diana offered up her most evil smile and explained the situation.

The server was nonplussed. "You cannot just help yourself. This is a restaurant." Now the server was concerned that they observe the traditional customer/server roles? Unbelievable.

"I tried to get your attention. The salt shakers were more interesting than serving us." Diana's inner voice, the one that tried to keep her from getting into fights during the annual lingerie sale at Nordstrom, warned her to stop. She, of course, kept going. "Next time I'll send up a flare."

The server was interrupted before she could reply.

"Ma'am, is there a problem here?" The voice was confident, trust-inspiring, and directed to the server. It was also intimately familiar.

Angel. The flicker of candlelight from a nearby table bounced off her proffered badge and the server shot Diana a triumphant glare.

"Officer, I caught this woman stealing a beer from our cooler."

Angel regarded Diana with an amused twitch playing on her lips. "Really, Diana, are things so bad you can't afford to buy a beer?"

Diana didn't answer. This whole thing was ridiculous and cutting into her time with Cami.

"Well?" Angel tapped her badge, a sign that she was uncomfortable. Like every other cop Diana knew, she fell back into the role of police officer when unsure how to respond on a personal level.

"You shouldn't make your date wait while you play peacekeeper." Diana flicked a bored glanced at an annoyed-looking woman who'd stepped around the server.

A full year and a hot kindergarten teacher later and Angel still affected her. It had to stop at some point. She returned to her table and pulled the cap off the beer.

"Enjoy." She sat the open brew on the table in front of Cami and sighed. Why did everything turn into such a circus?

The server continued to glare, a triumphant smile on her face. It was an unsettling combination. "I'm adding that to your bill." She went back to her salt shakers.

Angel slid into the seat next to Diana without invitation. Her date was not with her. Diana looked around and saw the woman across the room sitting at a small table for two, glaring at Angel. "Scooch over." The booth was shaped like a horseshoe, with a continuous bench going all the way around. Diana worked her way around to Cami's side. She didn't want to see Angel, but this gave her a good excuse to run her hand along the inseam on Cami's jeans.

"What do you want, Angel?" She aimed for civil, but it came out sounding hostile.

"I saw you causing trouble. Couldn't pass up the opportunity to say hi." She stretched across the table and offered her hand to Cami. "Hi. I'm Angel. The evil-bitch ex."

Cami flinched but took Angel's hand. "I'm Cami. I haven't earned a title yet."

Yet. It was a small word with big intentions and Diana liked the way it sounded when Cami said it. She rested her hand on the table next to Cami's and stroked the back of it with her fingers. Cami made her hope for more. She wanted the future to fulfill its promises when she looked at her. It held all the safety of home, suffused with heat. Angel had been different. They'd burned hot and fast. Supernova. Until there was nothing left to feed the flame, leaving them with a legacy of long-spent lust and infidelity.

"Angel, your date is waiting." It was time for Angel to go. Diana wanted to get back to Cami.

"Okay, Di." Angel plastered on a forced smile. "You just looked happy and I wanted to be close to that again." She sounded wistful.

"I am happy." And Angel should be, too. She was the one who wanted out, who said monogamy was burdensome and boring.

Angel turned back for one final question. "When did you start bringing dates here again?"

Ouch. Shoot to kill, that had always been Angel's motto. Namaste was their joint discovery. They'd stumbled across it one weekend while searching for a guy they'd found on craigslist with a vintage Wonder Woman comic. Angel was a freak for that stuff. They never did find the guy, but the restaurant became a favorite stop for the two of them.

Diana chose not to answer Angel's question. It was none of her business if she decided to bring a date here. Clearly Angel had no reservations about doing so herself.

Angel departed, leaving Diana to explain. Cami cut in first. "So, that's your ex? She's beautiful." No hint of jealousy or fear in Cami's voice.

"She is." Diana's eyes followed Angel across the room to her own table. She moved with fluid grace and confidence, her long, black hair swaying as she walked. She looked back at Cami. "She's got nothing on you." It wasn't terribly sentimental, but Diana definitely meant it.

The tips of Cami's ears flooded with pink and she shifted in her seat. "I can't believe they haven't brought our food yet."

Silence crept into the lull and took over the conversation. Diana was okay with that. It felt good to sit next to Cami and let the residue of her investigation—the pain of Mona and Ali—fall away.

Diana started to move back to the other side of the table. Cami's hand on her thigh stopped her. "Stay."

Easily one of the most beautiful words ever spoken, orgasmic events excluded. Namaste was not the most forward-thinking establishment, but at that moment Diana didn't care. She placed her arm around Cami's shoulder and pulled her tight. "God, it's been a rough week." All the frustration and despair she'd uncovered summed up in one insufficient sentence.

Cami covered Diana's cheek with her palm. "Tell me about it?"

Diana liked the way Cami asked. It was an offer to let Diana purge, without any expectation beyond a desire to listen. She didn't ask with the intentions of fixing it or forcing Diana to let it go. She simply wanted to know more about Diana's life.

Diana didn't spend a great deal of time in morbid introspection. The combined weight of Mona and Ali rested heavy on her. She seldom got to hear another woman's darkest secrets, the crimes committed against her, let alone two separate women in such a short period of time. She was at a loss for what to do.

"The case I'm working on, it's…got a lot of baggage attached to it."

Cami circled her thumb over Diana's palm, a gesture Diana found calming, almost relaxing. Almost. "Do you want to talk about it?"

"Trust me, you really don't want these images in your head." Even if she couldn't find the goddamned katana, there was no way Diana would let that kind of ugliness touch Cami. She was goodness and light. And she needed to keep it that way.

"Come on." Cami slid out of the booth and pulled Diana along with her. "I'm taking you home."

"But we haven't eaten." The protest was halfhearted. Being alone with Cami held great appeal and Diana was ready and willing to follow her anywhere.

"We can eat later. Right now I just need to hold you."

Diana dropped a fifty on the table. It would cover the two beers, the food they didn't eat, and still leave a generous tip for the lousy service. And it was the smallest bill Diana had with her. Cami was halfway to the door and Diana wasn't going to wait for change.

❖

Color and context. That's what the designer said when they picked out her furnishings. She'd wanted simple, understated, but not stark and barren. Diana was sure they'd achieved her goal, but still she was nervous. This wasn't the first time she'd brought Cami here, but last time they'd gone straight to the bedroom. She wanted Cami to be comfortable. And naked. But that would happen later.

"Come on in." Diana dropped her keys on the table in the entryway and looked around. She tried to see the place like Cami would, visiting for the first time. The building was part of the city's reclamation project a few years back, and Diana had picked it up at a decent price. It wasn't literally falling down, but it was in desperate need of repair. The plaster had crumbled in many places, leaving the brick beneath exposed. Diana liked the look, like the past refused to be buried any longer. After much debate, she'd convinced the contractor to simply remove the damaged plaster, seal the wall as it was, then paint over it. She'd chosen a deep cream infused with a faded brick red.

Cami ran her hand over the rough surface. "Beautiful."

Diana breathed a sigh of relief. If the rest of the apartment passed muster, she'd be able to relax and enjoy Cami's company.

Several paintings from local artists hung on the walls, accentuated with soft track lighting. Cami focused on the only print in the collection. *La Danse a la Campagne*—The Country Dance—by Marie Laurencin. It depicted two women embracing casually in a traditional dance, the long lines of their bodies leading the viewer naturally to their legs. A female minstrel played a stringed instrument in the background.

Cami's smile held a hint of shyness that confused Diana. She led her to the soft brown leather couch and invited her to sit. "You are full of surprises." She laid her hand softly on Diana's cheek. Instead of the soft reassurance the same action had promised in the restaurant, this touch was full of reverence and curiosity. "What else are you hiding?"

Diana swallowed hard. "What do you mean?"

"This place," Cami waved her hand in an encompassing circle, "is not what I would have pictured for you."

"You don't like it?" The answer mattered more than Diana was willing to admit.

"I like it a lot, actually. I just picture you as bright colors and possibly circus music."

Diana pulled her brows together. Circus music? That did not sound good. "Are you serious?" She tried hard not to sound outraged and insulted. She wasn't sure it worked.

"It's not a bad thing. You just do everything to an extreme. I expected your home to reflect that in some way."

"Hmm." Diana thought about what Cami said. True, she charged through life with a take-no-prisoners approach, but when she came home at the end of the day, she wanted to relax and recover. She wrinkled her nose. "Do I really remind you of circus music?"

Cami laughed, full and uninhibited. "No, not really." Her laughter faded and she traced the line of Diana's jaw. Diana trembled, her skin begging for more of the gentle touch. Cami pulled her close and brushed a whisper of a kiss over Diana's eyes. "I can't describe the music I hear when I see you. No, not hear. I feel it." She pressed Diana's palm against her chest. "Here."

Diana tensed her jaw and held perfectly still. She knew if she looked in Cami's eyes she'd be lost. It wasn't exactly a proclamation of love, but it was close enough. Her instincts were at war. One voice told her to grab on to Cami with all her heart. The other screamed for her to run away. Now. The conflicting messages rampaged through her nervous system.

"Diana," Cami pressed her lips to Diana's ear, "take me to bed."

The walk up the stairs seemed to take forever. Cami was here, in her house, on her way to her bed. She deserved to be more than a prolonged one-night stand. Diana wondered if she could be the one to give her what she needed.

❖

    Light streamed in through the window, making Cami's naked skin glow. Diana watched as her lover slept, suppressing the need to kiss the exposed curve of her hip. For the past year, Diana had slept alone in the king-size bed. Now, with Cami so close, she didn't want to do it again. She eased out of bed, careful not to disturb her. It was a little early for phone calls, but she wanted to get this one out of the way before Cami woke up. Her family deserved to know that she was going to miss their weekly get-together. Once Cami's eyes fluttered open, Diana planned to make sure she was happily occupied for the rest of the weekend.

Chapter Seventeen

When she pushed the door buzzer at South Lake this time, Diana wasn't asked to identify herself. Apparently, she had visited the shelter often enough to be granted access, no questions asked. She wasn't entirely sure what she was doing here first thing on a Monday. Her excuse—the polite apology for their interruption at dinner last Thursday—was a thin rationalization. The real reason lay somewhere between curiosity and a hunch. Ali Sandoval wasn't like anyone she'd ever met, and Diana felt sure she knew much more than she was saying.

She stepped inside and scanned the reception area. Ali was nowhere in sight. The women working there didn't look up until Diana asked, "Ali in her office?"

A distracted nod was all she was granted.

The door to Ali's office was slightly ajar and Diana pushed it open and stepped inside. As the door swung shut behind her, she realized that Ali was indeed in her office. Naked. At 8:30 in the morning.

Ali swung around, her eyes full of accusation. "What are you doing here?" She pulled on her slacks and zipped them. "I just finished working out."

"Hi. Um…" Diana knew it was rude to stare, but she couldn't look away. Ali's torso was laced with fine white lines that stood out in stark relief against her olive complexion.

She took several paces forward, her eyes fixed on the exposed skin. The lines were a crisscrossed pattern of scars. She traced her finger gently over the longest of them. Ali trembled beneath her touch, but didn't move away. Diana was close enough to see her own exhaled breaths bring bumps to the surface of Ali's body.

"What happened?" She forced herself to meet Ali's gaze.

Her eyes were filled with remorse and fury. "Ricardo." A one-word explanation that said everything.

The tick, tick, tick of the clock on the wall grew louder, more distinct until it crowded out all other sound except Ali's ragged breathing. A small voice in the back of Diana's head told her she shouldn't be doing this. The level of intimacy was too great, yet she couldn't stop herself. Seeing the road map of Ricardo's sadism carved over Ali's body was too much to ignore. She wanted to smooth away the ridges and kiss away the pain.

"How could he do this to you?"

"What else would he do?" Ali's answer was emotionless, a question rather than a sarcastic defensive rejoinder.

A shiver ran through Diana. The longer she searched for this sword, the more she learned about the darkness in the world. Ali's history was proof that there were places where Ricardo's behavior, and that of Charles Stewart, was not only accepted, but expected.

Diana held Ali's challenging stare as long as she could, before letting her gaze slide back down Ali's body, searching out old grievances. Her hands followed, gently evaluating and cataloging. The white lines varied in size and texture. Some she could barely feel with her fingertips. Others were hard and unforgiving. She wanted to block out the image but couldn't take her eyes away.

Hot tears trickled down Diana's face. She dropped to her knees and pressed her lips to Ali's abdomen. It was unthinkable, the torture she'd endured, to the point of unbelievable. With the cruel evidence covering her body, there was no denying her past. Diana wrapped her arms around Ali's waist and hugged her hard, her cheek pressed tight against her belly. After a few moments she felt the rigidity leave Ali's body. Her hands pressed against the back of Diana's head, bringing her closer.

"Tell me about this." Diana traced a series of lines, four in a row, a fifth one cutting across them diagonally, like a permanent score sheet. The scars rested low on Ali's abdomen, almost disappearing into the waistband of her slacks.

Ali didn't look down. "I was thirteen. Ricardo invited several of his business associates to his home for a celebration. It lasted a week. Each line represents a man who borrowed me." The words were devoid of emotion.

Diana was prepared for steel and ice, but the nothingness tore at her insides. She pressed a chaste kiss to each of the five marks, just like her mother used to do when she injured herself as a child.

Slowly, she worked her way around Ali's torso. She stopped at each mark and listened to Ali's simple recounting in horrific detail. When every visible abuse had been reported, she rose to her full height and pulled Ali into her arms.

"You didn't deserve this." Her guts churned and she forced her morning bagel to stay down. "That man's a monster."

The heaviness in the air gradually dissipated and Diana reluctantly released Ali from her embrace. She wanted to say she was sorry, but words were inadequate. Even though her sentiment was genuine, everything she thought of saying seemed forced and trite. Ali had suffered so much and she stood there unfazed. It was Diana, not Ali, whose face was streaked with tears. Ali remained composed.

"How can you stand coming here every day, seeing these women after what you've been through?" Diana asked.

A flicker of emotion crossed Ali's placid face. "How could I not?" She turned away and resumed dressing. When her blouse was buttoned, she faced Diana again. "So, what brings you by here this morning?"

Diana marveled at Ali's control. With the protective barrier of her clothing restored, she was ready to pretend that nothing had passed between them. The moment had been fleeting, and Ali was the one who'd exposed herself, yet Diana found it difficult to move on so quickly.

"I came by to apologize for Thursday night." She blinked her tears away and checked her face in the mirror. Blotchy as all hell. Damn. "I knew Brigitte was upset, but I didn't think she'd crash in on us like that."

"No need to apologize. I enjoyed myself. The two of you are something else."

Diana wasn't sure if that was a compliment or not. "Thanks…I think."

Sounds of activity in the reception area crept into Ali's office, reminding Diana of the mountain of work waiting for her at Carter and Lowe. Still, she didn't want to leave Ali without saying more.

"If you need anything, I'm here." She touched Ali's arm. It was the kind of suggestion made at funerals and weddings. No one expected to be taken up on the offer. It was understood. Still, Diana lacked the words to convey her wishes any other way. "For real."

Ali lifted Diana's hand and pressed her lips into the soft part of her wrist. The gesture was strangely intimate and familiar, but without the charge Diana would have felt if Cami had been on the giving end.

There wasn't anything left to say. Diana exited the office quietly, without a good-bye. All normal observances of tradition, including a formal departure, were just beyond her grasp, hiding behind a cruel tangle of white lines and bronze skin. The more she uncovered as the investigation progressed, the less Diana wanted to find the sword. Whoever had used it to kill Charles Stewart had done the world a favor. Who was she to lead the police to that person's door?

Ali studied her profile in the full-length mirror. She'd always hidden her past beneath a veil of pretense and fabric. Diana had accidentally stripped that away with a poorly timed entrance and an understanding touch. Everything she kept well guarded was laid bare for Diana's insistent exploration. Ali had waited for her emotions to catch up. The expected rush of panic never arrived. She felt safe, known. There had been love, without passion or the need to dominate, in Diana's kisses. The experience took her into unexplored territory. She'd been kissed many times, in many different ways, but after her life collided with Ricardo's, she'd never been kissed with permission. And the act had never brought her anything but pain. Diana filled her with warmth. She felt cared for, respected, without a hint of pity or judgment. She knew that if Diana had been able to, she would have taken away all the scars—and the memories of their creation—with her probing touch and gentle kisses.

The physical scars never went away, but they hid nicely behind her clothes. Their pattern was so deeply ingrained in her self-perception she forgot all about them most days. They were a part of her, as familiar as the breath that filled her lungs. Ali unfastened the buttons that held her top closed and slid the shirt from her shoulders. Her stomach was no longer damp with Diana's tears, but she could still feel them sliding down her skin, carving out their surprising message of kindness and healing.

Ali traced her fingers along her flesh, trying to recreate the path Diana had taken. The scars she'd kissed tingled. Chills followed her fingertips. She tried to see her body as Diana would. She couldn't. The pain of her past had been buried too deep to make the trip to the surface safely. Her heart simply wouldn't release the pain long enough for her to mourn her lost childhood. If she did let down the walls, she feared that she would never regain control.

Diana had cried for her. Unashamed and uncensored. Never before had someone done that. Ali had stopped crying for herself a long, long time ago. Her soul ached for more, like a parched desert stretched out for miles, cracked and abandoned, unaware of its need for rain. Now awakened, that need would be hell to bury again. Ali dared to hope Diana was her sanctuary on the horizon.

The three-inch stack of Charles Stewart's personal phone records was waiting on the corner of Diana's desk when she arrived at work later that morning. Traci, Charles's wife, had been reluctant to produce the documents until Diana reminded her that the insurance policy mandated client cooperation in any investigation. Without her compliance, no settlement would be issued. Diana wondered at Traci's hesitation in sharing the records. Even with the threat of nullifying the contract, Traci hadn't been fully willing until Diana pointed out that all she wanted was to find the sword. Nothing more. She'd have to mention that to Oscar next time she spoke with him.

Diana made a cursory pass through the pages, crossing out known numbers like Charles's office and Traci's cell phone. Then she started in earnest, looking for unfamiliar numbers and patterns, paying special attention to the day before his murder. If there was a phone call linking Charles Stewart to her thief and his murderer, Diana would find it. The monotonous task also kept her from thinking about Mona's endless cloud of smoke and the bright white lines mapping Ali's body. She wasn't sure whether she felt relieved, irritated, or excited when the phone rang and Cami's velvety voice filtered into her ear.

"Di, it's Cami." She sounded unsure. This was the first time she'd called Diana on her office line, rather than her cell.

Diana rolled her neck from side to side, working out the tension from sitting too long. This wasn't an unwanted phone call. It was Cami, and Diana was more than willing to make time for her.

"Hey," she said softly. "How are you?"

Normally, she never wasted time on niceties like that, preferring to get to the meat of the conversation right away. With Cami it was almost enough to hear her breath on the other end of the line, close enough to touch. Almost.

"I miss you. This weekend didn't last long enough."

The observation made Diana's tummy do back flips. She'd forgotten how overwhelming the getting-to-know-you phase of a relationship could be. Or maybe she'd never known. She tried to remember if she'd felt this way with Angel. She didn't think so. This extreme tension and the need to be with Cami every minute of the day were unfamiliar to her.

"I agree. Our time together was way too short." She hesitated. If it were possible, she'd crawl through the phone to be with Cami. Still, she didn't want to push for too much. Her feelings for Cami placed her on uncertain ground, and she wasn't sure what the rules were for frequency of dating. "Want to get together again next weekend?"

"Do we have to wait for next weekend?" Cami asked.

Diana thought she heard her gulp, almost like the words came out before she had a chance to think about it and once they were out she thought better of it.

"No, we don't have to wait. I'd love to see you tonight. Hell, I'd love to see you right now." Diana pictured Cami stretched out on her desk, her head thrown back, sweat glistening on her skin in the moment before climax. "I just meant do you want to lock ourselves in my apartment and not come up for air next weekend, too?"

Normally she didn't expose this much of herself; she'd never wanted to. Cami made her feel safe, wanted, desired. She made all the ugliness of Diana's work disappear with the curve of her lips. Diana wanted to press herself into Cami, merge with her, and never let her go.

"What about your family barbecue on Sunday? I don't want you to miss it two weeks in a row."

Diana considered Cami's words. The tone wasn't presumptuous, insinuating. Simply observant. Her parents would be relieved that she'd met someone who made her crave a picket fence and a two-car garage. There was no reason not to invite her.

"My plans for you involve lots of naked time, but I guess I could let you get dressed long enough for us to make the trip to Norwood Park." It wasn't the most straightforward invitation, but it felt right.

"Did you just invite me to meet your family?"

"Yes." It came out as a cross between a squeak and a yelp. So much for smooth.

Cami's smile reached through the phone and caressed Diana. "I'd love to."

Diana exhaled in relief. She gathered strength from knowing Cami was willing to brave her family. "Careful what you ask for. My family can be a little overwhelming."

"We'll compare notes after you meet mine."

And with that one sentence, all pretense was stripped away. They were negotiating the terms of their relationship, carefully, trying not to spook one another. Diana wondered if Cami was having the same internal struggle, the one that screamed at her to run away and hold on tight all at the same time.

"I'm looking forward to it." Diana continued to run her eyes over the data in front of her, a silly grin on her face, reading the numbers more out of habit than actual interest. She knew she'd have to go through the records more thoroughly when she finished her conversation.

"But about tonight?" She let the sentence hang there, hoping Cami would fill in the blanks.

"I want to cook for you in that amazing kitchen of yours."

When Diana had shown Cami her kitchen on Friday night, Cami's eyes lit up. Apparently all the stainless steal surfaces were delightfully overwhelming for her.

Cami went on to explain all the delicious things she planned to do to Diana in the kitchen. Some involved food, most didn't, and Diana almost missed a brief, incongruous incoming call the night Charles Stewart was murdered. It had lasted no more than a minute, just long enough to establish a connection and therefore earn a spot on the call log. The number was naggingly familiar and it took a moment for Diana to place it. A glance at a business card tucked into the Stewart file confirmed that the call originated from the South Lake Domestic Violence Shelter.

Warmth spread through Diana. At least Ali was taking an interest in Mona and providing some ongoing support. With her help, maybe Mona would be okay. Ali was an inspiration. Enduring a childhood like hers would have stopped many people from going on to become productive adults and make a difference in the lives of others. Ali's example gave victims of domestic violence a reason to hope.

"Di, you with me?"

The question snapped Diana's attention back to the phone. "Sorry, baby, this case has my head running in fifteen different directions. What were you saying?"

Holy hell! She'd just called Cami "baby." Diana's respiratory system instantly fell to its knees. Incredibly, Cami responded like nothing had happened. Maybe she thought Diana used the same endearment for every woman she dated. Hell, maybe she thought Diana *dated*.

"I'll let you get back to it. My break is almost over anyway."

The words sounded clipped, almost formal, as though Cami was hurt. Who could blame her? Diana's lack of concentration was less than flattering. She wanted to pull Cami through the phone and hug the tension away.

Diana glanced up at her open office door. No one was around. "Do you really have to go?" She dropped her voice to a low, intimate level. "I haven't told you what I have planned for dessert."

Cami's response was a breathy half laugh, half growl. "Damn, the kids are coming back in from recess. I really do have to go." This time Diana heard reluctance and disappointment. Cami wanted more.

"Oh, but I have the most delicious things planned involving my tongue and your cl—"

"Hold that thought," Cami said. "In two seconds this room will be filled with six-year-olds and I need to be able to walk."

Diana squeezed her thighs together, an unsuccessful attempt to bring her own escalating passion under control. Cami distracted her on a cellular level, eclipsing everything else, including work. Just the sound of her voice, soft and sweet, coming through the phone line was enough to jump-start Diana's libido. Add the image of her in a Catholic schoolgirl uniform having difficulty walking...damn. Diana was a goner. Not that Cami wore a little plaid skirt to work, but in Diana's fantasy she did.

"See you tonight?" Diana murmured.

"God, yes." Cami sounded rushed and heavy, like a woman on the edge. Diana stayed on the line, unwilling to break the connection, until Cami disconnected the call. After work—no, after dinner; she was civilized, after all—Diana would take Cami to the edge and over it. But first she had to find that damned katana.

Chapter Eighteen

The smell of sweat and chlorine greeted Diana as she stepped through the double doors into the gym where she and Braxton sparred. She rarely took advantage of the lap pool, but the scent made it impossible to forget a large body of chlorinated water occupied the adjoining area. Diana looked around for her mentor. It was a few minutes before six a.m. and for once, Diana had actually arrived first, assuming, of course, that Braxton wasn't waiting for her in the changing room, which was an annoying habit of hers.

Diana stepped around the corner, half expecting to see Braxton fully changed and flexing her muscles, impatient to get started. She loved Braxton's company and the edgy tension they often shared in the locker room. It was a place where they were allowed to be naked and appreciate one another without pretense or expectation. Still, as much as she usually enjoyed watching Braxton change, she didn't feel that interested this morning; in fact, she appreciated having solitude.

She changed her clothes and started tightening the laces on her trainers. She felt fuzzy and unfocused, unable to think about her workout goals or the tasks awaiting her at the office. Cami had spun a web through her body and mind that held her captive. Every time she tried to break free, she was reclaimed by memory and longing. They'd spent the night before curled up on the floor in front of her fireplace, facing one another with a bowl of strawberries and dipping chocolate between them. The image made her smile; it was so clichéd, bordering on absurd. Cami inspired Diana to strive for increasingly Harlequin moments. If she wasn't careful she'd end up scaling trellises and quoting poetry in her quest for romance-novel perfection. Bleah.

The firelight had tripped over Cami's body, hypnotizing Diana with the soft play of light and dark. She traced the patterns with her tongue, amazed that this beautiful woman willingly spread herself out, open and inviting, for Diana to explore. It was perfect. The press of Cami's smooth skin against her own, chocolate sauce and strawberry juice mingling with the light sheen of sweat as Cami arched and screamed Diana's name.

With her hand on the back of Diana's head, holding her tight in place, she'd exhaled, "God, I love you." Not "I love the way you make me feel." Or "I love it when you do that."

Words like that can't be taken back. Diana wondered if Cami even realized what she'd said. Did she mean it? Beyond just that moment and into forever? That was how Diana defined love. It wasn't fleeting. It didn't show up for a few moments a day and disappear when the people involved got bored with one another. Love, if it was real, was tangible, solid, and strong enough to span a lifetime. She'd seen that with her parents and she wouldn't settle for anything less.

She had no idea what those three words meant to Cami. Was a declaration of love her natural response to a particularly shattering orgasm? Diana didn't think so. They'd shared plenty of those and managed to avoid false confessions of devotion. Cami's words had to mean *something*, but what? Did she feel the way Diana did, that love was precious and rare? A prize worth fighting for and protecting at all costs.

Her soft avowal had hung in the air, clinging to the drops of sweat on their bodies, living in the crackle from the fireplace. Diana had choked down her response, refusing to give purchase to a half-conceived emotion, unsure if it was real or just a response to the moment. But she'd barely been able to hold herself back. She was overwhelmed, confused, and at a loss for what to do with the building tide of emotion threatening to pull her under. One thing was certain, she and Cami needed to talk. A quiet night, no distractions, and fully clothed.

All Diana had to do was figure out what she wanted to say. Did she love Cami? Hell, she barely knew her. Still, she was undeniably drawn to her, like the ocean to the moon. When they weren't together, she couldn't stop thinking of her. When they were together, she couldn't get close enough. Visions of Cami, of them together, five, ten, fifteen years in the future popped into her head at the most inopportune moments.

She would be reviewing data and suddenly picture herself and Cami exchanging gifts next to a Christmas tree. Or the two of them lying together on the beach sipping margaritas. Or toasting their anniversary, her family singing out cheers in the background. For every wanton fantasy, she had another that involved a house, two-car garage, white picket fence, and growing old together.

Her father had proposed to her mother two months after they met. He said it was like being struck by lightning or hit by a bus, depending on the morning. Either way, he knew right away that he couldn't live without his future wife and there was no reason to delay the inevitable. Did those images of life with Cami mean the same thing for her? Should she just give up and buy a ring now?

"Sugar, those shoes ain't going to tie themselves." Braxton dropped her bag on the bench next to Diana. A quick glance at the wall clock confirmed she was more than a few minutes late.

"What happened? You oversleep?" Diana kept her tone light and playful. "No, wait, I know. Jake tied you to the bed and wouldn't let you leave until you recited *Cyrano de Bergerac* from memory."

Nothing short of being physically restrained could explain Braxton's tardiness. It just didn't happen.

With an eye roll over the reference to her least favorite play of all time, Braxton said, "I was just caught up in a little discussion with Jakey."

The fine lines around her eyes were etched just a little deeper and her words didn't hold the same humor she normally conveyed. More than that, though, when she said Jake's name it sounded flat, bordering on stark. Her husband was normally the high note in any song for Braxton.

Diana looped her shoelaces together and cinched them tight. "Anything you want to talk about?"

Braxton changed her clothes in silence. When she finished, she closed her locker door and faced Diana. "Shug, I appreciate it. Really, I do. And when I'm ready, your door will be the first one I knock on." She squeezed Diana's shoulder as she walked past her on the way out the door.

Their workout was uneventful and ended early. Braxton seemed as unfocused as Diana, and that was a surefire recipe for injury. Finally they collectively threw in the towel and headed for the showers. Diana watched Braxton as she dressed quietly. Not a single quip about Diana staring at her. Something was very wrong and they were both clearly in need of a distraction. Work would do the trick, no doubt. When they reached the elevator, Braxton pushed the Up button.

Diana, however, called for a car going down. "I have a promise to keep," she explained. "You should come with me."

She wasn't trying to be vague, she just didn't know how to explain what she was planning. Braxton wasn't Catholic, so she might not understand Diana's feelings about the pledge she'd made a few days earlier.

To break her promise would be blasphemous. Her grandmother, God rest her soul, had looked past Diana's lesbianism. She didn't understand it, but she didn't see it as evil. She simply wanted her granddaughter to find love and be happy. The gender of her partner was of little consequence. But breaking a promise about visiting the grave of a young Catholic woman who had reached a point where life offered no options? That would be unforgivable. Nana would make the trip down from heaven just to smack Diana upside the head if she made a mistake like that.

Not one to follow along blindly, Braxton asked, "A promise to who to do what?"

"Remember Rosa Dominguez?"

"Don't make me ask for every detail. I don't like it."

That wasn't entirely true. Braxton gloried in a difficult interview, proud that she could wrangle the tiny details out of unwilling subjects. But Diana wasn't a stranger and Braxton obviously wasn't in the mood to jump through hoops. "I promised her neighbor that I'd visit her grave. I haven't done it yet."

Braxton stared at her. "What the hell are you talking about?"

The elevator doors slid open, but neither of them moved toward the stale interior.

"I promised that woman I'd go," Diana said. "Look, it's a long story but you'll just have to take my word for it. I don't have a choice. I have to go."

Another elevator arrived, this one going down.

"Okay," Braxton said as she stepped into the car. "Let's go chase your ghost."

❖

The main entrance at Calvary bore testimony to the age of Chicago's oldest Catholic cemetery in mottled gray tones. Imposing and inviting, it promised salvation to those who were worthy, the chosen children of God, and damnation to those who weren't. An arched car gate was flanked by two smaller man gates, with a Celtic cross perched at the highest point.

They followed the winding road past the old-money mausoleums toward the rear of the cemetery where the graves were denoted only by small, church-issued markers.

Diana pointed toward her family plot, located between the imposing and the obscure. "Nana is over there."

It'd been too long since she'd visited with the woman who'd taught her that God's love couldn't be defined or contained in rules written by men and that family loyalty trumped any other obligation in life. Once she figured out where exactly her relationship with Cami was going, maybe she'd bring her out and introduce her. Maybe.

She consulted the plot map. "Slow down. We're close."

Braxton pulled up next to a row marker. If they got lucky, Rosa's grave was to their right, thirty or forty feet. Records for the plots in other areas were impeccably maintained. The plots donated to the needy by the church were another matter entirely. The need for accuracy was not so great. After all, who visited society's forgotten citizens?

Diana climbed out of the car, but Braxton didn't move.

"Are you coming?" Diana leaned down to look in the window.

"You go." Braxton rested her head against the steering wheel. "I'll wait here."

The look of defeat on her face tore at Diana. Whatever had happened with Jake wasn't as simple as a disagreement over what to watch on television. It was serious, but she wasn't going to pressure Braxton for details. When she was ready, she'd talk. Diana hoped.

"Okay, I'll be right back." She closed the passenger door and headed off in what she thought was the right direction.

The map detailing the location of Rosa's final resting place was drastically inaccurate. After a great deal of frustrated swearing, followed by hastily executed signs of the cross and numerous Our

Fathers, Diana found the grave several plots farther down. The marker was small, nondescript, buried in leaves from last fall that no one had cleared away. They had the rotting brown-black hue showing they'd been covered over by the winter's snow and subjected to the harsh sun beating down this summer. Diana swept her foot over the grave, clearing away the debris to allow the choked grass beneath it a chance to take in the still strong late summer sun. She moved methodically, talking as she went.

"Hello, Rosa. My name is Diana Collins and I'm here because..." She didn't know the ending to that sentence. Why was she really here? "Because I don't want to disappoint an old lady who reminded me of my grandmother." She clasped her hands behind her back and fidgeted from foot to foot. "It's awful what happened to you, but you ended up in a beautiful place." Calvary, by any standard, was beautiful. It held a tragic, gothic charm that Diana found comforting. "My grandmother, the grand lady herself, is resting just over there. Next time I come to see her, I'll visit you again, too."

What did she just promise? Fuck it all. Diana looked around. Typically, husbands and wives were buried next to each other. Sergio's grave wasn't there. Had she asked to be kept away from him? No one would blame her for that.

"I work for an insurance company," Diana said. "And we're trying to find your husband's killer. Well, that's not entirely true. We're trying to find a really expensive sword before we have to pay out for it." An idea struck her. "Do you know who killed him? Is that why you couldn't go on, even though he was dead? Did you feel guilty?"

Was Rosa somehow involved in her husband's death? Or had she figured out who killed him and been bound not to reveal the killer's identity? Diana knew she wouldn't have been able to hold that kind of secret in; the guilt would kill her.

Diana found herself listening intently, as though she would hear an answer in the unnatural quiet of the cemetery. A graveside service ended several sections over and the quiet purr of engines reached her across the distance. A breeze caught the leaves she'd flicked aside, piling them up once more. When she shoved them more firmly aside, her toe hit something solid and she bent down expecting to find a rock, or perhaps a fallen tree branch. Not even close.

She unearthed the top of a shoebox-sized package partially buried next to the simple steel marker. It was wrapped in plain brown paper, discolored by the weather and decomposing leaves. The sides of the package sagged, like the weight of the lid was too much to bear.

Diana wanted to open it but didn't. That would be a ticket to hell. Even though the box lay somewhat aboveground, she was pretty certain her grandmother, and therefore God, would frown upon her plundering the grave. The box could be something accidentally left behind after a night of grave knocking by neighborhood teens. Diana doubted it. They usually limited their activity to the larger headstones. Or maybe it was a box of gardener's tools, forgotten by the groundskeeper the last time he'd worked in that area.

There was another possibility. "Did someone care about you, Rosa? Did a friend come and leave a few mementos for you?"

Diana lifted the box clear of its shallow hole and brushed off the earth and leaves. It would be wrong to open the box, she knew it, but she was bursting with curiosity. She had to know what was inside. Braxton was a self-proclaimed agnostic and could peek inside without the threat of eternal damnation. Fire and brimstone were laughable to her.

"Listen, Rosa." Diana tried to reason through her plan. If it sounded okay spoken aloud, then she'd do it. "Whatever's in this box isn't going to help you there. I'm just going to have my friend Braxton look in it for me. If it belongs with you, I'll return it. If not, I'll make sure it gets to the right people."

She'd done it again. When would she stop making promises to or about this dead woman? Hopefully Braxton would accommodate her.

She managed to make it all the way back to the car without tearing off the lid. No small feat. After claiming her seat inside the Mercedes, she held the box out to Braxton. "I found this on her grave."

Braxton looked the package over but didn't touch it. "What's in it?"

"I don't know. You should open it." Diana set it on the middle console between their seats.

"Why me and not you?"

"Because I found it on the grave of the wife of a serial killer's victim." The description sounded convoluted, like she was at a Southern family reunion with her brother's uncle's wife's first cousin twice removed.

The gray shadows in Braxton's eyes brightened as she carefully removed the brown paper from the outside and lifted the lid. "Holy shit."

"Sweet Jesus." Inside the box lay a hunting knife that must have belonged to a giant. Diana estimated it to be around eighteen inches long.

"Is that what I think it is?" Diana forced herself to breathe.

"A big fucking knife? Yes, that's exactly what it is."

"Rosa's husband, Sergio—"

"Filleted with a big fucking knife," Braxton completed with satisfaction.

Diana's head spun with the implications. The knife had been wrapped up like a present and left for Rosa. There was no way to be sure it was the weapon used to kill Sergio without forensic examination, but the clench in her guts told her otherwise.

"We have to take this to Oscar," she said.

Chapter Nineteen

"Tell me again why we can't just deliver this to the station house?" Braxton asked for the third time as she guided the Mercedes to the top level of the parking garage.

Diana sighed. "Because if we take it there, we'll spend hours answering stupid questions while some overdressed monkey in a suit goes to Mona's house and scares the crap out of her."

The knife sitting between them, coupled with the common factor of South Lake, might not be enough for the task force to get a warrant to search Traci's and Mona's homes. But it would definitely pique their interest, resulting in another visit to the other widows and Mona.

Diana wanted to be the one to confront Mona. The longer she thought about it, the more convinced she was that Mona had the katana. The only question left was when and how did she get it? Diana didn't give a rat's ass about catching a serial killer. She just wanted that fucking sword so they could finally close out this case. She'd gone over all this with Braxton more than once, but Braxton was being disagreeable. She argued that they'd done all the legwork and should turn over the knife and leave the risky stage of the investigation to the police. If Mona had the sword, collecting it should be easy, even for law enforcement.

Oscar was already waiting when they pulled into the parking spot closest to the roof access elevator. Diana left the box in the car when she went to meet him.

"Okay, what's so goddamned important?" He was not in a good mood.

"Have you guys made any progress at all with your serial?"

"Nope. Even after you established the shelter as a common link, we haven't been able to break through." Oscar's eyes held the hard edge of a streetwise Chicago cop. "Nobody wants to talk to *us*."

The last word dripped with disdain and implication. The shelter women wouldn't talk to cops, but opened up to Diana and Braxton without resistance. That obviously rankled.

"I have something for you, but I want you to give me something in return." Diana hoped her preemptive demand wouldn't send Oscar straight back to his elevator without so much as a "fuck you."

He stiffened. "Don't jack me around, Collins."

Christ, he was treating her like a common street informant. She didn't like it one bit. Still, she was pushing in a way that would make her father cringe. "I found the knife that killed Sergio Dominguez. Or at least I think it is."

Oscar's mouth dropped open. "You have it?"

"How about I show you?"

As Oscar examined the weapon, Diana said, "I think the killer gave it to Rosa as an offering to show that she's safe from his reach now. If that's true, then Mona Stewart has our missing katana." She rushed on, refusing to pause long enough for Oscar to respond. "I want to be the one to ask her. She'll tell me the truth…I hope. If I'm right, I'll turn it over to you immediately."

Silence stretched between them, taut and frayed, ready to snap at any moment.

"Have you lost your mind?" Oscar's voice thundered out, vibrating Diana to the core. "I can't sit on a piece of evidence this big."

"We'll go there right now. All you have to do is walk back to the precinct, slowly, and do your job. Protocol dictates that you should visit the victims' wives in order, right? By the time your people finish with Lora, Susan, and Traci, we'll be done at Mona's."

It was the least he could do in exchange for the major break. Without her hand-feeding them evidence, they wouldn't know about the shelter, or have a way into Siger Enterprises, and they certainly wouldn't have the knife.

"Mona won't talk to you," Diana reminded him. "You said it yourself. I'll have more chance of getting the katana if she's hidden it."

Oscar replaced the knife in the box with a grunt that wasn't a yes, but it also wasn't a no. Diana took the nonanswer as permission to proceed.

"You got anything on the killer?" he asked.

"No, how about you guys? Any suspects?"

He shook his head in frustration. "You'd think we'd have this bastard in handcuffs by now, what with finding the common link between the women, but we don't even have a single solid lead."

"You really think South Lake is just a coincidence?"

Diana was amazed at the task force's willingness to overlook a pool of potential suspects simply because of their gender. There was little point in tracking dead-end leads, and statistical norms were hard to escape, but if evidence pointed in a certain direction, it had to be followed, eyes wide open. Eventually the answer would show itself. When would law enforcement stop underestimating the capacity of a righteously pissed-off woman?

"You know the statistics. Serial killers are men. All the employees at the shelter are women." Oscar held up a hand when she started to argue. "Sure, there are exceptions, but why chase an improbability? We ran background checks on all the women. Parking tickets, shoplifting, that kind of thing. So we're looking at males with some kind of connection to the place."

"There can't be many of those."

"More than you'd think. Husbands of all the employees. Drivers and staff of services the place uses on a regular basis. Plus they operate these *treatment* groups, guys who teach abusers what it's like to be on the receiving end. Straight out of the Old Testament, eye for an eye kind of people."

Diana raised an eyebrow. Did he really believe that was where they'd find the answers?

"Believe me, I know, Collins." He shook his head, disgust clear on his face. "Feels like a big circle jerk to me, but it's not my party. Hell, the only reason they're still letting me play is because I keep showing up with neat party favors like this one." He hefted the box to illustrate his point.

"Maybe the knife will provide DNA," Diana said in a conciliatory tone.

"I owe you a beer if it does." Oscar started back toward the elevator, calling, "Go find your sword."

❖

"I've been wondering how long it would take you to show up here." Mona stood in the open door to her apartment, effectively blocking Diana and Braxton from entering. She appeared to be sober and in control.

"If you knew we'd be back, why didn't you just call me?" Diana asked.

"It was more fun to see if you would figure it out on your own." Mona stepped out of the way. "Come on in."

The apartment was free of the haze of smoke Diana had come to associate with Mona. The clutter that had dominated the kitchen had been tamed. The countertops and table were clear and clean. The scent of patchouli burned a trail around the room, obscuring the clinging veil of stale French cigarette smoke.

Diana sat down at the kitchen table. Every other discussion between them had taken place there, no reason this one should be different. "You look good, Mona."

"Thanks. I finished my last bottle of rum three days ago and didn't have the energy to go out for a new one."

There was more to it than that, Diana was certain. But she didn't ask Mona to explain herself. As long as she was sober and on the road back to okay, that was all that mattered. "Tell me, what was I supposed to figure out on my own?"

Mona quirked her head to the side. "If I tell you that, then you won't have figured it out."

Diana thought back to her first meeting in this apartment. Mona's emotions had been shredded, but despite her distress signs of strength were apparent. Today the insecurities were stifled behind a mask of cockiness. Diana didn't like seeing Mona crying, but she wasn't sure this version was an improvement.

"We want the sword, Mona," Braxton cut in abruptly, her patience tested. She was still standing, scanning the room in a constant loop.

"What makes you think I know where it is?"

"Because we know everything," Braxton said. *When in doubt, give the interview subject the impression there's nothing left to hide.* Most people spoke truthfully if they thought they would be caught in a lie.

Diana had to hand it to her colleague. Braxton's face was impressively placid, almost bored.

"You can talk to us or talk to the cops," she continued, like it was immaterial to her or Diana.

After several moments of uncomfortable silence, Mona said, "All right. I have it." She stood. "It's under the bed."

Diana looked around the one-room apartment. Not a bed in sight.

Mona crossed to the low sofa and lifted the dust cover, explaining, "It's a futon."

She dragged a long box from beneath and sat it gingerly on the table. Weak with relief and hardly able to believe they'd solved their case, Diana exchanged a quick look of triumph with Braxton. Tomorrow they'd wrap up the paperwork on this godforsaken case and her life could return to normal. She could go home and get lost in Cami for a few hours and start thinking about what really mattered to her.

She reached to open the lid.

"Shug." Braxton issued a quiet warning. The last thing they needed was Diana's fingerprints on another piece of evidence.

"I'll open it," Mona said.

Braxton peered over Diana's shoulder and let out a long, low whistle as the contents were exposed. Diana had recovered a lot of merchandise in her years as an investigator, but she'd never seen that much deadly, shiny, and sparkly all in one place before. Her intention to deliver the weapon to the police station evaporated at the sight of dried blood on the blade. She pulled out her phone to call Oscar as Braxton took picture after picture with her digital camera.

When Oscar picked up the phone, Diana didn't bother with a greeting. "It's here, but you need to come get it."

"Make up your mind," he grumbled. "You wanted to collect the sword, why the sudden change of heart?"

"It hasn't been cleaned."

The katana was no longer a coveted prize that she had to chase down. It was the embodiment of death. The length of the blade had traveled inside Charles Stewart, forcing his life from his body. She didn't want to be anywhere near its deadly legacy.

"Don't touch it." Oscar disconnected the call and Diana assumed that meant he was on his way.

Mona's comment about framing the sword and hanging it on the wall echoed in her mind. At the time Diana had dismissed the words as angry bravado; now she wanted to know why Mona hadn't turned the sword over as soon as she received it. Did she really have a blood thirsty streak?

"How did you come to have this?" Diana asked.

"It arrived in the middle of the night." Mona sounded defensive. "I was going to call you."

"It *arrived*?" Diana repeated. She avoided the question about *when* it had arrived. The thought that it'd been in the apartment the last time she'd visited made her stomach rise up in protest. She didn't want to know if Mona had concealed the weapon from the beginning. Questions about timeline were best asked by the police.

"On my doorstep. Like a present. There was even a card." Mona tapped her fingers against the table, a rhythmic tattoo against seventies-era Formica.

"Do you still have that?"

Mona took the only framed photograph of her family—Charles, Traci, and Mona—off the wall and stared at the image. "He looks so normal, harmless even." With a practiced move, Mona slid an envelope from behind the matting and returned the portrait to its place on the wall.

"Don't you want to read it?" Mona's voice was almost taunting as she held the envelope out to Diana, daring her to take it.

"You know we can't touch it."

Mona shrugged and pulled out three sheets of paper. Two small newspaper articles and a piece of plain white paper. She set the latter on the table and smoothed her hands over the surface. One sentence was written there in bold, black letters:

HE WILL HAVE NO MORE VICTIMS

Diana read the message and commented, "So, the killer fancies himself a protector of some sort?"

It wasn't a hard conclusion to draw. The common link between the victims made the protector angle an obvious supposition, and the note solidified the idea.

"It made me feel...powerful," Mona said wistfully. "Like I had my very own guardian angel watching over me, one who isn't afraid to get blood on her hands."

"Her?" Chicago's finest assumed it couldn't be a woman, Mona Stewart assigned female gender without a thought.

Mona pulled herself from her introspection. "What?"

"Her. You said her." Diana leaned into the table. "What do you know?"

"Nothing." Mona shook her head. She looked confused, not devious. "It just couldn't be a man."

"Why not?"

"Because a guy wouldn't care enough about me to do this."

"To do what?" Braxton asked.

"Kill to keep me safe." Mona spoke with reverence. Apparently she regarded her would-be savior with a gleam of hero worship.

Diana had battled with the need to bring a killer to justice weighed against the good the vigilante had done by eliminating men with a singular, evil need to dominate the women in their lives. In theory, the concept of a dark warrior protecting fair maidens comforted Diana like a story out of a book. Faced with the grim reality, she wasn't at all sure how she felt.

CHAPTER TWENTY

The leather-bound scrapbook felt good in Ali's hands, heavy and substantial, a carefully compiled testimony of the work she'd done to stop Ricardo and keep the four women safe. Logic told her that killing those men didn't really impact Ricardo, but in the moment, the breath of time before she made the fatal strike, the man before her each time had been Ricardo. His death felt good, but hot, sticky vengeance always gave way to cold, ugly reality. At some point after the heart stopped beating, Ali would see the event for what it really was—the death of a stranger in a foreign country. The red-tinged haze would fade, leaving her disappointed and overwhelmed with obligation to the woman left behind.

Page one of her scrapbook contained a small obituary summarizing the life and death of Sergio Dominguez. He had been an impromptu gift from the Fates. She hadn't planned to end his life. Rosa had left South Lake without saying good-bye. Ali went to her house to talk her into returning. Instead of Rosa, she found Sergio, drunk and out for blood. He didn't care who he extracted his pound of flesh from, his wife or Ali. That was a mistake.

A black cloud hung around Sergio. He was dangerous, but that night he was altered and unpredictable. It was only a matter of time until Rosa returned, and Ali knew that would be fatal for her.

"Bitch," he said when he saw Ali standing on his doorstep. "What did you do to my wife to turn her against me." It wasn't a question but a judgment.

She met Sergio's hard gaze. "It took no persuasion from me to convince your wife to leave you." She pushed into the house and Sergio swayed back on his heels.

"Come right in." He smiled, a predatory sneer.

It wasn't smart, putting herself in front of a man like Sergio. But she needed to be there, or Rosa would surely suffer the full brunt of his alcohol-enhanced need to dominate. "Tell me," she asked, "have you always been a coward?"

This was what being in the United States had taught Ali. Men like Sergio and Ricardo were afraid and they expressed it with violence and pain.

"*Pendeja.*" Sergio drew his hand up across his body.

It was never a straight-on punch with guys like him, always a backhanded slap that exploded just below the eye. Everything else from that night was bathed in red. Ali had snatches of memory, the glint of steel, the outrage in her attacker's eyes, the spray of hot blood covering her. Later, her hands still wrapped in a death grip around the polished handle of the large hunting knife, she'd stumbled into her shower fully dressed.

As she watched the swirl of blood escape down the drain, what she'd done finally hit her. It was Sergio's blood, not Ricardo's, that covered her clothes and matted her hair. She felt hollow and victorious at the same time. Rosa was safe and Ricardo's time would come.

Ali turned to the second page. Unlike Sergio's death, Mikhail Petrov's had been planned, right down to the weapon she would use and the ways she would make him suffer. His wife, Lora, was a timid woman, ducking away from conflict with fear in her eyes. Her body held the lessons that had been meted to her at the hands of her loving husband. The day she checked in to the shelter and Ali saw the long, white scars, so similar to her own, she knew she would kill the man responsible.

She had tracked Mikhail for two weeks while Lora hid, tucked away from his violent temper at South Lake. Ali entered the house through a side door, never announcing her presence. Rather than taunting him, as she'd done with Sergio, she waited until he passed out for the night. He woke up strapped to a chair, his razor-sharp switchblade pressed to his Adam's apple.

Ali had been torn. She wanted to look in his eyes as he died, but she didn't want to be covered in evidence again. Compromise was found when she stepped behind him and tipped his head back. His eyes were wild with dawning comprehension, his scream stifled by the duct tape covering his mouth. She knew it was Mikhail, yet when she drew the knife across his throat, cutting deep from ear to ear, it was Ricardo's sadistic smile gleaming up at her.

The relief in Lora's eyes when she heard of Mikhail's death was golden. Ali wanted her to be frozen in that moment of freedom. That's when she'd decided to make a gift of Mikhail's switchblade to Lora, a sign that she no longer had to cower in his memory. Pleased with the decision, she'd wrapped the hunting knife for Rosa at the same time. After a few days it became obvious that Rosa no longer lived at her old address. A couple of well-placed phone calls and Ali learned she was dead. She'd delivered the knife to Rosa's grave hoping she'd look down from heaven and see it there.

Her next deserving candidate, Victor Delaney, had died on his back, defiant and belligerent to his last breath. He'd stood over the stove in the tiny house he shared with his wife, Susan. His culinary creation bubbled on the stove, the rich scent of beef and spices wafting through the room. Ali slipped through the back door and engaged the lock without a sound. She didn't want him to escape through a carelessly unsecured exit. He started when he saw her standing there, stock still, his gasp sounding over the quiet symphony of the sauce bubbling on the stove.

His precious set of knives rested on the small butcher block in the center of the kitchen. Ali selected the largest one, the chef's knife, and nodded in appreciation of the well-kept, sharp blade. Before focusing her full attention on Victor, she rolled the professional-grade protective case into a tight bundle and tied the flaps down. She didn't want him to have easy access to his toys.

Victor watched her, his muscles visibly tensed, ready for action, but his reflexes were dulled by the pint of vodka working its way through his system. Ali had watched him from the backyard, waiting until he'd consumed enough of the alcohol to dull his senses, but not long enough for him to lose consciousness. She wondered how long he would remain silent at her bidding. His voice was, so far, not impaired. And though wariness was clear on his face, he obviously saw the small woman as no real threat, even armed with the large knife he'd used as a weapon many times in the past.

Her appreciation for this dance between life and death had grown since she'd dispatched Mikhail, and she wanted to savor Victor's passing. She kept her voice low, infusing it with as much deadly intent as she could muster. She wanted to see fear in his eyes.

"This is the one you used to brand Susan." She twirled the long blade lightly in her hand, her gaze never leaving Victor's face.

"You're crazy." Victor lunged for her.

Ali dropped low to the ground and pivoted as he stumbled and flew over her. With satisfying precision, she cut him low and deep on the back of his ankle. He dropped to the ground and grabbed his leg, rocking and moaning in pain. Ali stood and stepped back as the pool of thick, red blood spread across the cracked linoleum. Victor lurched to his feet, all his weight on his uninjured leg. Gravity helped his heart pump the blood out of his body at an even greater rate.

"What are you doing?" The tremor in his voice told Ali he already knew the answer.

"You're a bad man, Victor." She used his name intentionally, wanting him to realize her familiarity with the details of his life. The simple statement didn't answer his question directly, but it was all Ali was willing to offer. Victor's face twisted with realization and outrage.

"Get out of my house." He also kept his voice low. Ali imagined it was out of habit from years of not wanting the neighbors to know what wrong things he'd done. She was grateful for his self-imposed separation from would-be witnesses.

Ali felt her mouth curve into a smile as Victor's body trembled. He wouldn't be on his feet much longer. Soon he would be dead and his wife would be free from the dark shadow he'd cast over her life. "I don't think so."

Victor reached for her, a lurching, staggering lunge that placed him off balance and vulnerable. As he toppled to the ground, Ali struck out with the razor-sharp blade at the other ankle. She moved out of reach before he could respond. The rich meat sauce on the stove bubbled and she turned the heat down a level. She didn't want it to scorch. The aroma reached out and invited her to taste it.

While Victor's life drained from his body, she dipped the spoon into his creation and lifted it to her lips. "Mmm. Victor, this is very good. But it's missing something."

Ali was not a cook. The sauce was intoxicatingly good, definitely not in need of any further meddling, certainly not from a rank amateur like her. She dropped to her knees next to him, no longer caring about the blood. It blanketed the floor, leaving no clear place for her to put her feet without stepping in it. She slipped the tip of the knife beneath the edge of his beer-stained shirt. It sliced through the material with ease.

"What are you doing?"

Ali sighed. "Victor, that's twice you've asked that question." She reached over him and grabbed the small onion off the butcher block. "The answer has been obvious both times." She placed the vegetable on Victor's chest and rested the sharp edge of the knife on top of it. "Tell me, how thin should I slice this?" She didn't wait for his answer before pushing down on the blade until it passed through the onion and cut into his skin. She pressed a little harder and pulled the blade swiftly toward her body, leaving behind a long, shallow wound. Victor gasped and struggled to get away. A single tear slid down the side of his face.

"Did Susan cry when you did this to her?" Ali asked in a conversational tone, the same one she used when checking out at the grocery store or ordering dinner.

She pushed the knife down through the onion and into Victor's chest several more times before standing again. She used the back edge of the knife and her hand to scoop the slices up. The hatchwork of cuts on his chest closely resembled the scars she'd seen on Susan when she checked into the shelter, but it wasn't quite right. It would take a little more effort to get it perfect.

Ali stirred the onion into Victor's sauce using the long knife. His eyes widened as he watched the blood trickle down the blade into the pot. She tilted her head to the right, eyes narrowed in concentration. Victor would be dead soon, but he still hadn't suffered enough to pay for the pain he'd visited upon his wife. Ali dropped back down beside the still-defiant man. She drew the knife along the soft skin of his belly and watched the blood bubble up to the surface in a thin line.

"This doesn't change anything," Victor spat, tendrils of spit and blood clung to his lip. "I still own you."

His face swam out of focus and was replaced by Ricardo's hard glare.

"No." The word barely crossed her lips, a brief, scarcely audible whisper, and she lifted the knife above her head and plunged it deep into the man's bloody chest. His body tensed and convulsed around the impact, then sagged. Ali pulled the knife out, her hands trembling. She held it for several moments, breathing deep, ragged breaths, waiting to make sure she didn't need to stab him again. Finally she stood and rinsed the blood from the knife. When she turned back around, Ricardo was gone and Victor Delaney lay dead on the floor. She left his dinner still simmering on the stove as she let herself out.

Displayed between the brief obituaries in Ali's scrapbook were pictures of the women she'd cared for from their first night at the shelter, their frail, damaged bodies exposed to harsh light and captured on film. Deep regret and sorrow haunted their faces. Their eyes were hollow and unblinking. Ali remembered that despair, the moment when she chose between sinking into the murky lake of Ricardo's sadism and kicking hard for the surface and fighting for life. She'd chosen to live, to escape and defy his reign, but her freedom was hard won.

Ricardo's men had tracked her mercilessly at first, granting not even a moment's reprieve during her flight. Her body and mind remained at high alert, on constant vigil against all that would bring her harm. It was time to escape or die trying. She recognized the same resigned determination in the faces of the women she now protected.

Ali continued flipping through the scrapbook. For the first time, she longed to share her accomplishments. Diana would understand. She said their deaths were just, deserved. Still, Ali couldn't take that chance, not when Ricardo was so close. Her opportunity to silence the demons had traveled to Chicago. She simply needed to rise to the challenge.

Ali closed the journal without looking at the pages dedicated to Mona and Charles Stewart. The taste of his death was fresh enough in her mind that she didn't need to revisit it. The deaths chronicled in her scrapbook had been righteous, a service to women not strong enough to defend themselves. She stepped out her front door, the first step on her way to face down the source of her own torment.

By the time Ali reached the hospital, the building was all but abandoned. She walked, head high, with purpose through the long corridors that led to Ricardo's room. She did not hesitate outside his room this time. Rather, she took a deep breath, braced herself, and pushed the door open with determination.

The quiet reached out and pulled her deeper into the room. The machines monitoring Ricardo's progress issued a beep periodically. Other than that and the low rattle of Ricardo's inconsistent breathing, the small room was shrouded in an eerie graveyard silence. Ali focused hard on the LED readouts on the various machines in the room, keeping her eyes safely off Ricardo.

She lowered herself into the only chair in the room. It sat in lonely vigil beside his bed, waiting for a loved one to occupy it. The wait would be long and unfulfilled. The only visitor this man would receive would be vengeance personified. Ali watched Ricardo's chest rise and fall, lost in the weak, arrhythmic cadence that made her wonder if this was the same strong, seemingly invincible man who'd held her captive for so long. Finally, when she could wait no longer, she stood and took the few short steps to his bed. The face, once beautiful in its evil intent, was sallow and thin.

Ali gasped. This couldn't be Ricardo. His father, perhaps. Or his grandfather. But certainly not the proud man from her past. She pressed her fingers to his neck, testing to see if there was any sign of the animated, fiery man she knew. His skin was cold, dry. It held none of the warmth she remembered. This was not the man she loved to the point of hatred. It wasn't her surrogate father, turned lover and torturer. He wasn't anyone at all. Just a hollowed-out mannequin of a man that lived only in her memories.

One hot tear trickled down her cheek, followed by another and another. She cried for the irrevocable loss of her family, her innocence, and her one sure chance for revenge. She left his room, confused and shattered. For the first time in her life, she turned her back on him as she walked away, the cold bands of fear slipping away from her heart.

CHAPTER TWENTY-ONE

The bullpen at Carter and Lowe erupted into shouts and applause when Diana entered through the double doors. Jeter poked his head out of his office and hurried over to greet her. "You're a hero."

Diana smiled and punched the air above her head in what she imagined was a suitable victory salute, à la Rocky Balboa. She didn't know what all the fuss was about, but that was no reason to not play along. "What are you talking about, Jeter?"

"Christ, Collins, don't you watch the news?"

She'd awoken that morning with Cami in her bed and more delicious things on her mind than the morning news. "Not today. What's going on?"

"The FBI announced that they recovered the murder weapons in the serial killer case they're working on. Someone in the department leaked the information that it was an investigator from this firm that actually led the authorities to them."

"No way." Diana was shocked. She didn't want credit in the media, she just wanted to protect the financial solvency of Carter and Lowe.

"Braxton's with a few select reporters now in the executive conference room. They're waiting for you to join them."

"What?" Since they'd finished their fieldwork yesterday and today promised a long, boring date with mountains of paperwork, Diana had dressed down. Way down. Jeans and plain black T-shirt. Not exactly press conference attire. She looked down at her low-top Docs and shook her head. "I'll change in my office, but these are the only shoes I have here."

"No, you look fine," Jeter said. "Just get in there."

He urged her toward the conference room. She was going to kill whoever had shared this little tidbit with the press. Right after she killed Jeter for pushing her into the lion's den. She hated reporters. Misquoted once was more than enough for Diana.

"Jeter, I'm sure Braxton can handle this on her own." Diana tried one last-ditch effort to stay on the right side of the conference room doors. She noticed Jeter wasn't running to put himself in front of the cameras either. "Or you could help her."

Jeter opened the door and gave her a gentle shove. "Go."

"There you are, sugar."

Braxton's crowd-pleasing smile didn't reach all the way to her eyes, but Diana was dazzled nonetheless. She was used to Braxton's milk and honey charm and it still melted her. It had an almost hypnotic effect on others, especially the press. As a result, she generally served as media liaison when the need presented itself.

Diana set her briefcase in an open chair by the door. "You didn't tell me you were having friends over this morning."

That garnered some polite laughter followed by a barrage of questions. Diana tried to ignore the volley of lights that went with it. Damn photographers.

"Now, now, folks, be patient. We'll answer your questions one at a time." Braxton's voice stayed low and sweet, but her meaning was clear.

The members of the press looked utterly charmed. Diana wished, not for the first time, that she had a sexy Southern accent of her own. "How about I just jump right in, unless you want to tell me what you've already covered?"

Diana knew Braxton would decline. It wouldn't impact the questions the press asked and it would waste time. Why prolong the experience?

"Ms. Collins, tell us what led you to the first murder weapon."

Diana hated being called Ms. She wasn't even thirty, for Christ's sake.

"I did what any investigator does. Remembered my training and followed my instincts. And it certainly didn't hurt having the best investigator in the company working with me." She smiled at Braxton. Her father had taught her to never take more credit than she was due and always give it freely. Braxton deserved far more than Diana could ever pay.

Diana counted down the questions with predictable ease until Braxton brought the conference to a close with a "y'all come back now" smile. Diana stretched the muscles in her face to relax the tension out of her jaw. It just wasn't natural to smile that much in such a short period of time. By unspoken agreement, the two women headed straight to Jeter's office. He was watching a telecast showcasing the interview.

"That was fast." Diana was amazed. There were no live feeds in the conference room. The IT department wouldn't allow it.

"Modern technology is an amazing thing, shug." Braxton sank into one of two oversized square leather chairs. They were ass ugly, in Diana's opinion, but they were unbelievably comfortable. Braxton assured her they were also very fashionable. Diana didn't believe her.

"I'll tell you what's amazing." Jeter was practically gushing. Diana wanted to shoot him with a tranquilizer gun—the big kind they used at the zoo. "You guys. You did great." He pointed to the screen. "And you looked great." Jeter really needed to find a new adjective. "Amazing" and "great" only went so far.

"Thanks, Jeter." Diana forced herself to issue the expected polite response. In reality, the only thing she was thankful for was that the investigation, barring some paperwork, was finally closed. "This case was pretty gruesome."

Jeter straightened the short stack of papers on his desk, aligning his pen perfectly along the top edge. "I think the two of you should take a long weekend, starting now."

"What the hell am I supposed to do for the next four and a half days?" Braxton did not sound grateful.

"Go home and talk to your husband." Jeter said it evenly, but the set of his shoulders told Diana that he was braced for impact.

Braxton stiffened. "Not an option."

"Then go talk to your therapist. Either way, don't come back here until Monday." Jeter turned his attention to Diana. "And you, go lock yourself in a room with your kindergarten teacher."

Diana's brain filtered through several smart-ass comebacks in rapid-fire succession. She discarded every last one of them. As irritated as she was that Jeter assumed a level of comfort regarding her relationship that she herself didn't have, Diana was planning to do exactly what he suggested. Granted, she'd have to let Cami go to work, but beyond that Diana simply wanted to hold her until the greasy film of tracking a serial killer was washed away completely.

❖

Diana stopped shy of knocking on Ali's apartment door. How would she explain her unannounced arrival? She was still working through the reasons in her head. She wasn't sure she could justify it to anyone else. When she'd left Carter and Lowe, she was bent on heading directly to Cami's apartment to await her return from work. During the short drive, Diana tried to reach Ali at the shelter. Even though it would upset Oscar, Diana wanted to share what they'd uncovered with Ali. The women at South Lake were her responsibility, after all. Diana reasoned that she had a right to know. Besides, she wanted to give Ali the opportunity to pursue their friendship beyond the constraints of her investigation. It was just after two on a Wednesday. Ali should have been at work, but she wasn't.

"Diana?" Ali's voice was sharp with curiosity and something else Diana couldn't identify. "What are you doing here?" Ali wore baggy trainers, a loose fitting T-shirt that clung to her perspiration-dampened skin, and had a towel looped around her neck.

"I wanted to talk to you." It sounded lame to Diana. She could only imagine how it must sound to Ali.

"How did you find me?" She held her body rigid, coiled tight like she was ready to pounce at any moment.

"You weren't at work, so I did an Internet search." Diana held up her PDA. "It led me here." She knew she was babbling, but the tangy scent of Ali's sweat combined with her hard glare knocked Diana off balance.

Ali's face softened. "Come on in." She reached past Diana and opened the door. "It's not much, but you are welcome."

Diana stepped over the threshold feeling like she'd passed an important test that she hadn't been forewarned about. She tried to relax, visualizing the tension draining from her body, down through the soles of her shoes. The farther she moved into the apartment, the deeper her sense of foreboding. The apprehension she tried to discard ricocheted off the floorboards and bounced back into her body with a vengeance. When the door clicked shut behind her, it sounded with finality.

"I hate to abandon you, but I need to clean up." Ali motioned to the couch, indicating Diana should take a seat. "Can I get you anything to drink while you wait?"

It was obvious to Diana, in spite of Ali's words of welcome, that Ali did not want her here. She searched for the right way to remove herself without offending her reluctant hostess. "I'm sorry. Coming here was inappropriate. I didn't mean to interrupt your workout." She made a move toward the door.

"No." Ali closed the gap between them with ferocious speed and touched Diana's arm. "Please, stay. It'll just take me a moment."

The look in Ali's eyes—fierce, demanding, almost pleading—left Diana spinning. She'd noticed the contradictions in Ali's demeanor, at once assessing, measuring for threat, and begging for a place of safe haven, during the first visit to South Lake. The extremes became more pronounced the closer she got to Ali—the aloof defiance, heart-wrenching compassion, and beneath it all, the faint whispers of hope. The last was what kept Diana reaching out, kept her rooted to the threadbare carpet even though good sense told her she should go.

"Please?" The word held actual intent, not just polite formality.

Diana lowered herself onto the couch. "I'll wait for you."

Ali excused herself with a small smile and left Diana unmonitored in her home. Only it didn't feel like a home, more like a place that served a purpose but would be easily left behind and forgotten. No artwork, no books on the shelves, no magazines on the coffee table, no signs of personalization save two small framed photos lost in the expanse of floor-to-ceiling shelving that covered one wall.

The muted sound of running water filtered into the room and Diana fidgeted, restless in her role as willing captive. Ali had deliberately guided her to the sofa, waiting until she was seated before retreating to the bathroom. The action itself wasn't suspect. After all, it was polite to see a guest properly seated. If her mom had done the same thing, Diana would have felt taken care of, looked after. With Ali, the effort felt restraining, as though Ali would only allow her to venture so far into her sanctuary.

Diana shrugged off her uncertainty, convincing herself she was being ridiculous, reading too much into simple gestures. Determined to step outside of her self-imposed restrictions, Diana forced herself to move from the couch to the bookcase where she inspected the photographs. They were faded, the colors muted to soft sepia by time and improper handling. The edges were rough, frayed, and there was a white crease, a deeply ingrained fold mark, that bisected the happy face of a young girl. Was this a picture of young Ali? The other picture was of a man and a woman, younger than Diana, gazing at each other with undeniable, tangible love for one another. Ali's parents?

Diana ached for what might have been, flooded with the senseless sacrifice Ali had been forced to make at such a young age. She wanted to hold Ali, like she had that day in her office, until all the pain faded. Diana moved away, sweeping her eyes over the apartment with greater scrutiny. She looked for a connection with Ali, a way to gain a greater sense of who she was. There had to be more here than the empty sterility present at first glance.

Nothing. Not even a discarded scrap to indicate a person lived here. No hastily scribbled grocery list, no half-completed crossword, no carelessly forgotten glass of water. She made her way to the dining area to continue her inspection. A large, leather-bound journal sat on one corner of the table, a rich, textured brown, so dark it was almost black. Diana smoothed her hands over the cover, recognizing pay dirt. If Ali's essence was anywhere inside these walls, it would be within this book.

The first few pages revealed newspaper articles about Sergio Dominguez, followed by pictures of a woman Diana assumed to be his wife, Rosa. Her body was covered with dark purple bruises and several white-lined scars similar to the ones on Ali's body. Diana skipped ahead a few pages and found a section dedicated to Mikhail and Lora Petrov.

There was nothing about Ali here, just a further display of her dedication to the women at South Lake. Diana glanced at the closed bathroom door. Any real revelations about Ali would come from her, not from poking about where she didn't belong. She flipped through a few more pages, not really looking at the images, until she came across a gruesome photo of a blood-drained man staring lifelessly up from the page. The full force of what she was seeing registered with a jolt. This wasn't a makeshift shrine compiled out of respect for the women, it was a macabre collection of victories. That was the only explanation. Where else would Ali have gotten a picture like that? It certainly hadn't been released to the press, and it lacked the precision, the focus on detail, of a crime scene captured by a police photographer.

Diana's heart slammed against her chest, eclipsing everything except the rush of blood through her ears and the harsh, uneven force of air through her lungs. Fear gripped her stomach and clawed up her throat. She closed her mouth tight, refusing to scream. She had to get out of this apartment. Now.

"Sorry I took…" Ali emerged, her eyes darting from Diana to the open album and back again. Lightning quick she was at Diana's side, closing the book, her hand coming to a rest firmly on the cover.

Sound and color drained from the room and Diana stood, afraid to move, afraid to even blink, inches from a murderer. Her brain raced for the quickest way out. She sparred regularly, was willing to go toe to toe with gun-wielding criminals, but she'd never tasted another's death at her own hands. She didn't think she could kill but was certain Ali could and had. That put her at a disadvantage physically. Clarity of thought evaded her. She couldn't see beyond the moment and the dark despair drowning Ali from within. Diana stared mutely at an unspeaking Ali as the minutes ticked by.

Ali ended the showdown. "Diana." Her voice was hesitant, unsure and she reached for Diana's hand. "Please, it's not what you think."

Diana projected calm, willing herself to speak, to sound reassuring. She had to convince Ali that she believed her, that she thought nothing about the content of the album. "It's *okay*, Ali." She gave her fingers a tight squeeze. "It's just a scrapbook. These women are important to you, of course you keep records about the important events in their lives." It sounded almost plausible. Almost.

Ali relaxed her stance. "Right." Heavy relief colored her words. "I knew you'd understand."

Awkward silence filled the room as Diana searched for a safe topic, one that would expedite her departure. She led Ali out of the kitchen, back to the neutrality of the living room. Nothing had been exposed there. Hopefully Ali would feel safe enough to let her leave.

"You never did tell me why you're here."

Damn. She'd intended to tell Ali about their progress, about the discovery of the weapons. She couldn't do that now. The words "aiding and abetting" were too deeply ingrained from her childhood. "I called the shelter. I was worried when you weren't there. I came by to check on you." It was something a friend would do, and it was just a shade away from the truth.

"Really?" Ali's voice was soft with wonder, like she didn't quite trust that Diana would care about her without an agenda.

"Yes." Diana glanced at her watch. "Now that I see you're all right, I really should go. My girlfriend is waiting for me." She said it too fast and the words took on an edge of fumbling desperation.

Ali regarded her, her lips drawn in a tight line. "He's here."

Diana was halfway to the door when Ali's words registered. "Who's here?"

"Ricardo."

The hair on Diana's neck prickled to attention. Ali turned toward the bookshelf and touched the picture of the girl reverently with one finger.

"He killed my parents. He killed my sister. He almost killed me." Her voice dropped to a whisper. "And now he's here."

The quagmire of the investigation, the drowning, sucking, thick quicksand of malevolence that threatened to engulf Diana at every turn all started with Ricardo Chavez.

"Ali, you escaped. You're free." Diana stopped. The words, as much as she believed them, bounced off the walls, empty and hollow.

"I'm not free." Ali squared her shoulders, a tense line of resolution. "But I will be soon."

Diana's stomach dropped. "God, what are you going to do?"

"You must understand." Ali faced Diana, her eyes pleading. "All the pain, the unrelenting agony that drags my heart across the miles to Colombia, the fury scratching and clawing in my belly, there's only one way to find peace from all that. It ends with his death. I've always known this, but I wasn't strong enough to do it before. Now I am."

"This isn't right." Diana shook her head, her arms hung limp at her sides. "Killing Ricardo won't make the nightmares go away. They'll only get louder and louder until they're all you hear."

"You're wrong."

Unsure if Ali was Catholic or not, but desperate for a lifeline, an anchor in a desperate sea, Diana said, "Come to confession with me, Ali. Talk to my priest. He can help you."

Ali seemed to shrink in on herself; her shoulders sank, her head dropped. Diana wanted to wrap her up and protect her, but how could she protect her from herself?

"If not a priest, then a counselor." She took a cautious step closer to Ali. "You don't have to carry this alone."

"They can't help me." Ali's eyes glinted with unshed tears, her voice final. "Will you stay with me?"

Diana considered it. What good could she really do? Ali needed professional help, someone who had been trained to deal with the depth of Ali's pain. One wrong word and she could send Ali careening off in the wrong direction. She needed to get Ali out of this apartment and to somewhere safe, a place where she couldn't hurt herself or anyone else, but Ali clearly wasn't going to go.

"I can't. I have someone waiting. She needs me."

Ali thumped her chest with her fist. "I need you." The words tore out of her in a sob.

"Ali," Diana spoke softly, soothingly, "you need help...more than I can give."

Ali didn't look up when Diana stepped out the door. A ribbon of ice formed around Diana's heart, chilling her, and all she wanted was Cami's touch to soothe the pain away.

CHAPTER TWENTY-TWO

Diana started shaking halfway to Cami's apartment, little tremors that soon gave way to full-body quakes. She pulled over, rolled down the windows, and sucked in the cool evening air. Her hands gripped the steering wheel, vibrating against it as she cursed the unfulfilled adrenaline in her veins.

She needed to do something besides run to Cami and hide. A man's life was at stake. As despicable as he was, Diana couldn't stand by and do nothing. Ali had refused counseling. That left her with only one option. Her heart settled back into place, the shaking eased, and Diana pulled back onto the road. A few blocks from Cami's house, when she thought her voice was calm enough to talk, she dialed Oscar's cell phone.

It rang four times before he picked up, long enough for Diana to think it was going to voice mail, and the shakes started to return. How would she report this to the desk sergeant? She could call 911, but they would put her on hold as soon as they realized it wasn't an immediate emergency. She was about to disconnect and call her father—he would know what to do—when Oscar answered.

"I need help." It wasn't how she'd intended to start the conversation, but when Oscar's voice came through the line, confident and sure, she felt like she was ten years old and in need of her Uncle Oscar's protection.

"Di? What is it?"

"Ali Sandoval, the director of the shelter, she's your serial killer." Even knowing the truth, it sounded surreal spoken aloud like that.

"How do you know?"

Diana parked in front of Cami's building and jogged up the stairs. She couldn't get to Cami soon enough. "I saw her scrapbook."

"Scrapbook? Where?"

"In her apartment." Diana threw open the door and stopped dead. The phone fell from her limp hand.

Ali was there, so close to Cami, leaning over the kitchen table, listening with rapt attention to whatever Cami was saying. Diana closed the door softly. Clearly leaving Ali alone had not been a good idea.

Ali looked up. "You dropped your phone." The strain from earlier was gone, leaving behind only the warm caramel of her South American accent.

"You're home." Cami rose and greeted Diana with a kiss on the cheek.

With a possessive arm around Cami's waist, Diana asked, "How did you get here?" There was so much to that question. How did she know where Cami lived? How did she get here before Diana? How did she convince Cami to let her in?

"Your friend stopped by to talk to you. I couldn't let her leave without a cup of coffee." Cami's warm smile was an oasis, something to cling to in the shifting emotional sand surrounding Ali.

"Cami, do you mind if I talk to Ali alone?" Diana scooped up her phone and clicked it shut.

Cami darted a glance at Ali, then back to Diana. "If you need to, sure. I'll wait in the bedroom."

"We'll only be a minute."

Diana waited for the door to close on Cami before wheeling to face Ali. "You have no right to be here."

Ali gestured to the chair Cami had vacated. "Please, we need to finish our conversation."

The deadly calm in Ali's eyes sent a chill though Diana.

"The conversation was over, Ali. I can't help you. And I certainly can't excuse you."

"You said you understood." The pleading for acceptance returned to Ali's voice, her composure no longer etched in granite. "You said that whoever killed those men did society a favor. What happened to that? Didn't you mean it?"

"Of course I meant it." Diana threw up her hands, frustrated that she'd ever said that and frustrated even more that Ali was holding it against her. "As an abstract concept. That doesn't mean I want to sit down to dinner with a killer." Diana knew in an instant she'd given too much up. She'd been careful not to let Ali know the conclusion she'd drawn from the pictures in her scrapbook. Then, in a careless burst of frustration, she'd forgotten her debilitating fear and turned loose her temper on Ali. Tormenting a serial killer was not a safe thing to do.

Ali stared at her, her jaw muscle twitching.

"Ali, you need to go. You can't stay here."

"Please, Diana, I need you to understand, to *really* understand what I did…why I did it."

Diana clenched her hands together in her lap. They had started to shake again and she didn't want Ali to see that. Earlier, in Ali's apartment, she'd been afraid, fixated on getting out. Now the threat had followed her to Cami, and her tenuous grip on control was slipping. She would do anything, *anything*, to protect Cami. But Ali seemed bent on explaining herself, converting Diana into a solid ally. She needed to focus on that, keep Ali talking and away from Cami, until she could figure out how to get her to leave.

"Ricardo took so much, they all took so much. I had to take it back."

"I know how those men died, no two the same. That took planning, forethought. You didn't just stumble into it."

Ali tilted her head to the side, a strange gleam in her eyes. "Not the same? They all died at my hands by their own blade. I wielded their power against them, used it to penetrate into their souls. I carved retribution out of them."

Diana felt the blood drain from her face. She'd been wrong. Talking to a priest wouldn't help Ali. She was too far gone.

"Their flesh yielded easily, split open, and spilled out red-hot absolution."

The low drone of faraway sirens grew in the background, muted by closed doors and windows, but Diana heard them coming, a screaming crescendo, closer and closer, until a look of recognition crossed Ali's face.

"You called the police?" Hurt and betrayal flickered in her eyes and was replaced with cold steel. "You've ruined everything," She spat the words out like hard bullets of judgment, her body already in motion.

And then she was gone, running out the door and into the night.

❖

Cami sat stone still on the edge of the bed, her face white and drawn. Diana kneeled in front of her and gathered her hands in a careful embrace.

"Cami, baby, she's gone." Diana smoothed her thumbs across Cami's knuckles, desperate for a connection.

"She's...I heard..." Cami shook her gaze away from the door and focused on Diana. "She killed those men, didn't she?"

Diana pressed her lips to Cami's palm, breathing in Cami's clean, citrus scent. She closed her eyes against the accusation in Cami's face and nodded. "Yes."

"She came to my home and I served her coffee." The words were a strangled mix of fear and disgust, like she should have been able to tell just by looking at Ali.

Diana moved to the bed, as close as she could get to Cami without crawling inside her, and wrapped her up tight in her arms, fierce and protective. "I'm so sorry." She kissed Cami's temple, then her cheek, then her lips. "So very sorry."

Loud pounding, a fist beating against the door, ricocheted through the apartment. "Dammit, Diana, answer the fucking door." Oscar's voice was raw with a desperation Diana had never heard before.

"Come on." Diana twined her fingers with Cami's. "We need to let him in before he breaks it down."

Oscar surged through the door, his gun drawn and ready. When he realized Diana was safe, his face crumpled and he pulled her into a crushing embrace. "Goddammit, Collins, don't do that again."

Uncomfortable with the show of vulnerability from a man she believed to be invincible, Diana drew back from the hug after a few moments. "How'd you find us so quick?" She tried to give Oscar something to focus on, the technical aspects of his job rather than the thought of his partner's kid in danger. As soon as he released her, Diana latched on to Cami's hand again.

"GPS. You drive a Mercedes. The hardest part was tracking down your boss to get the serial number." He looked around the apartment again, without the intense scrutiny of his first inspection. "So, where is she?"

"She ran out when she heard the sirens." It occurred to Diana that Oscar had never met Cami, yet he concluded immediately that she wasn't Ali. Braxton must have filled him in on a general description. "You need to get to her place, before she disappears."

"A car's already been there. She's gone."

Dread rose fast and sharp in Diana. "There's one other place you should look." She explained about Ali's relationship to Ricardo Chavez, about her expressed need to end his life. "I don't know where he is specifically, but she said he's here."

"Here in Chicago? Or here in the U.S.?"

Diana mentally added a third choice: Here in Ali's twisted mind.

"I don't know for sure, but the way she said it made me think Chicago."

Oscar's face hardened into the tough cop mask Diana was used to. "Get your stuff. You can't stay here tonight."

Cami's grip on her hand tightened.

"I need to stay with Cami."

"Diana," he drew her name out with the edge of forced patience, "I have a lot of work to do if we're going to catch her. And it's not safe here." He looked pointedly at Cami. "For either of you. Now get your stuff so I can walk you out. Take your girl to a nice hotel. Wine her and dine her. Show off that big expense account. Just get the hell out of this apartment." Oscar's voice cracked a little at the end.

It only took a few minutes for Cami to pack an overnight bag and they were ready to go. Diana wasn't worried about staying in the apartment. It was as safe as any other place in the city. However, this was a great excuse to spend a long weekend alone with no one but Cami and the occasional visit from room service. Diana locked the door on Cami's apartment, confident that Oscar was overreacting. Ali wouldn't be back.

CHAPTER TWENTY-THREE

"When do we get to meet her?" Grace's wicked streak tormented Diana from the other side of Chicago.

"Grace, this isn't funny. She could wake up at any moment." Diana glanced at the closed bedroom door, willing Cami to sleep just a little while longer.

"And I'm going to help you, but we, your loving family, want to meet any woman who has you this wound up."

"We? What are you? Spokesperson for the collective?" Diana pictured her sister-in-law with various computer components hardwired into her system. It made her giggle.

"I'm not going to help you until you answer my question."

Panic surged through Diana. Grace had to help her, or breakfast would be a failure and Cami would know what an abysmal cook she was. "Sunday." Now she'd be inundated with phone calls from her whole family. She'd wanted to bring Cami as a surprise, avoid the inquisition until the last minute. She sighed. "I'm bringing her with me on Sunday."

"That's more like it." Grace sounded satisfied. "Now let's talk about your menu this morning. You're trying to overcomplicate things. Forget about bacon and pancakes. You aren't a cook, and that's not going to change over the course of one phone call."

"I *knew* I should have called Rebecca," Diana grumbled. "She wouldn't be giving me this much shit."

The suite at the Hilton on Michigan Avenue, not far from Cami's loft, included a small kitchenette. During a fleeting moment of insanity, it seemed like a good idea for Diana to fix breakfast for Cami. Then the realization that she didn't know how to cook forced the phone call to her sister-in-law.

"Stop it. She'd be foolish enough to try to teach you how to cook over the phone. Now here's what I want you to do."

Soon Diana had a simple breakfast of fresh fruit, yogurt, and toasted bagels. It wasn't really cooking per se, but her intentions were good and the results were less likely to induce a heart attack than her original menu of fried pork products.

"Grace, I owe you."

Grace laughed. "Don't worry, you'll pay me back on Sunday."

"This is why I didn't want to tell you guys. I figured if we just showed up, you'd be too stunned to go in for the kill."

"Not a chance." The noise of Grace's busy office filtered back in, a sure sign she was getting ready to end the call. "Before I let you go, I wanted to fill you in on the cruise for Mom and Pop."

Diana fidgeted with the bouquet of flowers on the table, a fierce combination of tiger lilies, tulips, and carnations. She tweaked the position of several of the flowers until she was satisfied and then lit the red taper candles she'd set out. Candlelit breakfast. A little cheesy, but she wanted Cami to feel special. "What about it?"

"Nine grand, give or take. That doesn't include airfare or any activities."

Diana knew cruises to Alaska could be found for less. There had to be a reason Grace had selected this one. "What's special about it?"

"Mini-suite with a balcony on a high-end cruise ship. I know it's extra, but…"

Diana saved Grace from making her pitch about forty years being a rare and special thing. Diana agreed and she'd heard the speech too many times already. "Okay, so what about airfare and incidentals?"

Grace hesitated. "I was hoping that we could discreetly cover those without mentioning it. The price tag is high enough that the others won't question it. Don't you think?"

The last thing Brigitte needed was more expense to argue with Lucas about. "I think you are right on. Let me know my portion—and Brigitte's—and I'll write you a check." The bedroom door opened as she finished the sentence. "Got to go. Cami's up."

Diana met Cami halfway between the bedroom and the kitchen

table and pulled her into a tight hug. "Good morning." Cami's hair was loose and tousled, that sleepy, not quite ready for the day look. Diana loved her soft vulnerability of the moment and buried her face low in the curve of Cami's neck.

"Mmm, I could get used to this." She squeezed hard, then let go and pulled back, her arms still circling Diana's neck. "Did you cook for me?" The soft smile didn't quite erase the tiredness from the edges of her eyes.

"I did." Diana slid her hands down Cami's arms and laced their fingers together. She pressed her lips sweetly against Cami's. No pressure, simply the clear message that she was happy to be with her. "Just for you, but I'm not making any promises about taste or quality."

"It looks wonderful."

They walked to the table, holding hands, arms swinging gently between them. Cami stopped and drew Diana's hand to her mouth and kissed her fingers. "At some point today you're going to tell me about everything. I wasn't prepared for last night."

Diana considered Cami's words, the meaning behind them. The case was over, officially closed. No harm in talking about it, she supposed. "Deal." It felt nice, this early morning ritual they were sharing. She could see their lives falling together into a nice, agreeable pattern, and it didn't scare the living hell out of her. She squeezed Cami's hand. "Now sit down and let me feed you."

They ate leisurely, taking time to savor the meal, which turned out to be not half bad, and each other's company. The conversation was light and easy, as if by unspoken mutual agreement to save the heavy stuff for after breakfast. Cami took the first step, but it wasn't in the expected direction. "Di, there's something I've been wanting to discuss with you."

Diana reached for Cami's hand across the table. She knew she should say something, nod, anything to encourage Cami to continue. All she was capable of was staring silently.

"It's about that first night." Cami blew out a shaky breath. "I just want you to know that I don't do that very often."

Diana panicked internally, but tried for humor. "What? Take advantage of strange, drunk women?"

Cami didn't smile. "That's exactly what I mean. I don't do that. Well, I did do that, but I don't normally." Cami's words sounded more like an internal monologue rather than a conversation Diana was supposed to participate in.

Of course she didn't do that. Cami was, for all intents and purposes, a nice Catholic girl. "Cami, it's okay. I'm not sorry that you did."

This time she smiled. "No, I'm not sorry, really, just unsure where to go. Diana, I like you, a lot. Is it possible to build a relationship on a prolonged one-night stand?"

"Is that what this is?" Ouch. Diana thought there was more here than world-changing, sometimes acrobatic sex. "A prolonged one-night stand?"

Cami squeezed Diana's fingers. "No. Not for me."

This wasn't how Diana pictured this conversation going, but Cami had set the tone. It was up to Diana to keep up. "You said you don't do that, the one night thing." Diana's heart pounded hard against her chest, beating out a screaming rhythm of "don't tell, don't tell, don't tell." She had to. "What if I did?" She kept it carefully in the past tense.

Cami looked resigned, yet hopeful. "Have you, since we…"

"No." Diana rushed to erase any doubt. "Only you. All I want is you." Oh, hell. Did she say that out loud?

"Good." She stroked her finger lightly over the back of Diana's hand. "I don't care about before. But for the record, you're not allowed to do it again."

"Okay." The simplest words pull people through treacherous conversations, and just like that, Diana felt the shift as their relationship moved to yet another level.

Diana divided the morning paper into sections and handed half to Cami. She kept the front section for herself but gave Cami sports. Halfway through her portion, she came across a small, almost innocuous, article. Ricardo Chavez had been stabbed to death in his room at the University of Chicago Medical Center night before last.

She closed the paper, careful to match the original fold lines, without finishing the article. She already knew more details than the reporter, and a wave of nausea rolled through her. Ali had exacted her revenge.

"What's wrong?" Cami probed Diana with her eyes, concern clear on her face.

Diana recounted the details of her investigation, starting with the missing sword, meeting Mona, then Ali, and ending with the death of

Ricardo. As she spoke, she settled into the warmth of having Cami care for her, worry about her, and her insides melted. She'd found home, and it had nothing to do with the walls around her.

❖

The family had already assembled by the time Diana and Cami arrived, half an hour later than expected. Russell spotted them first and threw his whole body at Diana, then at Cami.

"Ms. Michaelson," he said with the delight only a child can manage, "What are you doing here? I missed you on Thursday and Friday. The whole class did. We were worried. Are you all right?"

Diana laughed as she watched Cami try to decide when to jump in and answer one of Russell's questions. As confident as she was in her classroom, this was a different setting altogether and Cami was obviously a bit off her game. Diana scooped Russell up and swung him around before setting him on his feet again. "One question at a time, mister. It's nice that you were worried about your teacher, but you still need to remember your manners."

Russell nodded solemnly. "Yes, ma'am." He turned to Cami with a shy smile. "Are you my Auntie Di's girlfriend now?"

Shit. Give the kid one question and he goes straight in for the kill. Diana regarded him with a mix of reprehension and admiration. He was going to be a great investigator one day.

This time Diana's father rescued Cami from the question. "Diana, introduce us to your friend."

The entire family stretched along the edge of the patio like a damn reception line. Diana wasn't sure if they thought it was a wedding or a funeral. She wanted Cami's inaugural meeting with the family to be less formal, but managed to conjure up the manners that she'd reminded Russell about moments ago.

Diana gave Cami's hand a reassuring squeeze and started down the line. By the time they reached Brigitte, baby William on her hip, Cami had relaxed considerably. "You're Brigitte." She touched the baby and looked over at Lucas, who was holding their two-year-old daughter. "You have a beautiful family."

It was the perfect thing to say and Diana loved Cami for it. She hadn't shared the difficulties Brigitte and Lucas were having adjusting to the demands of two small children. Cami just instinctively knew what Brigitte needed to hear.

"Diana, we need to talk." There was a stern underpinning in her father's voice that let Diana know this was a nonnegotiable request.

"Pops?" Diana cast a sidelong glance at Cami.

"She'll be fine." He motioned for her to follow him into the house.

Cami laid her hand on Diana's forearm. "I'll just hang out by the pool. If I'm lucky, Brigitte will let me play with her beautiful baby."

Her dad slid the patio door shut behind Diana and handed her a beer. He took a long pull of his own, then said, "Oscar called me." He let the sentence hang in the air awhile before continuing. "He said they're not catching any breaks in the search for Ali Sandoval. The FBI thinks she left the city."

Diana noticed the careful switch from Oscar to the FBI. "What does Oscar think?"

"Oscar's worried about you. And that worries me."

That was a fair statement. She'd be concerned if the roles were reversed. "Have you told Mom?"

He looked out the window, his face serious. "Parts of it. She knows you helped figure out who the serial killer is. She's very proud." He flicked his eyes back to Diana. "So am I."

"I don't think Ali's a threat." She'd spent a lot of time thinking about it over the past few days, more out of concern for Cami than anything else. She watched Cami in the backyard, smiling and laughing with Brigitte, the children running between them. Ali wouldn't come back. She just couldn't.

"I hope you're right." He took another swig of his beer. "Cami seems nice. We're glad you brought her."

"I wanted her to meet you guys, see my life." More important, see their future, everything that Diana hoped for them. Her family summed up everything she had to offer, what a commitment from Diana really meant. She wanted the same kind of happiness, enough to span a lifetime, that her parents shared.

"She's a welcome addition." He patted Diana on the back.

"Thanks, Pops." Diana slipped out the door. "Now I'm going to rescue her."

Diana settled her arm around Cami's shoulders and dropped a light kiss on her mouth. "How you doing?"

Cami laughed, light and easy. "They have a lot of questions."

"They'll be relentless until they figure out where you belong."

"Is that all they want?" Cami sobered and wrapped Diana in a loose hug. "That's easy. I belong right here." She punctuated it with a kiss, not passionate, but definitely possessive.

Diana pulled her in a little tighter. "Yes. Yes, you do."

EPILOGUE

It was a cold, moonless night in Wicker Park and Ali turned up her collar against the wind. The dark outline of two women moved across a lightened window several stories up.

Diana.

And Cami.

When Ali needed her most, dared to trust and hope, Diana had chosen the wild-haired blonde over her. She stood in the dim circle of light cast by the street lamp long after the windows in Diana's apartment went dark. The glimmer of hope that her bloodlust would ever be sated died with Ricardo. Diana had been right about that. The nightmares had gotten worse, not better.

With new betrayal hardening inside her, Ali climbed into her car. She drove until the night lights of Chicago dissolved to a flicker in her rearview mirror. She planned to drive until the entire damn city was nothing more than a bad memory, leaving Diana to fade into a faint imprint on her subconscious, like fingerprints on skin. With enough time and patience, she'd find a way to carve Diana out of her nightmares, too.

About the Author

Jove Belle grew up in southern Idaho and now lives in Portland, Oregon, with her partner of thirteen years. When she's not writing, Jove dedicates her time to chasing her four-year-old around the house, making silly faces at the baby, and being generally grateful for the crazy carnival ride of life.

Books Available From Bold Strokes Books

Love on Location by Lisa Girolami. Hollywood film producer Kate Nyland and artist Dawn Brock discover that love doesn't always follow the script. (978-1-60282-016-6)

Edge of Darkness by Jove Belle. Investigator Diana Collins charges at life with an irreverent comment and a right hook, but even those may not protect her heart from a charming villain. (978-1-60282-015-9)

Thirteen Hours by Meghan O'Brien. Workaholic Dana Watts's life takes a sudden turn when an unexpected interruption arrives in the form of the most beautiful breasts she has ever seen—stripper Laurel Stanley's. (978-1-60282-014-2)

In Deep Waters 2 by Radclyffe and Karin Kallmaker. All bets are off when two award winning-authors deal the cards of love and passion… and every hand is a winner. (978-1-60282-013-5)

Pink by Jennifer Harris. An irrepressible heroine frolics, frets, and navigates through the "what ifs" of her life: all the unexpected turns of fortune, fame, and karma. (978-1-60282-043-2)

Deal with the Devil by Ali Vali. New Orleans crime boss Cain Casey brings her fury down on the men who threatened her family, and blood and bullets fly. (978-1-60282-012-8)

Naked Heart by Jennifer Fulton. When a sexy ex-CIA agent sets out to seduce and entrap a powerful CEO, there's more to this plan than meets the eye…or the flogger. (978-1-60282-011-1)

Heart of the Matter by KI Thompson. TV newscaster Kate Foster is Professor Ellen Webster's dream girl, but Kate doesn't know Ellen exists…until an accident changes everything. (978-1-60282-010-4)

Heartland by Julie Cannon. When political strategist Rachel Stanton and dude ranch owner Shivley McCoy collide on an empty country road, fate intervenes. (978-1-60282-009-8)

Shadow of the Knife by Jane Fletcher. Militia Rookie Ellen Mittal has no idea just how complex and dangerous her life is about to become. A Celaeno series adventure romance. (978-1-60282-008-1)

To Protect and Serve by VK Powell. Lieutenant Alex Troy is caught in the paradox of her life—to hold steadfast to her professional oath or to protect the woman she loves. (978-1-60282-007-4)

Deeper by Ronica Black. Former homicide detective Erin McKenzie and her fiancée Elizabeth Adams couldn't be happier—until the not-so-distant past comes knocking at the door. (978-1-60282-006-7)

The Lonely Hearts Club by Radclyffe. Take three friends, add two ex-lovers and several new ones, and the result is a recipe for explosive rivalries and incendiary romance. (978-1-60282-005-0)

Venus Besieged by Andrews & Austin. Teague Richfield heads for Sedona and the sensual arms of psychic astrologer Callie Rivers for a much-needed romantic reunion. (978-1-60282-004-3)

Branded Ann by Merry Shannon. Pirate Branded Ann raids a merchant vessel to obtain a treasure map and gets more than she bargained for with the widow Violet. (978-1-60282-003-6)

American Goth by JD Glass. Trapped by an unsuspected inheritance and guided only by the guardian who holds the secret to her future, Samantha Cray fights to fulfill her destiny. (978-1-60282-002-9)

Learning Curve by Rachel Spangler. Ashton Clarke is perfectly content with her life until she meets the intriguing Professor Carrie Fletcher, who isn't looking for a relationship with anyone. (978-1-60282-001-2)

Place of Exile by Rose Beecham. Sheriff's detective Jude Devine struggles with ghosts of her past and an ex-lover who still haunts her dreams. (978-1-933110-98-1)

Fully Involved by Erin Dutton. A love that has smoldered for years ignites when two women and one little boy come together in the aftermath of tragedy. (978-1-933110-99-8)

Heart 2 Heart by Julie Cannon. Suffering from a devastating personal loss, Kyle Bain meets Lane Connor, and the chance for happiness suddenly seems possible. (978-1-60282-000-5)

Queens of Tristaine by Cate Culpepper. When a deadly plague stalks the Amazons of Tristaine, two warrior lovers must return to the place of their nightmares to find a cure. (978-1-933110-97-4)

The Crown of Valencia by Catherine Friend. Ex-lovers can really mess up your life…even, as Kate discovers, if they've traveled back to the eleventh century! (978-1-933110-96-7)

Mine by Georgia Beers. What happens when you've already given your heart and love finds you again? Courtney McAllister is about to find out. (978-1-933110-95-0)

House of Clouds by KI Thompson. A sweeping saga of an impassioned romance between a Northern spy and a Southern sympathizer, set amidst the upheaval of a nation under siege. (978-1-933110-94-3)

Winds of Fortune by Radclyffe. Provincetown local Deo Camara agrees to rehab Dr. Bonita Burgoyne's historic home, but she never said anything about mending her heart. (978-1-933110-93-6)

Focus of Desire by Kim Baldwin. Isabel Sterling is surprised when she wins a photography contest, but no more than photographer Natasha Kashnikova. Their promo tour becomes a ticket to romance. (978-1-933110-92-9)

Blind Leap by Diane and Jacob Anderson-Minshall. A Golden Gate Bridge suicide becomes suspect when a filmmaker's camera shows a different story. Yoshi Yakamota and the Blind Eye Detective Agency uncover evidence that could be worth killing for. (978-1-933110-91-2)

Wall of Silence, 2nd ed. by Gabrielle Goldsby. Life takes a dangerous turn when jaded police detective Foster Everett meets Riley Medeiros, a woman who isn't afraid to discover the truth no matter the cost. (978-1-933110-90-5)

Mistress of the Runes by Andrews & Austin. Passion ignites between two women with ties to ancient secrets, contemporary mysteries, and a shared quest for the meaning of life. (978-1-933110-89-9)

Vulture's Kiss by Justine Saracen. Archeologist Valerie Foret, heir to a terrifying task, returns in a powerful desert adventure set in Egypt and Jerusalem. (978-1-933110-87-5)

Sheridan's Fate by Gun Brooke. A dynamic, erotic romance between physiotherapist Lark Mitchell and businesswoman Sheridan Ward set in the scorching hot days and humid, steamy nights of San Antonio. (978-1-933110-88-2)

Rising Storm by JLee Meyer. The sequel to *First Instinct* takes our heroines on a dangerous journey instead of the honeymoon they'd planned. (978-1-933110-86-8)

Not Single Enough by Grace Lennox. A funny, sexy modern romance about two lonely women who bond over the unexpected and fall in love along the way. (978-1-933110-85-1)

Such a Pretty Face by Gabrielle Goldsby. A sexy, sometimes humorous, sometimes biting contemporary romance that gently exposes the damage to heart and soul when we fail to look beneath the surface for what truly matters. (978-1-933110-84-4)

Second Season by Ali Vali. A romance set in New Orleans amidst betrayal, Hurricane Katrina, and the new beginnings hardship and heartbreak sometimes make possible. (978-1-933110-83-7)

Hearts Aflame by Ronica Black. A poignant, erotic romance between a hard-driving businesswoman and a solitary vet. Packed with adventure and set in the harsh beauty of the Arizona countryside. (978-1-933110-82-0)

Red Light by JD Glass. Tori forges her path as an EMT in the New York City 911 system while discovering what matters most to herself and the woman she loves. (978-1-933110-81-3)

Honor Under Siege by Radclyffe. Secret Service agent Cameron Roberts struggles to protect her lover while searching for a traitor who just may be another woman with a claim on her heart. (978-1-933110-80-6)

Dark Valentine by Jennifer Fulton. Danger and desire fuel a high-stakes cat-and-mouse game when an attorney and an endangered witness team up to thwart a killer. (978-1-933110-79-0)

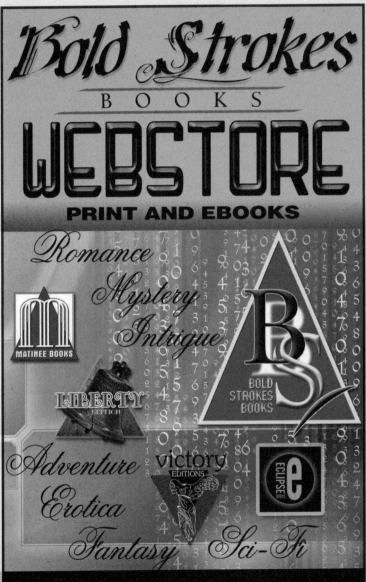

Bold Strokes

BOOKS

WEBSTORE

PRINT AND EBOOKS

Romance
Mystery
Intrigue

MATINEE BOOKS

LIBERTY
EDITION

B
S

BOLD
STROKES
BOOKS

Adventure
victory
EDITIONS

ECLIPSE
e

Erotica
Fantasy *Sci-Fi*

http://www.boldstrokesbooks.com